P1

"*Food Fight* is a heartfelt and hilarious look at life through the eyes of a picky eater. Linda B. Davis portrays Ben's hopes and fears as he learns to navigate middle school while keeping his selective eating disorder a secret from the rest of his class, especially the school bully. A must-read for anyone who has ever fought their own battles with both fitting in and being themselves."

-Shannon Schuren, author of *Where Echoes Lie*

"Linda Davis has a knack for zingy dialogue and depicting multi-faceted sixth-grade characters, but the story behind her book *Food Fight* goes much deeper. Protagonist Ben suffers from ARFID (Avoidant/Restrictive Food Intake Disorder). Typical middle school fare like pizza and ice cream literally makes him sick, and he uses humor to divert attention away from himself and his eating habits. But keeping his secret strains friendships with his classmates and worse, a hopeful first crush goes haywire. Davis's pacing moves right along and yet never diminishes Ben's emotional journey to self-acceptance, striking a pitch-perfect balance for middle-grade readers."

-Kimberly Behre Kenna, author of *Artemis Sparke and the Sound Seekers Brigade*

"Davis gives the reader a realistic and sympathetic portrayal of what it is like to be a picky eater in middle school. With a convincing cast of characters, she creates a lively and timely look into the life of a student with ARFID (Avoidant/Restrictive Food Intake Disorder) and the challenges he faces. An important and well-written debut novel."

-Joyce Burns Zeiss, author of *Out of the Dragon's Mouth*

"This debut novel pairs a unique subject (selective eating disorder) with a smorgasbord of universal middle grade themes including tolerance, bullying, acceptance, empowerment and self-esteem. Well worth the read!"

-Naomi Milliner, author of *Super Jake and the King of Chaos*

FOOD FIGHT

Linda B. Davis

Fitzroy Books

CONTENTS

Published by Fitzroy Books
An imprint of
Regal House Publishing, LLC
Raleigh, NC 27605
All rights reserved

https://fitzroybooks.com
Printed in the United States of America

ISBN -13 (paperback): 9781646033430
ISBN -13 (epub): 9781646033447
Library of Congress Control Number: 2022942676

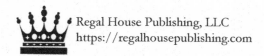

Regal House Publishing, LLC
https://regalhousepublishing.com

To all those becoming experts in being themselves

1

No Such Thing as a Free Lunch

I've been eating the same lunch since first grade: a plain bagel, a handful of pretzels, and two Hershey's Kisses—pretty normal, and impressive only in terms of its exact sameness day after day. My school lunch has never varied. Not even once.

I've eaten most of those lunches with my best buds, Josh and Nick. They know my routine, and I don't think they give it much thought. What they eat changes every day, and no matter what their mothers pack, they'll eat it. Tuna. Roast beef. Egg salad. Leftover lasagna. Josh and Nick are eating machines.

Some people—including my mother, who packs my lunch every morning and writes BEN SNYDER across each brown paper bag—think what I eat is a problem.

But lunch has never been a problem for me.

Until today.

Everybody knows that where you sit on the first lunch of middle school will determine your spot in the social hierarchy for eternity. And it's complete chaos in here. As new sixth graders, we're all scrambling to decide who to eat with and where to sit. From the other side of the floor-to-ceiling windows, I bet the cafeteria looks like an aquarium during a feeding frenzy.

Josh has managed to snag a table in the back. A few other kids are already sitting with him. I meet up with Nick as he's coming out of the cafeteria line, and we head over together. When we show up, Josh waves over a few more guys, who plop down with their trays like we've all been eating together forever. I recognize most of them from after-school sports, but until today we haven't all gone to the same school.

I grab a seat on the bench next to Josh, and suddenly I'm facing down the first curveball of my day: a kid with a square face and pug nose is headed straight for our table. I can't come up with his name, but I haven't forgotten his cheap shot at club soccer tryouts a couple of weeks ago—I still have the bruise his cleat left on my calf.

"Make room," he says, dropping his tray on the table between Josh and me. His Styrofoam cup of fruit catapults into the air and crash-lands onto his pizza in a disgusting, drippy heap.

For some reason Josh slides away from me, opening a space for that kid.

He sizes me up as he sits down. "Hey, I remember you and your daddy longlegs."

I laugh along with everybody else. I've been getting ribbed all day about how much I grew over the summer. It's getting old. I don't mention that he didn't make the team. The dirtiest players are usually the slowest.

My smile feels hard on my face, but I guess it looks pretty normal because another guy named Alex high-fives me as he grabs the seat on my other side.

"What's up, Ben?" he asks. "Haven't seen you since pee wee soccer."

"Yeah, go Bumblebees," I say, and we all crack up.

We go on like that for a few minutes, laughing and remembering what teams we played on together. This must be what Principal Wright was talking about during our assembly this morning when he said, "Seize the opportunities to widen your horizons at Crestwood Middle School."

I've crossed paths with most of these guys for years, but since we're all at Crestwood now, I'll be seeing a lot more of them.

It's no surprise that Josh has already collected enough people to fill out our lunch table. All summer he rambled on about all the kids from other elementary schools we were going to meet this year—and he's off to a strong start. Ever since this morning on the bus, he's been acting like an exaggerated version of himself. He's even sporting a new haircut and a shirt I've never seen before. I don't get why he's trying so hard. Everybody always likes Josh.

But I wish he'd mentioned his plan to invite all his new friends to sit with us. And I'm wondering if any of them have noticed I'm the only person at our table who isn't eating pizza off a navy-blue plastic tray. The brand-new thrill of buying a hot lunch is lost on me but big-time for everyone else.

Conversations about our upcoming Labor Day plans and our afternoon classes zig and zag across the table. I call out my schedule, and right away that loser kid says, "I've got Butler for fifth-period science too. Heard he talks too much."

Lucky me.

I'm relieved when Alex changes the topic. "Who's had history? Did you hear about that Abner Farms place? It's gonna be awesome!"

"Should be a fun day," I say, thinking back to what my cousin told me about the spring field trip sixth graders take to learn firsthand about colonial living. But Alex is strangely excited about something that won't happen for at least eight months.

"No, that's what I mean," Alex says. "It's not just a day trip. This year they're doing something different. It's an overnight. In October."

Suddenly everyone's talking about tents and campfires, and it's clear that half the table has already heard about the trip in the history class I haven't had yet. I'm picturing Josh and Nick and me kicking back in our own tent without any parents. It sounds amazing.

A few seconds later, as I'm tossing a pretzel into my mouth, the pug-faced kid has turned in his seat to face me.

"Man," he says, sneering. "*That's* the saddest excuse for a lunch I've ever seen."

I squeeze my empty bag into a ball. "Whatever," I say, shaking my head. His tray is splattered with sauce-covered fruit and mangled pieces of pizza. It looks like a crime scene.

"My grandpa eats better lunches." His laugh is sharp and angry like a dog's bark. "And he doesn't have any teeth."

This kid is seriously annoying. I want to snap back more than anything, but I don't. I've met plenty of people who have all sorts of opinions about what I eat, and I know from experience it's always better to laugh it off.

A couple of other guys start chuckling too, which doesn't surprise me. Everybody loves a joke when it's not on them. What does surprise me is Josh. He's laughing the hardest. And the loudest.

As we're leaving the cafeteria, I nudge Nick. "You know that kid?" I ask, nodding back at the table.

"Darren?" Nick asks.

I nod. I'm about to say that he's a real BW, which is what Josh and Nick and I say when we don't want to call someone a buttwipe out loud. It never stops being funny.

But before I can, Nick says, "Yeah, that kid's hilarious."

I pretend to laugh along with him. But it bugs me all the way to science class.

2

APPLE OF MY EYE

I'm the first one to show up for science class, arriving even before our teacher. I take a seat at a table in the middle of the room and wait. The noise coming from the hall suggests that unlike me, most people are squeezing every last second of fun out of lunch. That jerk Darren ruined lunch for me, and I'm going to have to face him again any second.

I watch the door, hoping to see a familiar face walk in, but the only person I recognize is Olivia Slotnick. I sure don't want to be associated with her, so I look away and pretend to be fascinated by a model of the solar system on the other side of the room. I must protect myself from exposure to Olivia's over-the-top weirdness, which will be more contagious than the bubonic plague on the first day of school.

After Olivia sits down—front and center, where she will use her super-smarts to antagonize our teacher—a girl I've never seen before walks into the room. Her smile is so sparkly and fresh that she could star in a toothpaste commercial. Right away, I'm mesmerized. She chooses a table in the row ahead of mine, and I consider relocating to the spot next to hers. But before I can make my move, Darren pushes past a couple of kids talking near the door and beelines right over to her. Obviously they already know each other, and I have to look away—like I do when I see a dead raccoon in the road.

When class starts, I monitor Mr. Butler's attendance-taking with the concentration of an air traffic controller all the way through the end of the alphabet so I can learn her name.

Lauren Walters.

I barely pay attention to anything Mr. Butler tells us about

sixth-grade science until he mentions lab partner assignments, which will be made later this week. I spend the rest
of class focusing all my mental energy on hoping Lauren and
I will end up together. And then, for good measure, I spend
some more energy hoping that neither one of us will end up
with Darren.

3

FEAST OR FAMINE

Lauren never resurfaces in any of my other afternoon classes. Fortunately, neither does Darren. By the end of the day I'm worn out, but my last period teacher, Mrs. Frankel, is far from tired—which is pretty amazing because it looks like she's been teaching history since the Dark Ages. Just as class starts, someone in the back snickers something about "Mrs. Frankenstein," and I bet she's probably heard that about a thousand times.

She introduces herself and tells us she doesn't put up with any *shenanigans*, as she likes to call them. To prove it, she walks back to the corner of the room where the Frankenstein comment originated and asks, "Is there a problem back here?" in the kind of disapproving teacher tone that freaks people out. But it seems like she's fair and has a decent sense of humor. She'll probably do a good job of making history interesting, possibly because she's witnessed a lot of it firsthand.

"I'd like to walk you through what we will be doing this year," she says. "I'm sure there will be numerous questions, but I'd like you to save them until I finish."

That sounds like a complicated way of saying we're going to be loaded down with a lot of homework.

She holds up a textbook and talks for a while about tests and projects and then launches into a boring lecture about what she will expect from us. After what feels like forever, she looks up and says, "Some of you may have already heard about our upcoming field trip."

I've been so distracted by Lauren all afternoon that I'd forgotten about Abner Farms.

Right away, kids start whispering to each other. Mrs. Frankel waits for us to settle down and then begins. "As I already mentioned, sixth-grade curriculum includes study of the Revolutionary War. Traditionally, we set aside an entire day for the sixth-grade class to participate in an experiential learning event to focus on this important period in our nation's history. We partner with a great organization called Abner Farms in rural Wisconsin, just an hour or so north of here."

She pauses, seemingly irritated with us already.

"Well, this year, the powers that be have decided to make this a longer event by taking advantage of Abner Farms' camping facilities for a three-day stay."

I can tell by the way she says "powers that be" that Mrs. Frankel is not psyched, which seems weird. I thought teachers loved field trips. Everyone else is, though, and some kids are high-fiving each other like they are personally responsible for this development.

"Quiet, please. Usually this field trip takes place in the spring, but another school's cancellation has created an opportunity for us. Our trip will serve as an experiment of sorts, to determine whether adding an overnight component enhances the learning experience." She rolls her eyes toward the ceiling, and it's pretty clear she doesn't believe this will enhance anything. I guess spending three solid days with us is not appealing to her.

Turning to her white board, Mrs. Frankel writes *Thursday, October 7 – Saturday, October 9*. From the corner, Tiffany and Claire, girls from my elementary school, are already whining about a travel soccer tournament they might have to miss. Now that I think about it, I'm going to have to miss a soccer game too.

Lifting a stack of papers from her desk, she continues. "I'm passing out information for you to share with your parents, a packing list, and a permission form." Mrs. Frankel looks like she has more to say, but at least fifteen people are raising their hands with questions.

I scan the packet of papers as soon as it hits my desk. Abner Farms Colonial Village and Campsite promises to take us back in time to the birth of our nation. The list of activities is almost a whole page long, and each one sounds better than the next—wood chopping, archery, crafts, and an orienteering course in which teams will use compasses and maps to find checkpoints in the woods. Everybody sleeps in colonial tents, and right away I'm hoping we can choose our bunkmates—but I decide not to ask Mrs. Frankel about that. I'm sure someone else will.

I read over the packing list, and a paragraph about contraband makes me laugh a little. Obviously no one had cell phones in colonial times, so we have to leave them at home. A threatening letter outlines expected behavior and is followed by a list of violations and the corresponding punishment. Almost any infraction seems to involve parents driving into the woods to collect their young criminal.

I'm imagining the smell of a campfire when I turn the page and see something that stops me cold.

Colonial cooking with six authentic meals.

My thoughts scatter in a hundred different directions like a bagful of marbles spilled on a tile floor. I force myself to read on, my stomach clenching with each nauseating word:

Arrival Day Dinner: Pulled pork over brown bread, glazed carrots, slaw, watermelon
Supper: Brunswick beef barley stew, succotash, red pepper cornbread, chocolate pudding
Morning Meal: Grits, flapjacks and eggs, sausages roasted on sticks

I have to stop reading after *sausages on sticks*.

I will be the only starving colonist at Abner Farms.

4

HAVE YOUR CAKE AND EAT IT TOO

Wanna help me find a baby picture to bring to school tomorrow?" my sister, Maddie, who's eight, asks as I walk into the kitchen. I've been upstairs trying to avoid thinking about my first night of sixth-grade math homework and the Abner Farms handouts.

She's sitting at the kitchen table surrounded by stacks of photos. A dozen are lined up in front of her. In each one she's wearing a different pink dress and grinning ear to ear. It's hard to believe that little bald head grew all the long blond curls she has now.

Randomly, I choose one and push it toward her. Mostly I'm focused on a photo on the other side of the table. It's a picture of me on my first birthday. I'm sitting in my high chair, laughing and rubbing birthday cake in my hair. I probably started out wearing clothes and a bib, but in the picture I've been stripped down to my diaper. White frosting is stuck in the folds of my chubby little arms and under my neck. I reach across the table and grab it so I can take a closer look.

Mom says I used to love birthday cake. And strawberries. And pizza. Apparently, I used to eat anything I could get my hands on.

I can't remember back that far. Without photographic evidence, I'd never believe I ate any of those things. It feels like for my entire life, I've only eaten the ten things I eat now. And honestly, I can't imagine that will ever change.

"Ick," Maddie says as she glances at the picture in my hand. "Who did that to you?"

"Ben did that to himself," Mom says, taking a pot off the

stove. "That's what happens at a baby's first birthday party."

I crack up at the look of disbelief on Maddie's face. It's like she's just learned I was raised by wolves. She's never seen me get anywhere near a birthday cake.

Before Maddie can ask any more questions, Mom hands her a plate of raw carrots, broccoli, and snap peas arranged around a mound of hummus and me a plate of sliced apple.

Carrying two bowls of steaming pasta, Mom follows us into the family room. Most nights Maddie and I eat in here. We sit on the floor on the same side of the coffee table so we can both see the TV. Maddie sits on a couch cushion so she can reach her dinner. I don't really fit at the coffee table anymore, but I make it work. I like to eat this way. With nobody watching me.

I flip past channels until I find one of those stupid singing talent shows Maddie loves so much. I'm too distracted to care about what's on. I keep thinking about that photo.

Gran says my eating went haywire after I choked on a penny I found on the ground at the zoo, but once when I asked Mom about it, she said the choking scared the grown-ups way more than it scared me. That was also the summer Maddie was born and I had four ear infections, so there was a lot going on. But none of those things seem like an adequate explanation.

What I do know is that most foods just don't seem like food to me—or like anything I'd ever put in my mouth and swallow. And most stuff grosses me out because of the way it looks or smells or sounds when somebody eats it—like oatmeal. I've never really been able to explain my strange eating habits to myself or anyone else. And I've pretty much given up on trying, since no one believes what I have to say about it anyway. I'm a one-of-a-kind eating oddity, as elusive as Bigfoot or the Loch Ness Monster. Sometimes it can be a pretty lonely existence.

As long as I can remember, I've never had a birthday

cake. Never stuffed myself with Halloween candy. Never tasted a burger straight from the grill. Or tried Gran's famous homemade baked macaroni and cheese. But the thing is, I'm content with what I *do* eat, even though there's not much variety. It definitely bothers other people, though. Mostly adults. Especially my parents.

Mom and Dad call me *picky*. I hate that word. It makes me sound like a pain in the butt. Or a whiny toddler. They're convinced I'm stubborn and my eating inflexibility is all in my head.

But it's real to me.

I'm startled back to reality when an especially bad singer takes the stage. Desperate to escape the noise, I rush through the rest of my buttered pasta and sliced apple. Just as I'm about to stand up, Mom comes back in. She has an irritated look on her face.

"Guess who your Brownie leader is this week?" Mom asks Maddie.

Maddie always loves a guessing game. She names five of her friends' mothers before Mom finally stops her and points to herself with what looks like fake enthusiasm. "Mrs. Jones has to fly to Arizona to take care of Bethany's grandma for a week. Apparently I was the only volunteer."

Maddie is oblivious to everything except her own excitement about this news. Her reaction is so joyfully out of control that you'd think she just found out she's going to Disney World.

As she dances around the family room, Mom looks at me. "You and Dad will be on your own for dinner on Thursday night."

The cruddiest parts of my day—Darren's obnoxious comments at lunch, Josh's quest for popularity, and the Abner Farms menu—reshuffle in my brain, making space for an even worse kind of disaster: a private dinner with my dad.

5

In a Pickle

It's the fourth day of school. I keep hoping that Darren and those other guys will find somewhere else to eat, but every day they head straight for our table like we've all been sitting together for years. Josh and Nick are more psyched about the daily invasion than I am.

Today I wish I sat on the end instead of right smack in the middle of the long table. I wish it even more when Darren sits right next to me.

"Hey, longlegs," he says to me and I nod. He starts pulling a bunch of random things out of his lunch bag and arranging them in a line. A baggie holding a monster-sized pickle. A brown banana. A huge sandwich with lettuce and alfalfa sprouts poking out like tentacles. A can of orange soda. And three Oreos.

I keep my food in my bag—something I haven't done at lunch in years. I don't need any more of Darren's comments. I catch him looking down at my lunch bag, staring at it for a second, and then looking up at me with a creepy grin. He opens his mouth to say something, but suddenly Nick yells from the other end of the table.

"Check this out!" Nick's face is inches away from his sloppy joe, which is the featured cafeteria item today.

"What?" somebody asks.

Without saying a word, Nick pulls a thick, long hair from his sandwich. Pinching it between two fingers, he dangles it in the air like a prize.

"Oh, man, I'm gonna puke," Alex says, and then everyone's laughing, including me. But the thing is, there's a distinct possibility that I might actually puke. I haven't even taken a bite of my lunch yet, but it feels like something is stuck in my throat, and I'm starting to gag.

I was already not feeling so great about what Darren's pickle might smell like once it hits the open air, but I'll handle it. The hair in the sloppy joe is the bigger problem. I stand up, not really sure what I'm going to do. The guys are still laughing, and I decide to walk over to the water fountain and chill for a second. I must look pretty green, because when I stand up, Darren takes one look at me and yells, "He's gonna hurl!"

Darren's announcement gets a lot of attention, and kids from a few different tables turn to see what's going on. I gulp some water and swallow it hard, forcing it to push down whatever was creeping up my throat, and while I'm staring into the water fountain, I make a game plan.

When I get back to the table, I yell, "Man, was that gross or what?"

Everybody laughs, and I figure I'm off the hook.

Honestly, I'm not even hungry anymore. But I take a bite of bagel and try to clear my mind. Some of the guys are talking about football, and I pretend to be interested. I can't get my head around it, but Nick is actually eating his sloppy joe.

Without looking, I know the pickle has come out of its bag. I inhale through my mouth, but the smell reminds me of pee, grossing me out even more. Then, if things aren't bad enough, Darren turns to me and exhales his hot pickle-urine breath at me. He's staring at my lunch bag.

"Thought you were goin' down a minute ago."

I turn to face him. "It's no big deal."

"Yeah," he says so quietly that I can barely hear him over the blare of the lunchroom. "Really nasty."

I don't know why he's bringing it up again, but it feels like he's up to something.

"Want an Oreo?" He pushes them in my direction.

"No thanks," I say, turning away from Darren and toward the debate about Big Ten football going on at the end of the table. I don't bother taking the rest of my food out. There's no way I'm going to be able to eat.

"Yeah, I didn't think so," Darren says.

I manage to ignore him for the last fifteen minutes of lunch, but he follows me over to the garbage can on my way out of the cafeteria.

"Hey, longlegs," he calls from behind.

I freeze for a moment, then drop my bag of uneaten lunch in the can and turn to face him. I look past his smug face to the other side of the cafeteria, where Josh and Nick are waiting for me. A sudden heat rushes through my body. "Quit calling me that."

"Chill, dude," Darren says, smirking like someone who's just cheated a little kid out of a quarter at a lemonade stand. He tosses his own bag past me and into the garbage can. "No need to get all wound up."

"Just cut it out," I say as I walk away.

But he's right next to me, heading toward Josh and Nick like we're all together.

His voice is quiet, almost like a whisper. "Why do they bother with a spineless freak like you?"

He can't be serious. I turn to look at him, and he shrugs like he's not completely sure himself.

"See you in science," Darren says, loud enough for Josh and Nick to hear before he walks through the cafeteria doors and disappears into the crowd.

"What was that all about?" Nick asks me.

"Nothing."

6

RECIPE FOR DISASTER

Shake it off.

I repeat it over and over again in my head, but the pounding in my ears and the angry storm rushing through my body gives me a strange, twitchy feeling that makes it impossible to take my own advice. So I fix my gaze on the window at the end of the hall and make my way to science class.

That Darren kid is bad news. And I'm pretty sure I'm the only one who sees it.

I had planned to hang out in the hall until Lauren arrived and then edge out Darren for the seat next to hers, but now my confidence is shot. I head to the far back corner of the classroom instead.

After a few minutes, Lauren shows up with a couple of girls. Today her long black hair is pulled up in a ponytail that swirls into a perfect coil and bounces as she moves. It's entertaining enough to temporarily distract me from my sour mood. Another girl has saved her a seat, and knowing that Darren has been edged out cheers me up a little. I decide to take it as a sign. Maybe the lab partner assignments will go my way.

Class starts, and Mr. Butler gets right down to business reading names and assigning lab partners. Right away Darren is paired with another boy, and I hold back a smile. My chances are improving. But then Lauren's name is called along with the name of one of the girls she's sitting with, and I try not to take their excitement personally while I start looking around the room to see who's left. I've been so focused on

Lauren and Darren that I haven't really considered any other possibilities for my own lab partner.

Right away I notice Olivia sitting by herself up front, and my heart skips a couple of beats while I try to convince myself it won't happen—my day is bad enough already. It couldn't possibly get worse. But my mind goes into overdrive anyway, hitting all the highlights on the tour of her breath-taking weirdness.

In kindergarten, she was the kind of kid who liked to wear costumes to school even when it wasn't Halloween. Mostly superhero stuff. At recess sometimes she'd wear a cape under her coat, and it would stick out at the bottom. Other times she'd ask Ms. Thomas to tie it over the outside of her coat. That's when Olivia seemed the happiest, when she was running across the playground with her red cape blowing behind her.

In first grade, she stopped wearing capes and started wearing orange. Orange dresses. Orange pants. It was pretty intense, especially against her red hair. In second grade, she used a fake French accent. And in third grade, something happened that was discussed so much it basically became true—whether it really was or not.

It was Josh who swore he saw it—but sometimes I'm not so sure. He said when he was in the far back corner of the school library, near the books about space travel, he saw Olivia sitting on the floor, leaning against a bookshelf, and picking her nose.

That was the day Olivia Slotnick became Olivia Snotlick.

The name followed her for years, trailing behind her in whispered voices like the red cape. Sometimes kids were more obvious about it, calling out, "Hey, snotlick, picked any good ones lately?" and other stupid stuff when they thought a grown-up wouldn't hear. At first, she'd raise her chin and say, "I do *not*." But after a while, she just walked away—probably because that's what her parents told her to do. We had an unusual number of special talks about kindness in third and fourth grade, and we all assumed it was because of Olivia.

By fifth grade, everybody pretty much stopped with the name-calling. I think we were all a little impressed with ourselves for being the oldest kids at Edgebrook School, and we bought into the message about "setting an example" for the younger ones that our principal, Mr. Edwards, drilled into us all the time. So instead of teasing her, everybody ignored her. Sometimes I think that might have been worse.

I wish I could say I never called her Olivia Snotlick or I never snickered behind her back or ignored her, but I did. And I wish I could say, now that I'm older, I'm way past that type of thing. But it's clear to me now that I'm not.

I know this because when Mr. Butler calls out our names together, my stomach drops like an elevator with a snapped cable. I want to beg him to give me anybody else. Or tell him I need to work alone. I do some quick mental calculations, estimating the number of days until the end of the school year and how many hours I will be forced to sit next to Olivia. And talk to her. And work with her. It's bad enough to have Darren on my case. But being associated with Olivia could completely ruin me socially.

As I trudge toward our assigned lab table in the back of the room, a couple of guys snicker. The loudest laugh is Darren's. This is becoming a seriously irritating day.

I slide my chair over toward the aisle and as far away from Olivia as humanly possible. She doesn't seem to care. She's too busy stacking up her folder and her binder and her science book in a perfectly symmetrical pile, which gives me a chance to evaluate just how strange she is these days.

I don't want her to notice me looking at her, so I take a few quick glimpses that don't yield anything too alarming. Jeans. High tops. Blue T-shirt with the word *Antarctica* or *Africa* or *Arizona* or something starting with an A. Bunches of curly red hair that have escaped from her ponytail. And one pretty cool friendship bracelet, which makes me feel better for a second. Because maybe she's normal enough now to have at least one friend. Or maybe she's completely friendless and strange enough to have made it herself.

As Mr. Butler rambles on and on about scientific method and classifying matter and other uninspiring things we're going to work on as lab partners this fall, I take another look at the bracelet. Lots of girls wear them—even some boys wear them for a couple of weeks at the end of the summer if they've been away at camp—but I've never seen one like this. It's extra wide, over an inch, and the design is a complicated series of interlocking gray and turquoise zig-zagging threads. Somebody worked on it for a really long time.

I turn back toward Mr. Butler and pretend I care about his endless list of projects and experiments—but out of the corner of my eye, I see Olivia is now looking at me. Right *at* me. Not casually glancing my way for a second. She's actually staring. I'm glad we're in the back so nobody can see what she's doing. I sit completely still like I'm in a horror movie and I don't want the bogeyman to find me under the bed, but she won't stop looking at me. Sweat is beading on my forehead, but I refuse to wipe it away.

Finally, after the longest five seconds of my life, I turn my head, just a little, and give her a look that says, *What's wrong with you?* Suddenly I'm not feeling so bad about how everybody treated her for all those years, because she is obviously a very peculiar person. I start to consider some drastic ways to solve my lab partner problem, like hacking into Mr. Wright's computer and changing my schedule. I could move math and English to the afternoon and put science and history in the morning. Or maybe I could fake a letter from my parents to the school board.

Then Olivia does the creepiest thing. She smiles at me.

I panic. And then I do the dumbest thing. I smile back.

7

EASY AS PIE

Good afternoon, class," Mrs. Frankel says as she pulls the door closed. "I have an important announcement."

I'm barely listening. I'm too busy trying to figure out how to fix my lab partner problem.

"I'm hoping some of you will consider running for student government." She pauses for a moment, and when she starts talking again, she's slightly more energized. "I can think of no better way to get to know your new classmates than by serving on our student council. If you're interested, please take an information sheet on your way out today, and declare your candidacy on the sign-up sheet in the hall."

"I hear Lauren Walters is running for president," someone behind me whispers.

Suddenly, my lab partner problems are old news. I know what I can do to change my own luck: I'll become vice president and serve by Lauren's side. I can already picture us presiding over important debates about educational policy, quietly conferring about the best ways to govern, and supporting each other during times of student council stress. It won't take long for her to realize how great we could be together.

As soon as class ends, I grab one of the student council flyers off Mrs. Frankel's desk and head straight to the sign-up sheet in the hall. Lauren's is the second name on the list to run for president—I've never heard of the kid running against her—but the vice president slots are all empty. I write *Ben Snyder* in neat block letters and step back to admire my work. My name looks pretty good there by itself.

Being Lauren's vice president will be even better than being her lab partner.

8

TAKEN WITH A GRAIN OF SALT

Where are we going?" I ask Josh and Nick as we get on the bus after school.

"Don't look at me," Nick says. "My mom's got a full house today 'cause my sister's nanny quit and—"

I cut him off. "Got it. Those kids are out of control."

Nick is the youngest of six—"a surprise," as his mother calls him. His brothers and sisters are all total adults, with minivans and kids and jobs. Usually his house is full of people—babies, grandparents, and cousins. It's total chaos, but in a cool way because everyone's always happy to be together. Nick has been changing diapers and warming up bottles for his nieces and nephews since he was a little kid himself, which has made him the most popular babysitter in our neighborhood. I bet he's going to have enough money to buy himself a car before he even gets his permit.

"They act crazier around you," Nick says. "Marissa told me she's gonna marry you."

"Just what I need," I say, laughing. "A four-year-old fiancée."

Josh rolls his eyes. "Let's go to my house. No rugrats."

"Fine with me," I say, even though I'd rather head home. My plan to be Lauren's vice president has turned my day around, but a monster headache has threatened to hit all afternoon, hovering close like impending thunder. That's the price I pay for dumping my lunch in the garbage. I seriously need to chill out and eat something before it balloons into a full-blown storm.

Josh and Nick don't ever come right out and say it, but

my house is always their last choice because my mom doesn't buy the kinds of things they like to eat after school: Cheetos, Pop-Tarts, chips and queso. To say our snack options are lackluster is an understatement.

When we get to Josh's house, his mom is strangely excited to see us. She's wearing a tennis skirt, and I try to remember if I've ever seen her when she's *not* wearing a tennis skirt. Tennis is the primary language spoken in the Callahan household. Their den is lined with trophies. Josh plays three times a week during the school year and every single day during the summer.

"Boys! It's so great to see you. Tell me all about Crestwood, because Josh hasn't told me a thing."

Josh hasn't looked up from his phone since we got off the bus. I don't think he's even heard her, and I'm pretty sure she's going to use that to her advantage.

"Ben, you're growing like a weed! And to think you were born with those perfectly straight teeth. I'm sure the girls are all fighting for your attention."

"Yeah, my dentist says I have perfect alignment," I mumble.

The combination of this awkward conversation and the gnawing hunger pulsating under my ribs is making me nauseous. I shoot Nick a look of desperation, hoping he'll jump in and save me, but he just shakes his head, his black spiky hair jerking back and forth like the crest of a tropical bird.

Mrs. Callahan turns to Nick, possibly worried she's hurt his feelings. "Nicholas, I bet you're going to have a growth spurt soon. Your father's a tall man—"

"Okay, Mom, this is getting weird. We're gonna do some homework," Josh lies. He stares at his mother until she backs out of the kitchen.

As soon as she's gone, Josh and Nick jostle for position— first in front of the pantry, then at the fridge. One of them tosses a new bag of pretzels in my direction and I rip it open, knowing it won't do the job. They've assembled a small feast on the kitchen counter—leftover fried chicken, barbeque potato chips, peanut butter crackers, trail mix, and a package of chocolate chip cookies. I might not be the best to judge, but this seems like a messed-up combination of food. But Josh and Nick go at it like it's a race, scarfing it all down in no apparent order.

I chew pretzel after pretzel, almost in a daze. I've witnessed their feasting ritual a million times, but for some reason right now it feels like I'm watching them from the wrong end of a telescope. I wonder what it would be like to get so much satisfaction from a food fest. I know Darren is getting in my head because I'm starting to feel like everyone else in the world, including my two best friends, are part of this exclusive club where eating is never a big deal. I'd love to be able to show up anywhere and be okay about whatever's put in front of me. But I don't think that's ever going to happen. It's about as likely as Josh and Nick deciding to start eating dryer lint at every meal.

Even with the pretzels hitting my stomach, I'm still nauseous. I zone out like I'm in a trance until Nick brings up the stupid hair from lunch.

"That was wicked gross," Josh says, wiping his mouth with the back of his arm.

Nick holds his hand in front of his face while he laughs. It seems like he started doing that when he got braces, which, honestly, I appreciate. The last thing I need is an upfront and personal view of what's caught in his steel trap. Everybody keeps saying how lucky I am to be able to avoid the pain of braces, but the best part for me is not having to deal with keeping them clean. I'd probably have to go on a liquid diet.

"Darren was lovin' it," Nick says. "He cracks me up."

This seems like a good chance for me to jump in. "What's his deal, anyway? He's kind of annoying."

"Darren's fine. He just likes to mess around with people," Josh says as he stuffs another handful of crackers in his mouth.

It didn't feel like Darren was "just messing around" with me today after lunch.

Nick nods. "Have you seen him do his impression of Principal Wright? It's spot-on."

"Well, he's not so great at soccer. He didn't make the travel team," I say, trying to sound matter of fact.

"Really?" Josh suddenly seems more interested. "His brothers were the best quarterbacks in the history of Shermer High. They both play college ball. Darren's got the jock gene."

"Oh yeah," I say, not really caring. "The Douglas boys. I remember them."

"Wait," Nick says. "Are you telling me those guys are named Duke, Drew, and Darren *Douglas*?" He can't hide his laugh behind his hand fast enough, and I catch an unfortunate look into his metal abyss.

"Sounds like dog names to me," I say, and I'm relieved when Josh and Nick laugh at my joke.

Darren might have been born into a high-achieving litter, but as far as I'm concerned, the only thing he seems to excel at is being a loudmouthed jerk.

Josh's phone lights up for the thousandth time, and within a second of picking it up, he's chuckling about whatever he's read. Right away his fingers are moving, and he laughs again.

Finally, he looks back up. "Do you guys know that tall dude, JT?"

Nick and I shrug. We've probably seen the kid around school, but we don't have Josh's abnormal skill for remembering every single name of every single person we've ever met.

But I know where Josh is going. Lately he's been talking about how we need to establish our *squad*. The first time he said it, Nick and I thought he was joking. "You mean like a cop car?" I had asked.

"No, it's a legit thing. Like your group—your crew, your buds. The people you hang out with and can count on. Brian has one."

Brian is Josh's older brother. He's sixteen and, according to Josh, the definition of cool.

Suddenly Nick was taking it all a little more seriously. "How many people do you need for a squad?" he had asked.

"More than three."

Finishing off the last of the barbeque chips, Josh drones on about how awesome JT and his friends are. JT is a twin—his sister Tiffany is in Josh's social studies class. But I barely listen. A heavy, tired feeling creeps over my body like a slow onset of the flu.

Three has always been enough for me.

9

NUGGETS OF TRUTH

I don't bother asking Dad where he's taking me for dinner. We're headed toward the mall, so there will be about a hundred options. I'll probably be okay with any of them—grilled cheese is pretty standard at most places. But I'd prefer a restaurant where I don't have to order it off the kids' menu. It's bad enough without Dad's eye roll.

Sports radio is saving us from having a conversation. During a commercial, he turns and asks me, "So how's your day been, buddy?" in a real friendly voice. But his eyes don't look so friendly.

When he calls me "buddy" I usually smile, remembering when he'd let me sit in the front seat of the car during what he called "Quick Coffee Runs." He'd wink at me and say, "Let's skip the car seat, buddy. Come up here with me." He never said, "Don't tell Mom." He didn't have to. I knew she'd be furious, even though Starbucks is only a few blocks away. When we'd get there he'd ask, "You want anything? Hot chocolate? Cookie?" But I always said no.

We never sat down inside, which was good for me because the smell of hot coffee makes me feel sick. Anytime I'm ever in Starbucks for more than a few minutes, that stink gets on my clothes and on my skin and I have to change my shirt when I get home. Really, I only liked the Quick Coffee Runs for the sitting-in-the-front-seat part. But now I'm too old to get excited about where I sit in the car.

Dad puts on his turn signal to make a lane change. It feels like everything's going in slow motion while I'm trying to figure out what to tell him about my day. I want to tell him it was a great day. I want to tell him I love being in middle school. I want to tell him I like the guys who we've been sitting with at lunch all week. But those would all be lies. So I tell him the one good thing that is true. I tell him about running for student council.

He doesn't respond, and I start to wonder if he's even heard me. Suddenly, he does the strangest thing—he makes a quick turn into McDonald's and parks the car.

"Good job," he says, unbuckling his seatbelt like this is the most normal place for us to have dinner. If he wants to reward me for my political aspirations, that's okay with me.

The relief of knowing what I'm about to eat is outweighed by a nagging uneasiness. Dad hates McDonald's, so this feels like it might be a set-up. But once we walk through the door and I'm hit with that distinctive McDonald's smell, I really don't care why we're here. Right now, I'm pumped.

If I had to choose only one place to eat for the rest of my life, it would be McDonald's. Any McDonald's. They're all the same. The food is exactly the same. And everything looks the same too. Same wrappers, same paper inserts on the trays, same napkin dispensers that always get stuck so you have to take about fifty napkins when you only needed four. There are no surprises at McDonald's.

Carrying our tray, I follow Dad to an empty table in the corner. He opens up the box containing his Quarter Pounder and inspects it. I'm sure he'll start in with his long list of complaints about this place any second now, so I start to eat right away before he can ruin my dinner.

I'm in my zone. Eating nuggets right here in McDonald's is the best because they're still hot and crispy. I always get the ten-piece. Honestly, ten is too many, but the Happy Meal six-count isn't quite enough.

My routine never varies. The first thing I do when I open a box of nuggets is take a quick inventory of the shapes. My favorite shape is the one I call "Louisiana" because it looks exactly like an outline of the state. Its official McDonald's name is the "boot." I like it the best because of the extra crunch around the tip where the toes would go. My least favorite is the round one—but I don't get those too often. The bell shape and the bow-tie shape are pretty much identical, but you can figure out which is which if you look hard. I know they all taste the same, but I still like the Louisiana ones the best. This box has four bells, two bows, three Louisiana's, and one round. Not bad.

I eat my nuggets first. Then I work on the fries. I eat McDonald's fries in the restaurant, or in the car, but not at home. By the time you get fries home, they're soggy. And no matter what you do to them, they never get their crunch back. I only really like the crispy ones anyway. The long, droopy ones are too mushy. When I eat at McDonald's, I dip my fries in ketchup. Only once per fry. And only in the ketchup from the packets. The stuff you squirt into the tiny cups is watery. My mom swears there's no difference, but she's wrong.

I'm halfway through my food before either one of us says anything.

"So how's the team shaping up?" Dad asks.

I relax a bit, settling into the same feeling I get when the seatbelt sign dings off on an airplane. We're flying in safe territory.

I tell him about playing forward and how I'm getting used to the new coach and new teammates. He peppers me with questions and follows up on everything, but in a good way. We go back and forth for a while, and I like the way he focuses on everything I say.

"Now that you're playing on the top travel team, I bet varsity soccer is in your future."

"You really think so?"

He reaches across the table and takes one of my fries. But instead of popping it into his mouth, he holds it between our faces.

I shouldn't have let my guard down.

"You know, dedicated athletes fuel their bodies." He points the fry at me as he talks, using it for emphasis. "You can't fill your body with this junk all the time and expect it to perform."

My gaze drops to the table. "I'm holding my own."

"Well, for *now* you are. But if you want to play in high school, or college, probably not."

I thought I shut him down on this argument a long time ago when I told him about what Usain Bolt, the Jamaican sprinter, ate in Beijing when he won three Olympic gold medals. Apparently he thought the food in China was weird, so he stuck with what he knew—chowing down on one hundred McDonald's Chicken McNuggets every day for ten days. Smart guy.

But I don't think this is the time to remind Dad about Usain.

He closes the box holding the rest of his Quarter Pounder and shakes his head in disgust. "This isn't even real food."

I wish an over-eager McDonald's manager would swing by and defend my nuggets with some impressive nutritional information about USDA-inspected white meat like they talk about on the commercials. But Dad would never believe it anyway.

I don't bother with a response. I've never been able to convince him of the virtues of McDonald's. He doesn't understand how much I count on this institution to never let me down.

Dad stares past me and sighs. "You're too old for this picky eating business."

I sit perfectly still, staring at the table. I want to fire off a bunch of snarky responses like he's the last one standing in a dodgeball game. I've got all the balls lined up on my side, ready to go.

Stop calling me names.

You think I have control over this?

Do you know how hard I'm trying?

But I don't say anything. I never do. He never listens to me when it comes to the way I eat, so why bother?

He pops the fry in his mouth and smiles like he has a great idea.

"Next time I'll take you somewhere that serves *real* chicken."

I nod along with his revolting descriptions of all the kinds of chicken available to the easy-going chicken-eaters of the world—barbeque chicken, buttermilk-fried chicken, spicy Thai chicken...

I hope there's never a next time.

10

WHEN LIFE GIVES YOU LEMONS

I'm back in my least favorite spot in the world—next to Olivia in science class. Even dinner with Dad last week was better than this.

"You might want to check number four," Olivia says, her mechanical pencil tapping on my homework.

I ignore her. Up front, everyone is laughing and having fun before Mr. Butler starts class. Being stuck back here with Olivia feels like some sort of undeserved punishment.

"Because it's wrong—like completely wrong."

I pull the paper closer to my side of our table and turn away, pretending to read what Mr. Butler is writing on the whiteboard.

"I mean, it's *your* homework. You can do it wrong if you want."

Like a nasty rash, being Olivia's lab partner has only gotten more irritating with time. She always has to be right, always has to double-check my work, and lately has started to take it upon herself to inspect my homework before I turn it in. I don't even know how she is so smart—she spends half of class reading novels she hides under our lab table.

"The average depth of the ocean floor is twelve *thousand* feet, but you wrote twelve *hundred*."

I grab my pencil and add a zero to the end of my answer.

"Thanks," I whisper, not looking at her.

"Aren't you gonna add a comma?"

"Aren't you gonna mind your own business?" It's out of my mouth before I can stop it.

Her reaction is loud enough to get everyone's attention.

"Just. Trying. To. Help."

Darren turns around first. He sits way up front, surrounded by the kids in our class who are definitely learning the least but making up for it by having the most fun. Darren has become their self-appointed leader. He hasn't bothered me much at lunch during the past couple of days because everyone's been busy guessing how the tent assignments at Abner Farms will work out. The permission slip asks for our requests, but there are no guarantees. If I had my way, I'd like a tent of three—Josh, Nick, and me. But the tents all have six cots.

Now here in class, Darren is making up for lost time. He won't let his fans down.

"Trouble in paradise, Mr. Vice President?" he asks in a concerned voice, triggering hysterics from everyone in his comedy club.

Everyone except Lauren. I have no idea if she's not laughing because she missed what Darren said or if she just doesn't think it's funny. Either way, it seems like a promising development. Up front, she swivels around in her seat, turning to look at Olivia and me. I'm momentarily paralyzed, desperate to make sense of the expression on her face and fighting the urge to slide off my chair and slip under our lab table into oblivion. But instead, I hold myself perfectly still and smile at her. After a second, she turns back around.

I'm pumped. Because good or bad, I'm finally on her radar. Now all I have to do is prove to her and the rest of the sixth-grade class that I should be her vice president.

"Quiet down," Mr. Butler says, not even turning from the white board. Darren seizes the opportunity to take one more shot at us by swiveling around in his seat and making a series of fake kissing noises. Everyone is fighting back explosive laughter—the kind that might be physically dangerous to hold in. Everyone but Olivia and me. And, thankfully, Lauren.

Darren's kiss noises remind me of the first day of school, when he was eyeballing my Hershey's Kisses as part of my "sad excuse for a lunch," but all the attention on my table is annoying. I can't figure out why I'm being lumped together with Olivia Snotlick. It must be the social demote of the century.

Olivia isn't bothered by any of it. I feel her staring at me—hard and critical like the way my mom inspects bananas before she puts a bunch in her grocery cart.

"So you're running for student council?" she whispers.

I nod without looking at her and wonder why she feels compelled to voice every random thought that bounces through her genius mind.

"So what's your platform?"

I turn to her, openmouthed. "*Platform?*"

"You know, your political agenda, campaign promises…"

Mr. Butler shoots us a look, but I lean in closer to her as soon as he turns around again.

"I'm running for vice president of the *sixth grade*. Not the whole country." I shake my head. "Plus, as of this morning, no one's even running against me, so I don't have much to worry about."

She sits back in her chair and crosses her arms. "It's never too early to take one's civic duty seriously."

"If you're so smart, why don't you run?"

I'm not sure she's heard me. But after a few seconds, she scribbles something in the top corner of her notebook and slides it over to me. *I have no interest in student council. My focus RN is on the environment.*

I want to respond with *You'd never win anyway*, but I don't.

At the end of class, Mr. Butler returns our lab assignments about erosion.

"Nice job," he says as he hands Olivia our worksheet, another hundred percent marked across the top. So far we each have a solid A-plus—thanks almost entirely to Olivia and her quest for perfection. Also, she's really smart. But I'd trade all those As for a spot up front with the normal people. Minus Darren.

The instant the bell rings, I'm out of my seat and headed for the door. I want to be gone before Darren slings any more comments my way.

But before I can escape, Olivia calls out from our table, "Ben, don't forget about the science fair meeting after school!"

I hate how she's just announced I'm on track to become a science nerd. Mr. Butler sent an email to my mom inviting me to participate based on some placement test I took last year. I guess it's kind of a big deal. As soon as Mom mentioned it, I said, "No way." But she convinced me to at least go to the meeting to see what it's all about.

I rush out the door, and I'm halfway down the hall when I hear my name called again. I don't even bother to turn around. I don't want any part of whatever weird thing Olivia wants to tell me next.

"Ben! Wait up!"

Finally I stop and turn around.

But it's not Olivia.

It's Lauren. And Lauren knows my name.

"Hi," she says, rushing up to me. "I'm Lauren Walters."

It takes every ounce of self-control not to say something totally stupid like "I know." And all that self-control is short-circuiting the same part of my brain that should be thinking of what I'll say beyond "Hi." For now, it's all I've got.

Fortunately, Lauren is talking a mile a minute. I can barely follow everything she's saying because I'm so distracted by how pretty she is up close.

"I wanted to introduce myself because, well, I'm trying to meet all the sixth graders in our class and learn their names. I figure it's a good place to start in getting to know people. Learning their names."

I nod. "Impressive. That's over a hundred names."

"And also, I wanted to meet *you* because *you're* running for vice president and *I'm* running for president, and it seems like we should know each other."

I nod again. For some reason, my second nod throws her off.

"I mean I really *want* to learn everyone's name. It's not just a gimmick or something for my campaign. I hope that's not how it sounds." She seems to be running out of steam.

"I didn't think that at all."

"Oh, good. You're making me feel better."

"Plus," I say, "if we both win, we'll be on student council together. So we should know each other."

"Right," she says, nodding so excitedly that now she looks like a bobble head.

I want to keep this conversation going forever. And I want to say something that will help Lauren ease off on the nodding. There's only one thing that comes to mind, and I'm just desperate enough to use it.

"So what's your platform?"

Lauren stops mid-nod. "What?"

"Your campaign. What's it about? What do you want to do if you win?"

"Ohmygosh. I have so many ideas. Mostly I want to start a peer-tutoring club. I'll tell you more about it at the election meeting."

Honestly, I didn't even know there was an election meeting scheduled. But I'm already looking forward to it.

11

Icing on the Cake

I spend the rest of the afternoon hyped up. A quick check of the flyer posted outside Mrs. Frankel's classroom brings me up to speed on the election meeting next week, during which we will review the campaign rules and have a chance to hang up our four school-approved posters. I'm still the only one running for vice president, but now there are a bunch of kids running for secretary and treasurer.

Before I can go home and start to think about my posters, I have the stupid after-school science fair meeting. At three thirty, I walk back into Mr. Butler's classroom, which is crammed with a crew of geeky overachievers, most with a musical instrument case dropped on the floor next to a humungous backpack. I take a seat at the back and pull out a packet of granola bars, sliding one out of the wrapper without making too much noise. I'll save the second one for later.

Mr. Butler is a completely different person with this audience. He's relaxed and makes a few science jokes, one of which I don't even understand. After he finishes his spiel about the incredible opportunity to begin our journey into the world of competitive science, I understand that if I want to survive middle school, I cannot be affiliated with this group of kids.

Reluctantly, I take his information sheet and shove it into my backpack, not caring if it rips. There's no way I'm going to do this. I'll tell Mom it's a firm *no*. I force myself to sit through Mr. Butler's endless explanation of how participation in the science fair works. Every single thing he says prompts someone to ask a ridiculous question. Just when

I'm sure we will be trapped here for eternity, Mr. Butler starts to wrap it up, promising to respond to any emails.

"Oh, and I almost forgot," he adds, oblivious to how painfully boring this is. "We have a record number of kids participating in the science fair this year, so I've decided to add two lunch meetings a week to help everyone stay on track, starting next Monday. We'll call it Science Fair Lunch Bunch."

A cheeseball name for an awesome idea—two lunches a week without Darren. It would be great to enjoy my lunch sometimes, rather than worry about what he's going to say next. Suddenly the science fair is super appealing. I'm in.

But I'm still desperate to get out of here. I tear out of Mr. Butler's classroom and head outside. The afternoon is still warm, and the sun feels good on my neck. I grab the other granola bar from my backpack and break off a bite.

Just as I start to chill out, Olivia is a few yards behind me, calling my name. I'm completely exposed, so I do the only thing I can. I turn toward her and slap a bored look on my face. A sudden wind gusts from behind, blowing her hair around her face.

"Hey, wait up!" She's carrying so much stuff that she moves in a lopsided gallop. When she gets to me, she drops everything on the ground but doesn't say a word. She's deep in thought, and I watch, mortified, as she reaches for her old-fashioned metal lunchbox, pops it open, and pulls out a cellophane package.

"Gummy bear?" she asks, like it's the most normal conversation starter in the world.

"No, thanks." I'm grateful no one is witnessing this. I hold up my granola bar as evidence that I don't need any handouts. "I'm good."

I turn and start walking again.

"Well, I need to talk to you, so can you hold on for a minute?"

I stop, take a deep breath, and turn back around. Olivia

is starting to load back up, hoisting on her backpack and jamming her violin case under her arm. It's probably better to cooperate. Otherwise she might follow me home.

"Okay, *what?*"

"I wanted to say, well, sorry for correcting your homework."

I'm beyond ready for this to be over, so I say the first thing I think of. "Don't worry about it."

Olivia's backpack slides off her left shoulder, but she doesn't seem to notice. She's just staring at me, openmouthed.

"See you tomorrow," I say, signaling the official end of our conversation. It's bad enough to have her monitoring my every move in science class, but harassing me in public is plain brutal.

Her backpack strap slips further down, past her elbow. She catches it in the crook of her arm, jostling a yellow plastic bag wrapped around her wrist. She sags under the weight of her belongings like an exhausted Sherpa.

"So, bye." My legs are jittery, ready to run away, but it's weird how Olivia isn't saying anything. Her expression seems to twist up into a question, but I'm not going to wait around all afternoon for her to spit it out. "*What?*" I ask.

Her cheeks turn hot pink, and suddenly I know the absolute worst thing is about to happen. She's going to start crying.

"Are you serious right now?" Her voice is angry, and I'm momentarily relieved that this is better than a cry-fest.

Now I'm the one staring. Olivia plants her hands on her hips, throwing the backpack and bags and violin into momentary chaos until it all settles back into place.

"Just forget about it," I say, realizing she's far stranger than I ever imagined.

"I'm not gonna forget about it. I'll stop telling you when *your* homework's wrong, but when it's lab stuff with *my* name on it too, well, then I can't let that go." She shudders, as if the thought of her name associated with a mistake is mortifying.

"Fine," I say.

"Fine," she says back.

"Okay, then, bye." I don't wait for her to say one more weird thing. I just walk away.

12

CHEESED OFF

I skulk into the kitchen, still fuming about my showdown with Olivia. I'm holding a bunch of papers from school about the election, the science fair, and Abner Farms. I'm hoping to add them to my mom's pile of mail without being seen, but she's sitting at the kitchen table, seemingly waiting for me.

"Anything interesting?" she asks as I hand her the stack.

"Yeah, I guess," I lie.

She picks up the papers, but the first one she reads is about the science fair.

"I'm gonna to do it," I say, eager for her to get to the more important stuff. I've read the Abner Farms handouts more than fifty times since I got them, and I've decided my chances of becoming a happy, carefree colonist are pretty slim.

Mom nods in approval and moves on to Mrs. Frankel's note to parents about the election. She's trying to act normal, but her expression of eager hopefulness is a dead giveaway. It's clear she's embarked on a fantasy trip into my political future and is picturing me sitting behind that huge desk in the Oval Office.

"You're running for student council?"

I nod. "I need some poster board for signs. But keep reading."

She waits for me to say something else, but after a few seconds, she gives up and swaps the election sheet for the Abner Farms packet. She studies the first page for a long time and then flips through the next couple pretty fast. But

when she gets to page four, where the menu is, she stops
reading and looks up at me.

"Crap," she says.

I start laughing because at our house, *crap* is the same as
a swear.

"Yeah," I say. "Crap."

Now we're both laughing.

"It sounds fun," Mom finally says. It's almost like she's
asking me a question.

"I know. Most of it." She's nodding. I know what she's
thinking, but she isn't going to say it out loud. "I think I'll
probably skip it, though."

"I can see why that would feel like a pretty good option."
She pauses. "If that's what you want to do, I mean."

Even though we were just laughing like ten seconds ago,
now I'm totally irritated with her. "Well, it doesn't really matter what I *want* to do. Obviously I can't do this."

"Ben, maybe—"

I don't even recognize my voice when I explode like a
can of hot soda. "Maybe *what*, Mom? Maybe if I just *tried*
cornbread and sausages on a stick I'd like them?"

"No, that's not what I was going to say. I meant—"

I cut her off and crank my voice up, maybe louder than
I've ever yelled before. "Thanks, Mom. You're just like everybody else! You think I want to be like this?" I simmer down
a bit and finish with, "Well, I don't."

"I know, I know," she repeats, like she really gets what I'm
saying. But she doesn't understand anything about what it's
like to be me. Not a thing.

"It's not like I *decided* to be someone who can't eat most
stuff." I want to sit down, but I don't move. "I can't change
my mind and undo it."

"I know you can't undo it, Ben."

"Well, it seems like everybody thinks I should."

Mom walks toward me, and I'm pretty sure she's coming

in for a hug. I cross my arms, and she stops as if we're in the middle of a twisted game of Mother May I.

"What I was trying to say is that maybe I can talk to someone at school, and they can help us make it work."

"No. You're not doing that."

"I'm sure there are other kids with medical concerns, like allergies, who won't be eating most of that stuff either."

I cross my arms tighter. "Well, that's different. No one thinks those kids are freaks."

My mom looks shocked. "Ben, no one thinks you're a freak. No one."

I shake my head and turn to walk upstairs. I know someone who thinks I'm a freak.

Me.

13

WALKING ON EGGSHELLS

"Mom tells me you're taking some school trip to a farm," Dad says from the family room as I walk by.

I'm on my way to the kitchen to get a glass of water. Normally I'd be in here watching the playoff game with him, but ever since I lost it with Mom this afternoon, I've pretty much been hiding out in my room.

Dad's eyes are glued to the TV, but I know he's waiting for me to say something.

Suddenly I understand exactly what it means to be a deer in headlights. I always thought that meant a deer was too dumb to move. Now I understand—it just can't decide which way to go.

I ignore his comment and head for a safer subject—baseball.

"Looks like a good game," I say. I've been following it online while I work on my posters. I attempt a casual pose, with my arms leaning against either side of the doorframe. I'm half in and half out of the room, ready to bolt if he mentions Abner Farms again.

"Bottom of the third," he says, not looking up. "We're at the top of the order."

Now I know the coast is clear, so I walk all the way in and plop on the far end of the couch, kicking off my shoes. I can get a drink later.

"Their pitcher's getting rattled," I say, relieved. Dad and I can talk sports forever.

"I know. I'd love to get another win while we're still at home."

My dad is the most devoted Cubs fan in the history of baseball, committed to a team that brought him years of misery before finally rewarding Chicagoans with a World Series win. You'd think breaking the curse would be enough for Dad, but now anything less than the championship is a disappointment. The fact that they've even made it to the playoffs again this year is a good sign. Last week, Dad let Maddie stay up forty-five minutes past her bedtime because the Cubs took the lead as soon as she jumped in his lap to say goodnight. He said Maddie was his lucky charm.

I'm about to say something about the score as they cut to a commercial, but Dad mutes the sound before it's out of my mouth. "So what's this farm thing?" he asks.

I'm trapped. I dig my heels into the couch and slide farther back against the pillows.

"I don't think it's an actual farm. It's more like a colonial experience, learning how people lived back then."

"Two nights, sleeping in a tent?"

"Yeah. Platform tents, so you're up off the ground."

I figure I've got about ninety seconds to fill before the game's back on and Dad has forgotten about Abner Farms. So I keep talking.

"And there's a bunch of activities, like archery and orienteering, where you do a treasure hunt using compasses. It sounds pretty cool. But most of the sixth-grade teachers are going as chaperones. And they're all trying to make it a learning experience, so I think we're going to have to do a lot of actual work, too, and—"

"Your mother's worried about what you're going to eat there."

I nod, even though it doesn't feel like he's asking me a question. He's sure not asking if *I'm* worried about it.

"I'll tell you what I told her." He turns to me and leans in, resting his forearms on his legs. There's a super-serious look on his face, and I imagine this is exactly how he looks right before he chews someone out at work. "This is the perfect time for you to snap out of this business. Sleeping in the fresh air, doing activities from dawn till dusk, you're going to work up a real appetite. And if your mother's not there pulling chicken tenders out of her purse, well, then you're going to have to eat what everybody else is eating. This is going to be great for you."

Anyone listening would think Dad is giving me a pep talk. He's incredibly convincing. But whenever he confronts me about the way I eat, it feels threatening—like he's determined to wear me down until I become what he wants me to be. These discussions always leave me believing that if he tries hard enough, I might disappear.

"Nuggets."

"Hmm?" The commercials have ended, and he unmutes the remote. Our family room is filled with ballpark sounds again.

"Nuggets," I repeat. "I eat nuggets, not tenders."

"Whatever. You know what I mean."

I'm glad he's not looking at me anymore, because my lip is twitching the way it used to when I was about to cry. I'm still wiped out from yelling at Mom, and any bit of energy I had left has dried up like a snake skin, brittle and chalky.

"I'd better go finish up my homework."

"Good thinking," Dad says, his eyes on the TV.

As I start to stand up, he thumps my knee a couple of times, the way he does when he coaches my basketball game and is about to send me out on the court. "Glad we talked this through."

"Yeah, me too," I say, but it comes out more like a whisper.

14

DON'T YUCK MY YUM

They're arguing about me again. It starts as soon as Dad gets home from work. Their hissing whispers float up the stairs from the kitchen, hanging in the air around me as I lie on my bedroom floor pretending to do my math homework. When the whispers get closer and angrier, I sit up and turn around so I can't see their faces as they walk past my room. Their door closes, and the water starts running full-blast from their bathroom sink. It runs for a really long time—like long enough for four or five people to brush their teeth. Whenever they fight, they run the faucet. I stand up and creep toward their closed door so I can hear them over the water.

Mom is doing most of the talking. "Let's just give this a chance. The way Dr. Roberts told us to."

"Told *you*, Barb. Remember, I wasn't there. You're the one who manages this eating business. If you'd listened to me at the beginning, we wouldn't be in this mess right now. And then we'd be able to sit down to dinner like a *normal* family."

"Seriously?" Mom yells. "I didn't create this. Can you *please* do what the doctor told us to do and keep your cool at the table? I want to see what happens if we're not all yelling at each other."

"I didn't yell at McDonald's the other night," Dad says, kind of huffy. And then the water goes off and I race back into my room. I grab my science notebook off the floor and flip through it like I'm searching for something important.

But neither one comes out for a few more minutes, so I slouch on the floor against my bed and stare at my feet, wondering if I should do something. For some reason my heart is racing like I've been running wind sprints even though I've barely moved.

My parents like to brag that they're more in love now than when they met in college, an idea I find pretty gross to think about. Mom claims it's because they have the same sense of humor, which I guess means they love the same dumb jokes. They do seem to agree on almost everything—which boring documentary to watch on the History Channel, what color carpet shows the least dirt, whether the lawn needs to be watered, and other critical parental stuff.

But there's one thing they've never agreed on—how to handle me with food. If they didn't have the same opinion about something that only came up every once in a while, like how to remove a splinter or how to plan a day at the beach, it might not matter very much. But eating is a huge, all-the-time deal. A lot of family time involves food. Even when it's not being eaten, it's being planned and bought and cooked or ordered and cleaned up. Eating isn't an occasional thing to disagree about.

I make most of that pretty tricky. I can usually tell when my mom and dad are trying to avoid having an argument about my eating, but sometimes their bottled-up irritation gets so intense that I can practically hear it sizzling around me.

I'm already dreading dinner tonight, because this argument sounded epic. It lasted longer than usual, and it sounded like Mom was telling Dad about some plan she's scheming. They've made zillions of attempts to get me to try new foods. Their methods basically fall into two categories—bribery and punishment. Neither works. They've tried tricks, mostly involving sneaking food I don't eat into food I do eat, which any kid with eyes wouldn't fall for. And they've tried threats, although the classic threat of no dessert will never motivate me because I don't eat dessert. Their efforts always end the same way—Mom looks sad, Dad looks mad, and I feel like I've lost another game I don't know how to play.

Tonight won't be any different. I can't imagine what Dr. Roberts, my pediatrician, has told Mom to try. He's so old that it will probably involve leeches or bloodletting.

After what seems like an hour, Mom peeks in my doorway and says, "Dinner's almost ready, Ben. Wash your hands and come downstairs."

I slink into the bathroom and wash my hands real slow. I might use up even more water than Mom and Dad did. So now I can add that to the list of problems I'm causing—lots of wasted water.

15

Too Much on My Plate

Dad's chair makes a scraping sound on the floor as he pulls it up to the dining room table, where we haven't sat since we played that epic, three-night game of Monopoly last winter. I slip my napkin out from under my fork. Maddie watches me and then does the same thing, but she drops her napkin into her lap without bothering to unfold it. She smiles at me and whispers the word "fancy" at the same time I'm thinking the exact same thing. This is a fancy dinner. Cloth napkins and the good plates and real glasses, not the short blue plastic cups we usually use.

"I feel like we're at a restaurant," Maddie says.

Mom heads toward the table with a covered platter. She sits down and says, "I thought it would be nice to eat together for a change."

Smiling, she lifts the lid off. "*Voila*," she says in a surprisingly fake accent.

I can't take my eyes off what she has uncovered—golden-brown chicken and green beans artfully arranged over steaming rice like a picture from a magazine.

It's completely disgusting.

I'm waiting for Mom to say something like, "Oops, I forgot your dinner, Ben." But she doesn't. I glance into the kitchen and notice the pasta pot isn't even out.

Dad picks up the dish, takes a huge helping, and passes it to Mom. She serves herself and Maddie, and then hands me the platter, but I don't make a move to take it. After a second, she smiles at me, like this is all totally normal, and spoons what looks like an enormous heap on my plate. I watch as the rice spreads out like it's alive. Reluctantly, I stick my fork into the piece of chicken and try not to watch as white juice oozes from the tiny holes where I stabbed it. There's no way I'm going to eat this.

"So what do we have here?" Dad asks, and Mom starts talking about this new recipe she calls "super-simple" because it has only five ingredients. When she mentions that one of the ingredients is lemon, I make a face.

"A very small amount of lemon," she says with a hard smile. "You can barely taste it. Plus, you like rice."

No I don't, I want to scream. The smell of rice reminds me of old cardboard boxes.

She's does this all the time, insisting I like rice when I've told her so many times that I don't. She always says the same thing, that I ate rice last year at Maddie's birthday dinner when we went to the Chinese restaurant near the mall. Mom had made me a grilled cheese before we left and said, "It would be nice if you tried something tonight, even if it's just a bite of rice."

I hadn't planned to try it. I really didn't even want to go, but once we got there it was actually pretty fun. Dad kept doing goofy things with his chopsticks like sticking them under his lip and pretending they were fangs and using them to eat invisible ants off the table. We were all laughing so hard that people at other tables were staring at us. I think we embarrassed Mom, but I liked it.

I liked having other people think we were the kind of family that could go out for dinner and have a lot of fun. So when the food came, I said, "I think I'll try some rice."

Mom got way too excited, and I knew right then I'd made a mistake. She put a tiny heap of rice in the middle of the huge plate with the Buddha face on it, and I spent twenty minutes eating the rice one piece at a time. I concentrated on picking up each grain of rice with those special rubber-band-ed chopsticks they hand out to kids at Chinese restaurants.

When I brought the chopsticks to my mouth, I put the grain of rice way back toward my throat so I wouldn't have to taste it, and then I swallowed it whole. I counted as I went. I swallowed seventeen pieces of rice that night—and even though my mom was trying not to make a big deal out of it, I think she was counting the bites along with me.

This has to be the tenth time she's tried to get me to eat rice since that night at the Chinese restaurant. It's never worked. I'm determined not to lose it, but I wonder what exactly my mom thinks I'm going to eat for dinner. There's nothing for me on the table. Not even a sliced apple. She and Dad are busy chewing and cutting and wiping their mouths like everything is fine, and no one even cares that I'm not doing anything but sitting with my hands in my lap. My right leg is bouncing uncontrollably, and I don't even try to stop it.

Suddenly Maddie slides off her chair and asks, "Does anybody want ketchup?" She walks back into the kitchen to open the fridge and then stands on her tiptoes while she tries to find it.

After a minute, Dad gets up and grabs the ketchup from the top shelf. He also grabs the barbeque sauce and the soy sauce, saying, "Barb, this chicken is so moist. Really good. I think I'll just spice it up a little."

Maddie shakes the upside-down bottle over her plate, and we all wait for the thick slurping noise that always comes before it squirts out.

"It *is* a little bland," Mom admits, reaching for the soy sauce. She looks a lot less happy than when dinner started. "I was hoping this recipe would appeal to everyone."

She's talking about me, the big dinner downer. So what I guess she's saying is that she made this lemony chicken because she hoped it might be plain enough for *me* to like. But it turns out nobody really likes it.

What did Mom think would happen? She knows what kind of chicken I eat.

Maddie nudges me under the table with her foot. "Want some ketchup, Ben?" she asks, in her softest little girl voice. I wish more than anything I could dip this chicken in that ketchup and eat my dinner. I think we're all wishing for that. But it's not going to happen.

I turn toward Mom. "May I be excused?"

Dad is the one who answers. "No, we're having a *family dinner.*" He doesn't look up from his plate.

Mom is staring at her plate too. I wait for her to say something, but she doesn't.

"Well, there's nothing I can eat at this *family dinner.*"

"There's plenty to eat." Dad's fork hovers over his plate, and he sits perfectly still—like a crocodile submerged in swamp water up to his eyeballs, ready to attack. He sets his fork down and looks at me. "*Can't* and *won't* aren't the same thing. You haven't even tried a bite."

"Bob." Mom's eyes bug out at him in some sort of warning.

"I'm. Not. Yelling," Dad says quietly. "And it's perfectly reasonable to expect Ben to eat perfectly good food." He turns back to me. "I thought we cleared this up the other night at McDonald's."

"I've told you before—I'm sure it *is* perfectly good food. I just can't eat it."

Dad shovels a huge bite of chicken in his mouth, I guess to demonstrate how easy it is to eat if you put your mind to it. He chews for a few seconds and swallows hard. I watch the lump of food slide down his throat, feeling like I've witnessed something private—like when you see a guy in a car next to yours picking his nose.

It's a stand-off, one we've had a million times.

I'm held hostage in his glare, but I refuse to back down and look away. Mom and Maddie fade into the background like they're not even at the table with us anymore. I wait, refusing to make a move, thinking of Harry Houdini being hoisted upside down in a straightjacket over his audience.

I need to conserve my energy.

I know exactly what Dad will do next, because his routine never varies.

His lectures about my eating always start with a few stories about his own dinnertime challenges when he was a kid—like how much he hated his mom's meatloaf or all the times he fed peas to his dog under the table. He tries to make me laugh, and I usually do. Somehow, he believes his old fear of meatloaf and peas makes him an expert in understanding what eating is like for me.

Next he talks about college eating, maybe telling the story of being forced to choke down twenty-five hotdogs as a fraternity pledge. If he's really long-winded, he'll include the tale of his first date with Mom. At the ice cream store, after Mom told him pistachio was her favorite flavor, he said it was his too. "I waited until we were married before I came clean on how much I hate pistachio," he likes to say. This part of his performance is supposed to make me realize I need to get my act together so I can go off into the world ready to eat like a "real man."

The final portion of his act is about the Real World, where adults have to do things they don't want to do all the time. Like go to work. And pay the mortgage. Obviously, eating stuff you don't like is easy compared to what most grown-ups do every single day.

I lean back in my chair and wait for tonight's show to begin.

"Have you ever seen powdered milk?" Dad asks. I shake my head. "Well, when I was your age, it was a thing. Remember, Barb?" He nods in Mom's direction. "It's milk that's been freeze-dried. You mix it with water," he says, like it's the most fascinating factoid in the world.

I nod. I have no clue where this is going. He's veering off his usual course.

"My best friend Billy had six brothers. His mom would have needed her own farm to keep up with all the milk seven boys can drink. So she used powdered milk. When I was your age, I slept over at Billy's house all the time. And in the mornings, we had powdered milk over cold cereal for breakfast."

He pauses for effect.

"Nastiest thing I've ever tasted. Or seen. Milk flakes stuck to your cereal is downright unappetizing. But I ate it. Almost every weekend. 'Cause I wanted to hang out with Billy and his gang of brothers."

"I don't drink milk," I say, looking straight at him.

Dad sighs. "I know you don't drink milk. It's not about the milk. Sometimes you have to do things that feel a little uncomfortable, you know, to get by—to fit in."

"At school, they tell us *not* to do things just to fit in. It's called peer pressure." I want to laugh at my own joke, but I'm sure he won't think it's funny.

In fact, now he's totally irritated. I can tell because he cuts straight to his Eating in the Real World finale.

"Ben, what do you think would happen if I took a client out for lunch and ordered a grilled cheese and asked twenty questions about the bread and the cheese and whether there's a tomato on the side? Might as well order a Shirley Temple while I'm at it."

I generally try to maintain a neutral expression during these showdowns. But tonight my stamina is off, maybe because I'm way too hungry. Or maybe because tomorrow I'll be back in the cafeteria and can already imagine what obnoxious comments Darren will throw at me. Either way, tonight I can't handle Dad's campaign to fix me. If he's right, I'm destined for a life of social isolation and career failure. All because of what I eat. And what I don't. Sometimes I try to explain or defend myself, but tonight I don't bother.

He must sense that I'm trying to tune him out, because he

shakes his head in disgust and says, "It's rude not to eat what your mother makes."

My response is out of my mouth before I can stop it. "If you stepped in dog poop, would you lick it off your shoe?"

Now Dad's face is blotchy. His hands clench and un-clench. "You will *not* compare your mother's chicken dinner to dog poop."

"I'm not comparing them. I'm just asking if you'd be able to eat dog poop, you know, to *get by*."

"Your disrespect for your mother and this food is com-pletely unacceptable." Dad's voice is shaky, like he doesn't trust it.

Mom tosses her napkin over her uneaten food. "I'll call you when your pasta is ready."

As I'm walking up the stairs, I hear Dad say, "I didn't yell. Came close, but I didn't."

16

DON'T CRY OVER SPILLED MILK

As soon as I get upstairs, I crack my window open. Even though we're two weeks into the school year, it feels like a summer night—warm and heavy with the hum of cicadas drowning out the dinner sounds downstairs. I'm edgy and irritated, and I can't tell if it's because I'm hungry or ticked off. Probably both.

I sit down at my desk to do some homework, but I'm too mad to concentrate. Dad was right. Nobody yelled. But even when he's not yelling, it feels like he is. Like he'd like to lift me off my chair and shake me until I follow his orders.

I want to go outside and shoot some hoops while it's still light. Sometimes the rhythmic beat of the ball slapping the driveway and the repetition of taking the same shot over and over again are the only things that help me get out of my own head. But there's no way I'm walking back through the kitchen and out the back door while Mom and Dad and Maddie are still at the dining room table, drowning their chicken in soy sauce and barbecue sauce and ketchup.

So instead I get back up and sprawl across my bed while I wait for Mom to call me back for my pasta. I keep imagining Darren yelling, "Trouble in paradise?" and suddenly I'm exhausted like a hundred-and-fifty-year-old tortoise who's been wandering around the desert his whole life looking for some shade. I try to nod off, but I know Mom is going to call me back down in a few minutes.

When she finally does, I pass Dad on the stairs. We don't even look at each other.

Mom is at the sink, starting the dishes. I don't say anything to her, either. I grab the bowl of pasta off the table and carry it into the family room, where Maddie is watching a stupid Disney show. Standing in the doorway, I scarf down the entire bowl in less than two minutes. It's hot, scorching my tongue, but I don't care. I don't even taste it.

On my way back into the kitchen, Mom says "garbage" without looking up from the sink. I'm glad to have an excuse to go outside. After I pull the cans to the curb, I grab my basketball.

I start with long shots, shooting from the worn-out spot where the sidewalk meets the driveway and working my way around the "horn," as Dad likes to call it. The crack of a bat echoes through my parents' open window upstairs, and the roar of the television crowd makes me guess it's a homer.

When I've made my lucky seven in a row, I move on to layups—alternating sides, picking up the pace, dribbling right, then left, then right again. I'm in my zone, finally focused entirely on my breathing and the beat of the ball against the pavement. I'm moving faster and faster, my arms and legs warm and loose. The television has gone quiet, and I feel my dad watching me from the window. I push even harder, but when I look up, he's not there.

17

Something Smells Fishy

I wake up to the smell of an apology.

Pancakes on a school day can only mean Mom is feeling bad about what happened at dinner last night.

I am too. I just don't know if I feel bad enough to go downstairs. I've been rehashing every aggravating thing that's happened so far this week. Between Dad and Darren and Olivia and the repulsive Abner Farms menu, I'm pretty much wiped out. If it weren't Friday, I'd tell Mom I have the flu.

But a day off wouldn't fix anything. Plus, the prospect of a pancake breakfast is too good to waste. Especially Mom's pancakes. Although honestly, I've never met a pancake I couldn't eat.

Never.

Mom used to call ahead to restaurants to see if we could special-order pancakes for my dinner. It was a fail-safe plan because in the world of pancakes, I'm surprisingly flexible. As long as they don't have butter or syrup or whipped cream or fruit on top or anything mixed into the batter, I'll eat them.

But at some point Dad decided I was too old to order pancakes for dinner. He also started saying how great it would be if I could apply my pancake adaptability to other foods, which he thinks should be easy. Thinking about Dad again gets me all riled up. I pull myself out of bed, yank my dresser drawers open, and slam them closed as I get dressed.

Downstairs, Mom greets me with a tentative smile. I glance over at the kitchen table, where a tall stack of steaming pancakes waits. "What's the occasion?" I ask, curious to hear her answer.

"A bit of a peace offering, I guess. I didn't like the way dinner went last night."

Just what I thought.

"Me either," I say, sitting down. "But Dad's the one who should be apologizing."

Mom sighs and sits down next to me. "You *both* need to show each other a little more respect."

My first bite is halfway to my mouth. I can almost taste it. But I lower my fork and turn to her. "*I'm* supposed to be respectful when *he's* on the attack?"

She stares down at my plate. "Dad and I are concerned about the trip to Abner Farms and how it's going to work for you. I think that's why he came on so strong last night."

"So you're on his side?"

We're in uncharted territory. Mom has never taken Dad's side when it comes to my eating.

"There are no sides here. We're both concerned." She sounds so much like Dad that I do a quick look around the kitchen to be sure he's not hiding in a corner calling the shots.

"So when Dad hassles me, it's because he's *concerned*?" I drop the fork and put my hands on the edge of the table. "And you're defending him? Dad's not worried about me going to Abner Farms. He told me I'll be just fine." She tilts her head like she's about to ask a question. But I don't let her. "Dad thinks I'll be so hungry I'll eat whatever they serve. Is that what you think too?"

"No. That doesn't seem like a great plan," she says quietly. She waits for me to say something, but I refuse to look at her. Finally she ends our standoff and says, "We have a month to figure this out. I still think we should start by talking to someone at school about the trip."

I push my chair away from the table, and it makes the same hard scraping sound Dad's chair made last night. In one quick motion, I stand up and grab my lunch bag off the counter. "I've got a better idea. Why don't I skip the trip? Then *nobody* has to worry."

Before she can respond, I shove the back door open with so much force that it ricochets back at me as I storm out. I didn't plan to say it. But maybe skipping the trip is a decent idea. These days I can barely get through lunch at school with food I *do* eat.

It's too early for the bus. I can't just stand around, so I pull a granola bar out of the stash I keep in my backpack and start walking while I try to forget about all those wasted pancakes. I'm hoping the fresh air will help me chill out, even though the same idea yesterday afternoon yielded no chill at all.

My mind races, playing a warped internal game of leap-frog as my thoughts jump from one irritation to the next. I feel like one of those stupid little robotic vacuum cleaners that can't stop running into walls. I keep getting caught off guard—even by Mom. I've got to be better prepared.

Especially for Darren and his lunchtime attacks.

I need a strategy for when people like Darren ramp up their questions and comments about my eating. Up until now, my go-to tactic has been all about avoidance—like being the last one to the table at a birthday party and the first one up and back in the bounce house. Leaving early. Faking a stomachache and heading to the school nurse if something gross is being served for a classroom celebration.

But none of that is working for me in sixth grade. I can ignore a lot, but I need some new defense. And maybe some offense too. Darren totally gets under my skin. And maybe that's why I get tripped up—I'm too focused on what *he's* doing to me instead of what *I'm* doing. I have to train myself to be a tougher opponent. I just wish I knew how.

In twenty whole minutes of walking, I don't come up with a single good idea. The worn red brick of Crestwood Middle School peeks through the treetops up ahead, and my stomach twists in on itself. I'm only two weeks into the new school year—way too soon for this kind of dread.

My own bus passes me on the street. I pick up my pace, wishing I wasn't lugging my backpack so I could run off some of my frustration.

And that's when it hits me. I need to think like an athlete. Shore up my weaknesses. Reduce my risks. Capitalize on my strengths. Be aggressive.

I can definitely step up my game.

18

COOL AS A CUCUMBER

The morning goes by without a hitch, and the first few minutes of lunch seem promising. I'm getting used to keeping my food in my bag and taking things out as I eat them.

Almost right away I'm lost in the talk about tonight's football game at the high school. We all decide to go. JT says he'll invite his sister and her friends too. And that means Lauren.

The conversation shifts to the NFL and fantasy teams. For a few minutes I feel like my regular self, making cracks about the teams that always stink, no matter who they've added to their roster, and the fans who complain that their loyalty is never rewarded.

I'm feeling so relaxed that I've momentarily forgotten about Darren.

But that doesn't last long.

He calls out from his end of the table, baiting me. "Hey, longlegs. Why are you trying to keep your lunch so top-secret? We all know what's in there."

A tingling sensation shoots up the back of my neck and fans across my face. I'm sure my cheeks and ears are turning fire-engine red. All the guys at the table turn to me, waiting to see how I'll react. I'm waiting, too, for Josh or Nick to jump in and stick up for me. But they don't.

"Wow. Nothing gets past you," I say, rolling my eyes at Darren. "You're a real genius."

I pull a pretzel out of my bag and pop it in my mouth to prove how much I don't care about what Darren has said. Everyone busts out laughing, and Nick shoots me an approving nod. Maybe he knew it would be better for me to handle it myself. Either way, I'm guessing Darren will back off.

But I'm wrong again.

"Good one," he says, his eyes cold. "And are you really going to the game tonight? Won't you be too busy with your *campaign*?"

I swear that kid travels with his own laugh track. Even Josh and Nick seem impressed at how quickly he has rebounded, which makes this whole conversation even more irritating.

For a second I can't get my head around the fact that Darren is attacking me from a new angle. Running for student government hasn't seemed like a very big deal. But now, like what's left of my lunch, the election feels like something I need to hide.

"Vice president is a *wanna-be* job. Like being runner-up in a beauty pageant." Darren is clearly pleased with himself, but this blitz feels like it's come out of nowhere. I need to call an audible.

"Just a heartbeat away from president," I say, hoping he's thinking about me in close proximity to Lauren. "Too bad we have to represent everybody. Even losers like you."

Darren's face flushes. The rest of the guys at the table seem impressed with my comeback, but I know it's only a momentary victory. I only planned to shake Darren off, like a Chihuahua who's been nipping at my ankles, but I might have gone too far. Provoking him might have been a bad idea. I'm sure I'll find out soon enough.

19

SWEET AND SOUR

In science class, I can barely follow what Mr. Butler is saying about the ecosystems of fresh water lakes. Even though I came out ahead at lunch, Darren's snide comments are on replay in my mind like an annoying song I can't stop hearing.

Olivia is visibly irritated about my lack of focus. If she elbows me one more time, I might lose it. I'm sure she's thinking ahead to our lab assignment—but honestly, she's probably going to end up doing the whole thing herself, whether I pay attention or not.

I force myself to tune in to Mr. Butler's babble about the impact of seasonal change on lakes just in time to hear him make a dorky science joke. "What do you call a snowman in July?" he asks and then immediately answers. "A puddle."

Almost everyone, including me, groans. But up front, someone laughs. It's a quiet, almost apologetic laugh that reminds me of tiny bells or baby birds. And I know without even looking up that this perfect sound was made by Lauren. Mr. Butler gives her an appreciative nod and goes back to his boring facts, and I go back to being completely distracted. But now I'm happy to be distracted. My thoughts are swirling in a hundred Lauren-related directions. I want to know everything about her. Her favorite color. If she's a cat or dog person. How she spends her weekends.

I close my notebook and put my pencil away a full minute before the bell rings, ready to race up front to her table so we can walk out together like we did before. My stomach is doing a tense, hiccupy thing, but I try to ignore it.

As soon as we're excused, I'm up and moving. Lauren

is still in her seat, gathering her stuff. I stop at her lab table and she looks at me up and smiles. Maybe it's my imagination, but I'm pretty sure she smells like something fresh and clean—like rain or laundry detergent or a new pair of cleats right out of the box.

"Hi, Ben," she says.

I love the ways she says my name. I'm about to mention tonight's football game, and ask if she's planning to go, when all of a sudden Darren is at my side. He nudges me a little, jostling for my position on the receiving end of Lauren's smile.

But I don't budge.

"Watch it," he says, as if I'm the one running interference.

"*You* watch it." I roll my eyes and turn back to Lauren. "So do you like football?" I ask her, wishing I could think of a stronger conversation starter.

Before she can answer, Darren sighs like he's completely exasperated. "Of course Lauren likes football. Our brothers played together. State champs."

I nod like I knew.

"Yeah, I'll see you tonight," Lauren says to Darren.

She definitely did not say it to me.

Darren is one heck of a magician. He made me disappear right before Lauren's eyes.

He launches into a memory of a great football moment in their shared history, and they walk out of class together with me staring at their backs.

I'm steamed—mostly at that lowlife—but I'm also mad at myself for letting him get away with it. I head to my next class with my eyes down. Walking takes some of the edge off, but I keep thinking the same thing—I might have underestimated Darren's abilities as a dirty player.

20

Eat My Dust

A few hours later we're at Josh's house celebrating the end of the second week of school. Josh and Nick are stuffing their faces with whatever they can get their hands on, and I'm eating pretzels.

The football game is looking like it's going to be a rain-out.

"Only eighty percent chance of storms in an hour," Josh mumbles, staring at his phone.

I glance outside. "What does it say about right now?"

Before he can even answer, a deafening crack of thunder rattles the kitchen windows, forcing him to look up. "This can't last all night. I'm sure it'll stop by kickoff."

His optimism is impressive, considering how dark it is outside. Nick and I exchange knowing shrugs. There's no stopping Josh when he has a plan. And there's no way he's going to let a little rain mess things up.

His phone vibrates again, and based on the way he sighs and slumps down in his chair, it must be devastating news. "Well, Lauren and Tiffany and Rachel can't go. Their moms don't think it'll be safe."

I'm just as bummed about not seeing the girls—specifically Lauren—but I don't let it show.

"Hon, it's *not* safe to be standing around outside," Josh's mom says as she walks into the kitchen. "You boys aren't going to the game either."

I'm waiting for Josh to push back, but surprisingly, he doesn't. He's plotting something.

"Well, can I have some friends over here instead? Inside where it's safe?"

Josh's mom seems confused. I'm pretty sure she's thinking what I'm thinking—that Nick and I are basically the sum total of who Josh hangs out with.

"I mean *other* friends—you know, who we were going to see tonight."

Mrs. Callahan crosses her arms. "A party?"

"No, just a few kids."

I can practically hear her mind buzzing. Mrs. Callahan has been through this before with Josh's older brother. She knows all the critical questions. "How many kids? Girls too? What time will everyone leave? Do I have to feed them?" Without waiting for a response, she starts firing off rules. "No one goes upstairs. The lights stay on in the basement. No R-rated movies. Everybody gets picked up by ten. And just snacks and drinks." Mrs. Callahan obviously knows more about hanging out with sixth graders on a Friday night than I do.

"Understood?" she asks, turning to leave. Then she stops and pivots back around. "And no more than ten kids max. Got it?"

Josh is all smiles like he's just won the lottery. As soon as she's gone, he starts rattling off names, and after each one Nick and I nod as if our approval really matters. Lauren and her friends make the cut right away. When Darren's name comes up, I hesitate for a second, hoping Nick might suggest we give him a pass, but he doesn't. I'm curious about where Darren fits into Josh's squad plan, but I don't ask.

"That's way more than ten," I say when Josh has finished. I've counted at least eighteen.

"Ten *plus* us," Josh says, beaming. "Don't worry. It won't be a problem 'cause everybody won't be able to come." After a few minutes of fast and furious texting, he looks up from his phone and says, "Okay, let's get to work."

I can't even imagine what kind of work we have to do to prepare for this not-a-party we're hosting in an hour, but

Nick and I drag ourselves out of our chairs and prepare to be ordered around. Honestly, watching football in the rain seems like more fun.

First, we clear the basement of any evidence Josh was ever a small child, including his SpongeBob stuffed animal collection and his superhero figures. Then we find all the balls for his Pop-a-Shot and take a bunch of junk off the foosball table. Finally, Nick and I sprawl across the couches while Josh vacuums up ten years of popcorn, crumbs, and dust bunnies.

It's almost impossible not to razz him about his newfound obsessiveness, especially when he tells us he's going to run upstairs to change his shirt. Instead, Nick and I roll our eyes behind his back. Josh's commitment to our social success is annoying.

For the first time all afternoon, I glance down at what I'm wearing. My clothes, like most other things in my life, are fairly predictable—jeans, cotton T-shirts, Sambas, and hoodies. My mom used to cut all the tags out of my clothes because I couldn't stand the way they'd scratch my skin, but I'm pretty much over that.

I fight back a smile, because I'm wearing a T-shirt—and over that is my new red soccer zip-up sweatshirt from the elite travel team I'm on. And Darren isn't.

Upstairs the doorbell rings, and we hear Josh's mom greet the first arrivals. All the voices are sing-songy, and my stomach does a little flip as the basement door opens.

Girls.

"Where's Josh?" Nick whispers. "Shouldn't he be down here with us?"

Nick and I both jump up from the couch, silently assess how strange it looks for us to be standing around doing nothing, and then plop back down. Fortunately, Josh's voice suddenly booms down the stairs, mixed in with the girls' chatter. When they all appear, I can't believe what I see. Josh is wearing a Hawaiian shirt, and his hair is slicked back with the obvious help of some sort of styling product.

It's going to be a weird night.

But that's the thing about Josh. Even with gel-soaked hair and his party shirt, he's a natural host—and the girls swarm to him like seagulls hunting down a hotdog bun at the beach. There are four of them—but of course the only one I'm focused on is Lauren. My plan is to capture her attention before Darren gets here. If I'm lucky, he'll be carried away by floodwaters on his way over.

Raindrops glisten in the curls of Lauren's hair, and I'm momentarily transfixed by the way they catch the light. She says a quick hi to me but then focuses in on Josh, laughing at every single thing he says whether it's funny or not. Her laughter is contagious, like a yawn, but in a good way. I must have a dumb look on my face because Nick elbows me hard. When I grunt in response, she looks right at me and laughs again.

My stomach drops in a rollercoaster kind of lurch. I look down, trying to decide whether she's laughing *at* me, which is too unbearable to even consider, or laughing *with* me in a friendly, encouraging way. But it doesn't matter because when I look back up, Darren is standing behind her. He's put his hands over her eyes in what I have always considered the most annoying and unoriginal prank.

"Guess who?" he asks, in his regular voice, which just confirms how stupid he is.

For some reason Lauren plays along, naming JT and Alex before finally saying Darren's name.

Grabbing her arm, he says, "Let's see how well you do in a game of foosball."

And then she's gone to the other side of the basement, where Darren wraps himself around her as an excuse to teach her to play. It looks ridiculous, but Lauren doesn't seem to mind.

Josh motions toward the Pop-a-Shot, like Nick and I should get a game going. I don't really feel like it, but there's no time to argue because more kids are bounding down the stairs. Some of the guys and I start a game, and I concentrate on making all my shots just in case Lauren happens to notice. But every time I look over, she's still totally absorbed in Darren. It's revolting.

After my turn, I spot Mrs. Callahan creeping down the stairs to do reconnaissance. There are way more than ten people in the basement. When the doorbell rings again, her face pinches up in a look of total irritation.

Now JT is taking shots. This time, a casual turn of my head yields something surprising: Darren is looking at his phone, and Lauren is staring right at me. When our eyes meet, she smiles. I can feel my neck turning the same color as my hoodie, but I don't look away. Darren slides his phone into his back pocket, and she's gone. I've lost her to that lowlife again.

Everyone turns to see who's next to arrive, but the collective anticipation temporarily sinks when we see it's Mr. and Mrs. Callahan, carrying bags of chips, big bottles of soda, and paper plates. They lay it all out on the bar, and Mr. Callahan does a quick check of the cabinets underneath to be sure they're locked. I'm guessing they feel a little duped—this is definitely a party. Mrs. Callahan's eyes dart from side to side, checking for rule infractions.

Josh is still surrounded by girls—they've essentially formed a ring around him. Tiffany and Rachel, who arrived first with Lauren, break off from the cluster and head to the bathroom. Once the other girls realize that two have left the pack, a couple more run in their direction. They all go in together, giggling hysterically. It's a pretty small bathroom. I don't know why they'd all want to squeeze in there at once.

The girls' movement has disrupted the equilibrium. When they come back out, everybody moves apart like a school of startled fish—girls toward the Pop-a-Shot, boys to the bar, and Josh bouncing between them. Darren and Lauren are still at the foosball table, and the way she tilts her head in concentration is pretty cute. She looks up at me and smiles again, rewarding me with a shot of adrenaline that makes me want to run around the basement like a wild puppy.

Time is moving both fast and slow. I hang by the drinks for a while, hoping all the dumb foosball is making Lauren thirsty, but in a few minutes I'm going to have to give up and join in a game of keep-away being played with one of the basketballs. The girls stay in clumps, and two more break off to go into the bathroom together. Josh is behind the bar, fiddling around with a speaker, and suddenly the basement fills with music. I've never seen him so happy.

A few minutes later, Mrs. Callahan comes down the stairs again—this time holding four huge pizza boxes. I take in a sharp breath like I've been kicked. What happened to the light snacks?

I'm in big trouble. Because when it comes to eating around other people, pizza is my kryptonite. No one believes I don't eat it. And life would be ten thousand times easier if I did, because there's no escaping the inevitability of pizza. It's everywhere. When I was younger, there were ways around pizza. Like at birthday parties when my mom would wink at me as she snatched the slice off my plate and ate it herself. But now I'm on my own.

I'm running through a list of possible excuses to get me out of here before slices are being dropped on plates. I could claim to have an early soccer practice tomorrow morning. But I know I won't bail—the benefits of a possible conversation with Lauren are outweighed by the likelihood of someone pointing out that I'm not eating the pizza. And that someone would be Darren.

A couple of girls rush over and start an assembly line of loading pizza on plates and handing them to Josh to serve. As he hands plates around the room like a governor doling out handshakes in the town hall, I'm sure he'll skip me—but suddenly I realize he has just dropped a plate in my hands. A puddle of saucy grease starts to form an outline around the slice, and I imagine it will seep through the bottom of the paper in about four seconds. I hand it off to JT, who's standing behind me, but as soon as I do, Josh hands me another plate.

"Here," I hand it back to Josh. "You can have this one."

But he won't take it.

"I'm gonna get rid of these empty boxes first and then I'll get myself a slice. You can have this one."

I'm about to laugh at his joke when I realize he's not joking. I don't know what he thinks I'm going to do with this piece of pizza. He knows I won't eat it. My expression is twisting up into what I hope looks like a question.

"It's cool," Josh says as he turns to deal with the boxes.

I don't have any idea what he meant by that, but I'm still stuck holding the plate. Maybe he's so preoccupied with his hair and the other guests that he's forgotten this basic fact about me. So I just stand there, holding my plate, feeling conspicuous.

My general response to food I don't eat is a polite *no thank you*. Honestly, most food doesn't seem edible to me. But I'm pretty good at keeping my thoughts to myself, even when the food being eaten around me looks gross or smells gross or sounds gross. Pizza is the trifecta of gross. And my observations about pizza are so messed up that if I went public with them, I could probably annihilate the entire industry.

A few feet away, Nick folds his slice in half and shoves it in his mouth. I'm pretty sure he didn't see what just happened with Josh and me. I try to look away before some sauce oozes out over his bottom lip, but it's too late. I can't escape the image of what's getting stuck in those braces any more than I can avoid the greasy plates and pizza-chewing going on around me. The girls take tiny little nibbles, like mice, but the guys all eat and laugh at the same time, exposing chunks of mushed-up pizza in their mouths. I start to feel sick.

So I do what I always do. I try to focus on conversation around me, but that's kind of hard to do without really looking at anybody while they chew. Mostly I try not to look at my plate, because it always feels like when I look at my plate everybody else does too.

"Aren't you eating?" Lauren asks, sliding up next to me.

From this close, I can see the small yellow flowers on her white shirt. I've got to optimize my chance to talk to her, especially since Darren has momentarily disappeared into the bathroom. Hopefully he'll get locked in there for the rest of the night.

She'll probably think it's suspicious that I don't eat pizza. I've heard it before. The worst is *unpatriotic*. Like not liking pizza means I'm not a Chicagoan. Or American. But it might be true. I've read a lot of official-sounding pizza-related statistics—like ninety-three percent of Americans have had a slice of pizza in the past month. And on average, Americans eat forty-six slices of pizza in a year. But I've never even had one.

"Nah, I'm not hungry," I say, knowing it doesn't sound believable.

She takes another tiny bite, a bite so graceful and delicate that I wonder if she's just eating air. I want to get rid of this plate, but not if it means taking one step away from Lauren. I have to start a conversation about something important— something so fascinating she'll follow me to our own little corner of the basement, where she'll hang on my every word.

"Yeah, I had a big dinner." I'm shocked at my lack of creativity. She nods. We are frozen in a tundra of piercing awkwardness.

Suddenly the back of both my knees are bumped, hard, from behind. I'm thrown off balance, and my plate flies out of my hand. I watch, horrified, as my uneaten slice of pizza slaps against the front of Lauren's shirt, leaving a tomato sauce trail across a few of those little flowers before landing upside down on the rug.

"Darren!" Lauren screams. "What's wrong with you?"

Her voice is biting and furious, but her expression confuses me. It seems like she's fighting back a smile. And her smile isn't directed at me. It's directed at him.

"I didn't think your daddy longlegs would give out so easy," Darren says, grinning at me.

A prickly heat rushes up my neck and face. But I don't respond to Darren. Instead I try to focus on Lauren. "I'm sorry about your shirt." I'm not sure she's even heard me.

My muscles are quivering in anticipation of the punch I want to throw at Darren. I force myself to take a few steps away from him so I can calm down. I watch Josh as he picks up the pizza and dabs a paper towel on the rug, probably hoping to get the stain up before his mom makes her next appearance.

I want to say something to Josh about Darren's BW move, but I don't know if he'd appreciate it. Josh seems too stressed about the stain on the rug. Also, I can't figure out why nobody is calling Darren out on what he did when they all saw it happen.

The girls gather around Lauren, taking in the horror of her wrecked shirt. Somebody says, "Let's go to the bathroom and try to rinse it out," and suddenly I know what to do. I unzip my soccer hoodie and hand it to her.

"You can borrow this."

"Ben, you're so sweet," Lauren says, finally smiling at me instead of him.

She disappears into the bathroom. A few minutes later she comes out wearing my hoodie, and the look on Darren's face tells me I've made the perfect move.

I'm definitely going to pay for it later.

21

Finger Food

"Ben, are you listening to me?" Mom asks from the front passenger seat of the car.

"No, sorry," I say, startled back to reality. I've been staring out the window, reliving my hoodie victory at Josh's house. I'm not ready to face Darren at school again tomorrow, but knowing I'll have two lunches a week without him helps a little.

"I was trying to tell you about Beth's cooking classes." Mom's voice has an edge to it. She's trying to sound real casual, but I'm not buying it.

We're headed to Aunt Beth and Uncle Pat's for our family's monthly Sunday dinner. Tonight we'll have a full house, because my older cousins are home from college for the weekend and Gran and Gramps have closed down their lake house for the summer. I love these family nights. There's always tons of laughing and goofing around. It reminds me of a loud, rowdy party where everybody acts like it's their own birthday.

The eating isn't serious either. People are always up and down from the table—checking the score of the game in the den, grabbing more drinks, or bringing stuff in and out of the kitchen. There's always something for me to eat, and nobody ever makes a big deal about it.

I finally answer from the backseat. "I haven't heard about Aunt Beth's class."

And I don't want to.

"She's all excited about a recipe she's making for dinner tonight."

I don't like where this is going. An uneasy feeling permeates the car like a bad smell. So far, this technically doesn't have anything to do with me. But I'm sure it's about to.

"And she's really wants you to try it—because, well, she kind of made it with you in mind."

I can tell this is the first time Dad is hearing about it too, because he looks over at Mom from the driver's seat and inhales a big, long breath through his nose.

"Well, I'm not eating it." My voice is a whisper, but I'm sure Mom has heard what I said.

She swivels around to face me. "You don't even know what she made."

"I'm not eating it." This time I'm a little louder.

"Don't you even want to know what it is?"

"No, not really."

"Well, *I* do," Maddie says. I can't tell if she's trying to help me by butting into our conversation or trying to make me look bad. Either way, I'm grateful for the distraction.

I think Mom is too. "Buttermilk chicken strips," Mom announces as if she's awarding prizes at a game show. "All natural. And super-crispy, the way you like 'em."

And that's what's so weird. Mom doesn't like the way I eat, but she's pretty much an expert in dealing with me and food. She knows exactly what I do eat and exactly what I don't. She understands the difference between penne and rigatoni. She remembers to buy extra boxes of Nature Valley Crunchy Oats 'n Honey Granola Bars when they go on sale. And most importantly, she knows there's absolutely no chance I'd *ever* eat something called buttermilk chicken strips, even if my aunt had been perfecting the recipe for a hundred years. Or if I was starving to death on a deserted island. Or if eating one strip would earn me a trillion dollars.

22

Spice Things Up

We're all sitting around the patio table, about to eat, and Aunt Beth starts pushing her fancy buttermilk chicken strips on me. Mom stays quiet while everyone at the table makes a point to tell me how incredible they are.

Gran holds one up and declares, "You don't want to miss out, Ben." I try not to watch how it wiggles in the air.

I keep saying *no thanks*, but somehow two end up on my plate anyway. They're bumpy and crooked like Gran's fingers. I stare at them for a few seconds, half expecting them to crawl away. Finally, I look across the table at Mom. She glances down at my plate and opens her mouth like she's about to say something but doesn't.

Instead she turns to Aunt Beth and smiles. "These are *fabulous*. Best I've ever tasted."

Now I know I can't even count on Mom. I want to say something rude or stomp inside to watch TV. Dad calls that *making a scene*, and I'm sure he'd tell me I'm way too old for that kind of behavior. But the thing is, there's nothing here for me to eat. I'm not going to eat these chicken strips any more than I'm going to eat the baked macaroni and cheese or salad or dinner rolls or green beans. I can't decide if Aunt Beth was so confident in the deliciousness of her chicken strips that she decided I wouldn't need any buttered penne, or if maybe she's being a little mean.

Just when I'm sure I can't contain my frustration for one more second, Aunt Beth stands up and heads inside. When she returns, she places a bowl of pasta in front of me. But it's not penne—it's elbows, glistening and slimy like a bowl of wet worms fresh from a puddle.

So I don't eat anything. This is the part no one understands. Even though I'm starving, I'm not going to eat at all. Not because I'm being disrespectful or babyish, but because I cannot put any of these things in my mouth and swallow them.

At the other end of the table, everyone's focused on my cousin Sally, who's chatting about declaring her major and other boring college stuff. I barely even hear what anyone is saying until there's a lull in the conversation and I realize all eyes are back on me and my uneaten dinner. I guess someone asked me a question that I didn't hear.

"Tell them, honey," Mom says, in an encouraging voice. I give her a blank stare. "About your class trip. To the colonial place."

I'm so relieved she's not asking me about the chicken strips that my thoughts go a little haywire. But after a second, I'm rambling about the platform tents and the archery and the orienteering competition at Abner Farms. The fact that I'm not honestly psyched about the trip doesn't matter. I just keep talking. Sally interrupts, saying the trip is *so not fair* since she didn't get to do anything like that in middle school. Gran asks if I'd like to borrow one of her good sleeping bags, and Aunt Beth offers to lend me her binoculars. But I'm too distracted by the puzzled expression on Uncle Pat's face to respond to any of them.

He plunks his elbow on the table and rests his chin in his palm. "Does this place have a colonial-themed McDonald's on site?"

Everyone stops talking and sits perfectly silent and still like we're posing for a picture.

About a million thoughts run through my head, tumbling over each other like they're caught in a riptide. I've always believed I was safe from this kind of treatment here at Aunt

Beth and Uncle Pat's house. But now it feels like an older version of Darren has invaded our family dinner, and I have about one second to decide how to react.

I force my face into something resembling a smile and look straight at him. "Yeah, I think they have a horse and buggy drive-through."

Laughter roars around me like I've said the most hilarious thing in the world.

Later I overhear Uncle Pat ask Mom, "Seriously, what's he going to eat there?"

23

STIR THE POT

When we get home from dinner, Dad heads straight upstairs with Maddie to get her ready for bed. Mom fills the pasta pot with water and sits down next to me. She slumps over the kitchen table, reminding me of how she looks sometimes in the morning before her first cup of coffee.

"I'm sorry I didn't stand up for you tonight."

It isn't one of those irritating fake apologies, like when she says, "I'm sorry you feel that way, Bob," to Dad when it's totally clear she's not.

"It's okay." I'm afraid she's going to start crying, so I look down at my hands.

"No, it's not okay," Mom says, staring at the table. "That was an ambush. And I should have known better."

"But Uncle Pat's right. There's no way I can go."

"Well, Dad and I think you can."

I jerk my head back up to face her. "You can't *make* me go."

"We would never *make* you go. But we're completely confident in your ability to go on this trip." She pauses, like she's thinking really hard. "If that's what you want."

A burning ache pulls at my throat, and I swallow hard to push it back down. I don't know where she's going with all this, but I don't trust a single thing she's saying.

I say, "You know as well as I do that what *I* want doesn't matter. Because that's never going to happen. I'm never going to start magically eating like a normal person. And it sure isn't going to happen at Abner Farms."

"Maybe we could use some help figuring it out."

I shake my head. She's about to go into high gear again, begging me to let her call the school and explain my "situation." She doesn't understand that the absolute last thing I need is to have all the adults at Abner Farms hovering over me like a bunch of mosquitos, asking nosy questions and making irritating suggestions about what I should eat.

"I'm having an idea." Her voice is so soft and uncertain that I'm sure it's going to be a shockingly bad one.

"Like what?"

"Maybe we should talk to someone who knows more than we do about the kinds of things that can be hard for kids your age."

"Like a *shrink*?" She bites her lip and, after a second, nods. I stare at her openmouthed, my head pulsating in an explosive mash-up of rage and hunger. "No way."

Mom stands up and walks over to the stove. Neither of us says a word while she drains the pasta, spoons it into a bowl, stirs in some butter, and places the bowl on the table. She lingers near me but doesn't sit back down.

I concentrate on shoving a monstrous spoonful of pasta in my mouth, silently daring her to remind me that they're hot.

"I don't need any more people poking around in my business. I'll figure it out myself."

She looks like she's about to say something but can't remember what it is. I keep eating, knowing she'll eventually sit back down and launch into a reassuring pep talk about how everything will be okay and she'll never make me do anything I don't want to do. But instead she turns and walks away, calling a tired *goodnight* from the stairs.

24

Out to Lunch

I'm still ticked off about the way I got hassled last night. Hopefully someone in my family will rob a bank or steal a car before our next family dinner and replace me as the biggest Snyder failure. At least I won't have to face Darren at lunch today because we have our first Science Fair Lunch Bunch meeting.

I wait until the last second to sneak into Mr. Butler's room, sliding through the door right before he pulls it closed. I'd figured these sessions would be pretty quiet affairs, with all the brainiacs eating in silence while they recharged for more high-level thinking. But surprisingly, now that I'm in here, I can see I was totally wrong. It's a pretty rowdy crowd. And maybe that's better, because I bet no one will even notice me. I grab a spot at an empty table by the door, thrilled to be sitting alone in the corner where I can savor my lunch and my solitude.

"Okay, glad everybody's having a good time. I'll give you a couple more minutes to visit, and then we'll get started," Mr. Butler yells over the noise.

On the other side of the room, Olivia is waving. It takes a second to register that she's waving at me. As I half-wave back, I realize she's the only other person sitting alone. Then her wave evolves into a *come on over* motion. I try to move my arms in a way that conveys *no thanks, I'm fine right here*, but I guess it looks more like I'm calling a runner safe at the plate. As soon as she yells my name, I shove my lunch back in my bag and walk over to the seat next to her. Trying to avoid her would never work. Olivia never gives up.

I'm sure she's going to nag me about something. But before there's an opportunity for her to irritate me again, Mr. Butler launches into a discussion about our developing passion for science. The only thing *I'm* passionate about is being able to eat without Darren breathing down my neck twice a week. Mom and Dad have no clue about my real motivation for doing the science fair, but they were thrilled I was doing it.

"Isn't this exciting?" Olivia whispers, and rather than disagree, I nod.

Now all I have to do is come up with a painless science fair project that I can execute with minimal effort.

And with minimal interference from my lab partner.

25

SUGAR AND SPICE

A short kid I've never seen before is standing outside Mrs. Frankel's classroom, blocking me from going into the election meeting.

"Ben Snyder?" he asks, staring me straight in the eye and holding out his hand for what turns out to be a fist bump. He's wearing a plaid button-down shirt, a leather belt, and dress shoes like he's on his way to a banking internship.

"I'm Albert Fisher. I was hoping to talk to you before the meeting. I'd like you to be my running mate."

"Huh?"

"I'm thinking if we run as a team, it improves our chances. I'm going to be class president, and I'd like you to be my VP."

He pulls his shoulders back and smiles a toothy grin. This is a kid who definitely watches too much cable news.

"Nobody's running against me, so I think my chances are pretty good already," I say, slipping past him and into Mrs. Frankel's room—where there are about ten kids.

Albert follows me, still trying to sell me on his idea, but I ignore him.

There's an empty spot next to Lauren. I grab it, smiling at her as I sit down.

"What was that all about?" she asks, nodding in the direction of Albert, who takes a seat in the front row.

I glance over at Albert. "Nothing. That guy's got nothing on you."

A list of candidates is up on the white board. Secretary and treasurer each have three or four contenders. Lauren and Albert are the only kids running for president, and I'm the only VP candidate. I guess most people don't go after the big jobs.

Mrs. Frankel shushes everyone and starts in on a long and boring explanation of the election rules, an overview of each position, and how our posters must be approved before we hang them. I barely listen and instead look around the room at all the other candidates and their posters. I'd bet anything that Savanna Simmons decided to run for treasurer just for the chance to turn all the Ss in her name into dollar signs on her posters. Mostly, I enjoy watching Lauren take furious notes about every single thing Mrs. Frankel says. It will be a breeze to be vice president for someone who's so responsible.

"I'm confident you're each familiar with the job description of the position you're running for, but I'm passing these out just in case."

I scan down to VP, which I'm sure will have the shortest list of duties. Everyone knows a vice president doesn't do much of anything except hang out with the president—a job I will excel at. As I read on, a sudden chill hits me like I've been pushed into an industrial-sized freezer.

The vice president will provide a brief update on class activities to the school board during meetings twice a year. School board meetings are broadcast on local cable television.

"Crap," I whisper.

Lauren looks away from her notes and glances at the sheet of paper I'm holding. "You knew about that, right?"

"Yeah. Totally," I lie.

Sweat drips down my back as I imagine reporting to the school board while our entire town watches. And if that's not bad enough, Mrs. Frankel throws out another public speaking zinger: we each have to make a sixty-second campaign speech in front of the entire sixth-grade class on Friday. Voting will take place that afternoon during lunch, and the results will be announced the following Monday.

"Mine's already written," Lauren whispers. "Is yours?"

I nod. Being almost-vice president is more work than I thought. Also, it seems like I shouldn't even have to make a speech since no one is running against me. In the spirit of democracy, I decide to keep that thought to myself.

A few minutes later, Lauren and I are wandering around school with our approved posters. I've pushed the school board meetings and the campaign speech to the very back corners of my mind. Lauren is super chatty, talking again about her plan to launch a peer tutoring program for the sixth grade and her commitment to learning every sixth grader's name by the end of the week.

"I just think if *I* make an effort to know someone, then *that person* will be more likely to get to know the *next* person. And if we all feel connected, we'll all want to help each other succeed. It'll snowball."

My face hurts from smiling so much. I could listen to Lauren forever. After we've passed a couple of Albert's posters, which are all identical and feature a huge photo of him wearing a jacket and tie under the words *Well-Suited for the Job*, I stop and come up with a great idea of where to hang Lauren's posters. My recent gain in height finally feels like a real asset, because I'm realizing that her glittery and inspirational campaign masterpieces would look great right above Albert's. And I'm tall enough to make it happen.

"Perfect," she says each time I hang one.

I like to think she's admiring me instead of the posters. Either way, I'm happy. And I'm even happier when she offers to help with mine.

My posters don't matter as much, but I do like them. *Vote for Ben—The only choice for VP.* They were a pain in the butt to make, but I kept reminding myself that all this hassle will be worth it when Lauren and I are on student council together.

26

Use Your Noodle

Sixty seconds is a seriously long time. I never thought so before I had to write this speech, but now I do. And it's an especially long time if you don't have anything in particular to say. Which is why it's a miracle that I have two hundred and seven printed words on a piece of paper I've folded and unfolded so many times since this election assembly began that it might disintegrate before I even get up to the podium.

Voting will take place right after this assembly during lunch, and the results will be announced Monday morning. Yesterday Principal Wright and Mrs. Frankel established the order of speeches using a system so low tech it's almost embarrassing—pulling positions from a hat. It was determined that candidates for secretary would go first, followed by treasurer, then president, and finally vice president.

So I got the very last of eleven spots, which I initially assumed was great news. But now that we're halfway through, I know it's actually a curse because everyone's already completely bored. From up here onstage, we candidates have a great view of every humungous yawn, blank stare, and sneaky whisper in the auditorium. Even Mrs. Frankel has closed her eyes a few times. It feels like time is grinding to a halt and that we'll never survive the last speeches and make it to lunch. I'd rather suffer through Darren's abuse in the cafeteria than be stuck in here.

Each sixty-second speech unfolds into its own small eternity of stammers and coughs and nervous laughter, from both the speech-giver and the voters in what feels like torture for all of us. My irritation keeps ratcheting up. My speech is just as mind-numbing as all the rest, and even though I'm guaranteed a win, I don't want to look like an idiot in front of everyone.

Finally it's Lauren's turn, and I sit up straighter and get ready to be wowed. I wish I could see her face, but as soon as she starts talking, I know she's destined for a lifetime of political greatness. She's on fire, outlining her plans for the peer tutoring program and describing her sincere desire to represent each one of her classmates. When she rattles off the names of each kid sitting in the front row like some sort of genius, everybody stops fidgeting and starts paying attention. It feels like Lauren's speech is over in an instant. I wish I could offer up my sixty seconds so she could keep talking, but instead I yell *Way to go* a few times as she walks back to her seat.

Now I can't wait to see Albert fall all over himself as he tries to compete with Lauren's performance. And whatever pathetic thing he does up there will only make me look better when I give the final speech of the morning.

Albert's up and hurrying across the stage as soon as his name is called—I'm sure because he's desperate to get the whole thing over with. Resting his arms on the podium, he pauses. I can only assume he's about to cry.

"*I* don't need to know everyone's name in order to be a great class president," he begins.

The room goes completely silent. He has our attention.

"What I *do* know is we're the best sixth grade ever."

A few kids cheer, mostly boys.

"Seriously. We're legendary. We're the smartest, most athletic class ever to set foot in this building."

Now everybody's cheering. Albert motions for them to be quiet, and for some reason they settle down. I'm wondering where he's getting his data. There's no way to prove a single thing he's said.

"And I don't know about you, but I'm fed up with being

treated like a baby. By the teachers, but mostly by the seventh and eighth graders."

Heads bob up and down like everyone's listening to the same song.

"We're not babies. And we need a president who can be sure we get the respect we deserve. Someone who knows how to *rule the school*."

Half the auditorium is standing now, yelling and screaming. It's like watching World Cup soccer on TV, minus the cowbells and thunder sticks. Just a few minutes ago, these kids were all half asleep with their mouths open. Now they're wild—stomping their feet and clapping to the chant of *Rule the school, Rule the school*. I'm pretty sure nobody has any idea what it means, but it goes on and on, getting louder with every passing second.

Lauren stares at her lap, her chin quivering. I'd do anything in the world to stop this riot if I knew how.

Finally Principal Wright walks up to the podium. "That's enough," he says into the microphone, using a tone I've never heard before.

Everyone shuts up.

Principal Wright turns to Albert. "I appreciate the passion, but you've used your allotted time."

Albert turns and swaggers back to his seat, a cocky grin plastered on his face.

"Ben Snyder is our last candidate today."

I force myself to keep a safe distance as I walk past Albert, because I know I'll punch him if I get too close. I don't understand what just happened, but I do know it was memorable. And I have about five seconds to come up with something even more memorable to steal some of his glory. The voters look agitated and jittery like they're ready for something big.

Bigger than my boring speech.

"Hi. I'm Ben Snyder, and I'm running for vice president."

My voice sounds weird as it ricochets off the auditorium walls. I take a breath and will myself to sound more confident. I glance over at Albert, who looks completely relaxed. "Well, *that* was really something," I say.

A few kids laugh. I'm sure I've heard Darren's obnoxious voice mixed in with the others, but I don't bother looking for him.

"What I have to say right now doesn't really matter."

Now they seem to be listening. I want to tell them to vote for Lauren. That she's responsible. And over-qualified. And nice.

But it could backfire. So I take the easy way out.

"So let's get outta here and go to lunch."

The crowd goes wild.

27

Couch Potatoes

Josh won't let this squad idea go. He texts all the time now, like he's on a critical mission to keep track of the entire sixth grade. It has to be exhausting to follow the movements of all those people—where they are, who they're with, what they're doing, and if it's fun—but Josh never tires of the job. It's not entirely bad—after all, he orchestrated the pizza party.

Today he's laser-focused on finding out what everyone else in the world is up to this weekend. He's glued to his phone, tapping away like a madman. Nick and I are sprawled across the huge couch in Josh's basement, balancing bags of pretzels on our stomachs while we watch two different college football games. It's a perfect Saturday. Especially since we're just watching and not talking to each other. Because I bet the only thing they'd want to talk about is Abner Farms. It's all anyone wants to talk about.

"Sweet," Josh says, standing up and grabbing the remote out of my hands. "Let's go."

"Go where?" Nick mumbles, not even taking his eyes off the TV.

"Mall. Everybody's going."

"Didn't we just see everybody yesterday at school?" Nick asks.

"Come on, we've got two close scores here," I beg, knowing it's a losing battle.

"And there are five more later. My mom will drive us. Let's get moving."

A few minutes later, Josh's mom drops us at the food

court entrance, and Nick and I follow him in like a couple of zombies. I hate the mall and avoid it the same way I try to duck away from Gran's kisses when she's all gooped up with lipstick. I was forced to do back-to-school shopping here last month, and when I refused to try on a third pair of jeans, Mom got crabby. We were back in the car in less than thirty minutes, with Mom driving home in a steely silence.

I can't remember the last time I've set foot in this part of the mall—it's been long enough that the entire place has been remodeled with glossy black tile and new tables. And all the food is fancy now, featuring stuff like chopped salads and falafel tacos. Even McDonald's is gone, replaced with a sleek fast-food sushi counter.

But as soon as we turn the corner, it's clear that nobody came for the food. At least half the class is already here, sliding tables together and calling out to each other. Josh scopes out Alex, and we head in his direction. Josh acts like he's the mayor of the food court, high-fiving every other person and hugging all the girls. Nick and I are pretty much doing the same thing, but we aren't enjoying it as much. All the yelling and squealing is already getting on my nerves.

I spot Darren right away, joking around with a couple of other guys. After a second, he glances over at me, and I hold his gaze until he looks away. I don't know exactly what message I'm trying to give him, but it feels important.

Rachel and Lauren are pulling chairs around a table and motioning us to sit down with them. I grab the seat next to Lauren, noticing how her eyes twinkle like Christmas lights. It's hypnotic.

"So do you like scary movies?" she asks me as if we're in the middle of a conversation.

"Sure, I guess."

"See, I *told* you," Lauren says across the table to Rachel and then turns back to me. "I personally *hate* scary movies. Well, maybe not hate. But I really don't like them, and I was

saying boys like scary movies—you know, more than girls—
and see, I'm right."

Lauren is so animated and bright-eyed that it's almost
tiring to watch her talk. Everything about her is shiny—her
earrings, her lips, her braces, the silver clip holding her black
hair off her face. If she gets even slightly more excited, she
might detonate. I'm mesmerized.

"So what's your favorite?"

"Favorite what?" I ask, not even sure she's talking to me.

"Favorite scary movie." Lauren bursts into laughter like
I've already said something hilarious and grabs my arm, I
guess to prevent her from falling off her chair.

I come up with a couple of titles, and she starts blasting
me with a thousand questions about movies and music. I
can barely keep up, and I'm thinking that playing basketball
would be a lot less tiring. Josh nudges my foot under the
table. When I look over at him, his smile is so big I think his
face might crack.

He's probably using this day to evaluate his stupid squad
plan again. Lately he's been consulting with Nick and me
a lot, asking us about different kids. When Darren's name
comes up, I don't say much. I know Darren's spot is probably
locked up. I don't care about Josh's squad project right now,
but something occurs to me when Lauren puts her hand
on my arm for the third or fourth time and I catch Darren
staring at me with dagger eyes from another table. It's pretty
clear that like the other night at Josh's house, Lauren's attention on me is getting under his skin.

Now her magnetic charm feels even more appealing. Maybe once she wins, she can make a presidential proclamation
that gets Darren kicked out of school.

"Are you going to eat?" Lauren asks me, jolting me out of
my epic daydream.

"Yes," I say before I've even considered what it means.

"Great." She grabs my wrist and pulls me out of my seat.

As soon as we're away from the table, Lauren says, "I really hope I win the election. I want to be president, but also, I think it would be fun to work with you."

"Me too," is all I can manage to say in return.

"What are you getting?" she asks.

"I dunno." I'm so blown away by what she just said that I can barely read the choices. I'm also starting to wonder why I said I was going to eat.

"Pizza?"

I'm not sure if she's suggesting we both get pizza or asking if I want it, but I shake my head and say, "I'm not too hungry. I'll probably just get fries."

"Will you share with me?" Lauren's eyes are huge, like this is the most important question of her life.

Things couldn't be working out any better.

Lauren pulls me over to a burger place, and as soon as I see the words "steak-cut fries" I hesitate. Steak-cut means super thick and mushy in the middle. I want to order them extra crispy, but I don't. The kid who's working the cash register has apparently been trained to entice his customers with extra toppings, and when we decline his offers of chili cheese and guacamole and bacon bits, he looks a little miffed. I take it as a good sign that Lauren doesn't want any glop on our fries either.

But she does like salt. As soon as we sit back down, she rips open a little packet and sprinkles it all over the fries in the paper basket.

I must have a funny look on my face, because she stops mid-shake and says, "Is salt okay with you?"

"Sure," I say, shrugging my shoulders like it's no big deal.

To prove how much it's no big deal, I take a crispy-looking one and pop it in my mouth, even though it's way too hot. Once it's in my mouth, I know it's also way too salty. The granules are stuck on my tongue and crunch between my teeth. The whole thing reminds me of learning to swim in the ocean when I was little. I grab my water and swallow the fry whole, hoping not to choke.

McDonald's fries are salted as soon as they're out of the fryer—while they're still scorching hot. I've watched it a million times from my side of the counter, and it doesn't seem to be a very scientific process. Just a couple of shakes from a tin create a little cloud of salt dust that floats over the fry basket, where it practically dissolves on contact. Then the basket gets a toss or two, which ensures an even distribution. McDonald's salt crystals are smaller than the regular kind of salt we have at home, and I think that's what makes their fries so perfect—the saltiness is barely there.

These fries are drowning in chunky, glistening salt bits. There's no way I can eat another one. Lauren has squeezed a grotesque amount of ketchup on a napkin. She motions to me to share it, which I would never do in a million years, but I thank her anyway.

I probably have less than thirty seconds before she realizes I'm not eating. I consider picking up another fry and just holding it or even dropping it on the floor. I wish she'd go back to bombarding me with a bunch of questions, because answering would give me something to do.

Josh is still on the other side of the table, deeply engrossed in a conversation with Tiffany about soccer, a shared passion I guess they've just discovered. If he'd look at me for a second, I'd do an exaggerated glance in the direction of our fries. It doesn't take much to get him going when food is involved. He's eaten me out of a lot of tricky situations. But I can't get his attention.

So instead I ask Lauren the first thing I can think of. "You have a lot of homework?"

As soon as I've said it, I realize how dumb it sounds.

She dips the tip of an especially long, droopy fry in her ketchup pool and scrunches her brow, as if she's thinking hard.

"Yes,' she says, brightening up. "But I did it all this morning. The science took me a long time."

I nod. She's giving me an opening, but I'm not sure I should take it. Do I really want to remind her I'm stuck in the back of class with Olivia?

Before I can decide how to respond, she adds, "I wish *you* were my lab partner. I'm always lost in there. You and Olivia are so smart—like definitely the smartest ones in the whole class."

For a glorious moment, I'm completely focused on the idea of sitting next to Lauren in Mr. Butler's class, up front and far away from Olivia. I picture myself as a spaceship, zooming off to explore new galaxies, and Olivia as the booster rocket, hurtling toward the ocean in a fiery ball. It's a cruel ending for Olivia, but she's holding me back.

"Maybe we'll get to switch next semester," I say, worried it sounds flat or like I don't really mean it.

As Lauren reaches for another fry and I try to come up with a way to rephrase how much I'd like to be her lab partner, Darren slips into the empty seat on her right. He still has the same nasty look on his face he had in Josh's basement, and my empty stomach lurches.

"So what's this?" he asks, his nose turning up like he smells something rotten.

"What's *what*?" Lauren flashes Darren the same shiny, perky smile she's been giving me for the past fifteen minutes. The exact same smile I thought was just for me, her future lab partner.

My mind is going into overdrive. Maybe Darren put her up to this whole thing so he could make me look like an idiot. And I totally fell for it.

"This cozy little french fry date is what's what."

Lauren is still smiling, but I have no idea what she's thinking. I want to get up and walk away before Darren goes in for the kill, but I'm frozen to my metal chair.

She slides the plate in front of him. "Here, do you want some?"

"Sure," he says, grabbing a couple. "I'm sure Ben here won't mind. He's sure not going to eat 'em."

There are probably fifty different things I could do or say that would decimate Darren, but I can't come up with a single one. Josh has followed Tiffany into the line for ice cream, and Nick is across the food court laughing with some of the guys. I have no backup.

Lauren isn't smiling anymore. "Why'd you say that?" she asks, looking straight at Darren.

He chuckles. "Why don't you tell her, Ben?"

For some stupid reason I start to laugh, hyena-like and way too loud. I know this isn't a normal reaction to complete mortification, but I can't stop. What is happening? Is my whole pathetic personal life about to be splashed across the food court?

But then something occurs to me. Darren's been watching me for a couple weeks now, and he's not a dumb kid. He knows there's something off about my eating, but he doesn't know what it is. And even though that's not funny, it makes me laugh even more.

"I'll tell you why he's not eating, Darren, since you're so *concerned* about it." Lauren's cheeks are turning pink. "I put too much salt on them. They're terrible." She slides the plate closer to him. "They're perfect for you."

There's no real glory in being bailed out by the girl you're trying to impress. But it feels like a huge victory.

28

That's the Way the Cookie Crumbles

It can't be true.

When the election results are announced during the Monday morning announcements, it turns out that Lauren has lost to Albert. Now I have to serve as his vice president. For the entire year.

People congratulate me in the halls between classes like I've actually accomplished something. They don't understand the scope of this catastrophe. How could a loser like Albert beat the most qualified candidate in the whole world? His failure as president is inevitable. But more importantly, the plans I had for Lauren and me are completely ruined.

I'm in my own head all morning trying to figure out what to say when I finally see her. I can't pay attention in math or English or Spanish. And at lunch I barely notice Darren's effort to irritate me. Instead, I tune him out as I count down the minutes until I will see Lauren.

I rush to Mr. Butler's room and then linger in the hall so I can catch her before class. I'm ready to be supportive and reassuring. I've even tucked a Kleenex in my front pocket in case she cries. Finally I spot her. She's surrounded by at least six other girls who flank her like bodyguards. They all eye me suspiciously, and when I smile at Lauren and open my mouth to say hi, they freeze and wait for her reaction.

"Can I talk to you for a second?" I ask, trying to give off a serious but warm vibe.

She nods to her friends, who pretend to walk away. But they're not going anywhere.

I'm feeling a little less sure of myself with this unexpected audience, so I try to consolidate my talking points. "You
got robbed. You totally should have won. I think we should
demand a recount or something."

"*We?*" she asks, her eyes wide in disbelief.

"Yeah. I think that's a thing they do in situations like this.
I can talk to Mrs. Frankel about it if you want."

She stares at me and blinks. I'm pretty sure she's touched
by my generous offer. I reach for the Kleenex. "Weren't you
and Albert in on this?"

"What?" I must have misheard her.

"In on it. Together. You know, by not giving real speeches
and just getting everybody all pumped up to go to lunch?"

Adrenaline blasts through my body like a herd of wild
horses.

"I wasn't *in* on anything. I decided at the last minute to bail
on my speech and say something memorable so *I* would be
who everyone was talking about at lunch. Instead of Albert."

She rolls her eyes. "I don't believe you even had a speech
to give."

My heart is pounding so hard it might escape from my
chest. How can this possibly be the same Lauren I shared
fries with on Saturday?

"Of course I had a speech to give. I don't even know that
kid."

"Well, you seemed to know him pretty well right before
the election meeting last week."

I shake my head. This can't be happening.

"And you never seemed very serious about the election
anyway. You didn't even know what the vice president does."

My mouth is open, but no words are coming out.

I want to know why she's attacking me instead of that
slime bucket, Albert, but I'm pretty sure asking would be a
big mistake. I glance at her friends. They all have an identical
smirk on their faces and are inching closer to us in a protec-

tive pack. I need to keep my cool. I had planned to save my best idea for the end of our conversation, but since things are going so badly, I decide to go for it now.

"What I wanted to talk to you about is getting your peer tutoring idea started."

"Are you kidding me?" she yells. "Now you want to take over my idea? Because you don't have any ideas of your own?"

Mr. Butler peeks his head out into the hall. "Everything all right out here?" he asks.

And as if this isn't bad enough, Darren suddenly appears out of nowhere, hovering at Lauren's side and looking concerned.

"Are you okay?" he asks.

She doesn't answer him. Instead she glares at me, and it's pretty clear she hates my guts. "I don't think you really care about being vice president."

Lauren stomps into class, and all I know is that she's absolutely right. But not for the reasons she thinks.

I'm even more alarmed later in the afternoon when I bump into Albert himself. He high fives me and says, "I'm going to insist my teachers call me Mr. President."

I don't bother to ask if he's joking. I say, "I think you and I should get together before the first student council meeting."

He looks at me blankly.

"To make a plan. You know, for a class project."

His laughter is shameless and loud. "You're kidding, right? Nobody expects us to actually do anything. We're in sixth grade."

As he walks away, all I can think about is how it will feel to stand in front of the school board and the cable news cameras with absolutely nothing to say.

After school I track down the other two members of our newly elected class board. I'm hoping they might have some ideas for class projects or school improvements. Treasurer Savanna Simmons tells me right away that she's a little over-committed but happy to attend our meetings and keep track of whatever money we make through fundraisers. And our secretary, Bridget Kane, suggests we do an anti-bullying campaign. Nodding in fake agreement, I try not to think about how much fun Darren would have with that.

I drag myself home and hide out in my bedroom, too discouraged to even look at my homework. I keep thinking about the way Darren acted in the hall. That kid's got a knack for showing up whenever I don't want to see him—like a roach.

I know I can deal with him, even at his worst. But every time I remember the anger in Lauren's eyes, I feel like I'm drowning. None of this has gone the way I planned, and now I'm stuck having to make good on my commitment. My motives about running for vice president were all wrong, and I can't blame Lauren for thinking I'm a self-serving jerk.

I have to prove that I'm not.

I just don't know how.

29

SALT IN THE WOUND

The election results were only announced yesterday, but it feels like a hundred years ago. All the energy I used to spend trying to find Lauren at school is now spent trying to avoid her. It's exhausting.

And Darren's eating it up. At lunch he's relentless in his retelling of what went down between Lauren and me in the hall. And he's even more excited to describe the hours-long text session he had with her last night.

Then for kicks he snatches my pretzels and eats a few, calling it a *trade* as he tosses a bag of Cool Ranch Doritos from his lunch in my direction. I slide the Doritos over and grab back my pretzels, but they're totally unappetizing after Darren's dirty paws have contaminated the bag. No matter what he does, he gets a lot of laughs—even from Josh and Nick, who never seem bothered by the fact that I'm the butt of every single one of his stupid jokes.

Sitting in science class, I'm waiting to see what Darren has up his sleeve next. He and Lauren arrive together, deep in conversation, but he calls out *Hey, longlegs* to be sure I've noticed them. If I could crawl into the snake cage behind me, I would. Even Olivia notices my dark mood. A few times she asks me, with genuine concern in her voice, if I'm okay. But I don't answer, and eventually she gives up and focuses on taking meticulous notes about erosion.

I zone out for the rest of the afternoon, dragging myself from class to class with a heaviness that makes me feel like I'm wearing Dad's winter coat.

Finally I slink into the house after school, hoping to escape to my room undetected. But Mom is at the kitchen table waiting for me.

"Have a seat, Mr. VP," she says, smiling.

Hearing those initials spoken aloud again makes me furious.

She's prepared a snack for me like I'm in kindergarten. I reach for a few slices of apple, sure this is some sort of trap but hungry enough not to care. She's sizing me up in that motherly way, trying to decide if I'm sick or if there's something else going on.

"How was your day?" she asks cautiously.

I shrug, knowing there's no way I would ever tell her what's really going on or how I'm feeling. No mom wants all the gory details about what a loser her kid is.

But she tries anyway.

"Anything you want to talk about?"

"Nope," I say, swiping the rest of the apples off the plate and standing up.

"I'm wondering if you've reconsidered my ideas about what you can do to manage your eating while you're at Abner Farms?"

I stare at her, incredulous. I can't believe she's bringing this up right now. She's been on my case for a solid week, begging me to let her call school and request special meals for me. She's convinced that if she doesn't take some action, I'm going to starve to death and the staff will have to orchestrate some sort of colonial funeral in my honor. If Mom had her way, she'd write "Please feed Ben a plain bagel every four hours" across my forehead before I leave for the trip.

If I leave for the trip. With the way things are going this week, it seems unlikely.

No matter what I say, she doesn't get it. In sixth grade, mother-ordered special treatment generates a loser status that can never be reversed. This is why I don't want *anyone* to know *anything* about me and food. And it's why every time she brings it up, I say the same thing: "I've got it under control."

But I don't.

And she knows it. A few days ago she started a new campaign to send me to Abner Farms with a few granola bars in my bag, even though every single page of instructions says *NO OUTSIDE FOOD OR DRINKS.* I wonder which one of us would get in more trouble if I got caught. Or if Dad found out. And if that isn't bad enough, she keeps bringing up the idea of sending me to a therapist.

Thinking back on my day reminds me of watching news coverage of a natural disaster. I'm too wiped out to add Mom's anxiety to my load, so I decide to negotiate before we're both sucked too far into her nervous vortex.

"Here's the deal," I say. "I'll go see a therapist. But you have to back off on your other ideas about calling school and sending me with contraband snacks."

I figure this is the least risky option if I'm trying to protect myself from the social repercussions of motherly interference. I try not to think about the possibility of having no social status to protect.

She considers it for a second.

"Okay. Three sessions."

"Two."

"Deal," she says, holding back a smile. "This feels like a good compromise."

I need to get out of here. I shove the last two apple slices in my mouth and head upstairs before I totally lose it. That was no compromise. It was a maternal version of the erosion we're learning about in science. She wore me down like a raging river cutting through the Grand Canyon.

30

TOUGH NUT TO CRACK

Moms can work pretty fast once they get their way—which is why I am sitting across from a complete stranger less than twenty-four hours after I agreed to her plan.

His office is actually kind of cool. A big picture of a volcano spewing chunky lava straight into the sky hangs on one wall, and a picture of a hundred hot air balloons hovering over a mist-covered field is on another.

He sees me looking at them and says, "Pretty awesome, right?"

I'm thinking he's awfully impressed with himself, but I don't respond.

"So, Ben," he starts, and for some reason I want to yell, *Hey—don't call me that.* But it doesn't even make sense. It's my name. I just don't like him saying it. Like we're friends.

"How are you doing today?"

I consider looking him straight in the eye, real confident, and saying, "Well, *Rob*, I'm doing just fine, thank you." I mean, he did introduce himself in the waiting room as Rob. But really, I've never called adults by their first names. Even my uncle Pat I call *Uncle*, not just Pat.

And besides, it's a stupid question. Obviously things are not so great if my mother has dragged me here to talk about what I eat—and mostly to talk about what I don't eat.

I don't answer. Nothing. It's like we're frozen. I'm still staring at the balloon picture, and he's staring at me, and I wonder how long we can stay like this. I can't wait to tell my mom she brought me to a worthless therapist who can't even get me to talk.

But it's weird, all this quiet. The air conditioning kicks on and startles me. I glance away from the balloons and look right at Rob, who's kicked back in his chair like he doesn't have a care in the world. He looks like he could stay in that position forever.

I say, "I'm sure my mom already told you everything you need to know." That should shut him up. But it doesn't.

He laughs a little and sits up straighter. "Yeah, your mom told me a little bit about you. But here's the thing: sometimes moms don't get it right when they tell me stuff. So I'm asking you."

I think for a second and decide maybe I'll give this joker a chance. But I'm not going to let him interrogate me. I've got to play some offense.

"Is there any kind of food you don't eat?" I ask Rob. I'm sure *me* asking *him* questions is somehow against the rules.

But he answers right away. "Sure, lots of stuff."

"Like what?" I need this guy to understand I'm not going be the one doing all the talking in here.

"Well, for starters, I don't eat meat."

I nod. "Vegetarian? Or vegan?"

"Vegetarian." He's nodding too, like we're in agreement. Which we're not.

"Do you not like meat, or you just don't want to eat it?"

"Great question." His enthusiasm is getting on my nerves, but I'm a little curious about his answer.

"Actually, I love meat," he says. "Pretty much any kind of meat. How 'bout you?"

"Nope, I don't eat meat."

And then he does another annoying thing. He asks me my own question. "Do you not like it, or you just don't want to eat it?"

"Both."

Rob nods, like he totally understands what I'm saying when it's obvious he doesn't.

"Anything besides meat you don't eat?" I ask.

Rob frowns. I can't tell if he's thinking or trying to out-smart me. Just when I'm sure he's not going to answer, he says, "Brussels sprouts. Eggs sunny-side up. Green jelly-beans. Oysters. Olives. Bourbon. And beef jerky. That's what I come up with off the top of my head."

I'm fairly impressed with his list. They all sound disgust-ing, so I go with the worst one.

"Oysters?" I ask.

"Yeah," he laughs. "Absolutely sickening. Have you ever watched anybody eat an oyster?"

I laugh a little too. He's smart enough not to ask if I've ever *eaten* an oyster.

I tell him, "Once my grandfather ordered oysters in a fan-cy restaurant on his birthday. Looked like huge snot balls."

What I don't tell him is that I had to go sit in the car because I was pretty sure I was going to puke. My dad yelled at me all the way home, saying I had been rude.

Rob might think he knows something about what the world of eating is all about for me. But there's no way he can help me with any of it.

I don't think anyone can.

31

BROWNIE POINTS

I'm in the kitchen filling my water bottle with the promise of a great Saturday ahead of me. I'm ready to take a mental break from all the aggravations of my week—Lauren's icy silence, Rob's nosy questions, and Darren's big mouth— and have some fun.

Just as I'm leaving the house, a text from Josh buzzes.

New plan—skate park!

We had agreed to meet at the basketball courts by school, so I respond with *???*

In less than one millisecond, it's followed by a text from Nick—*No hoops?*

Josh responds with *Alex says everybody is going 2 the skate park*

There are about a hundred things I'd like to text back. Like, *Who is everybody?* Or, *I thought you hated the skate park.* But it wouldn't matter. Once Josh has an idea, there's no stopping him.

I actually love the skate park. I tried to get Josh and Nick to go a bunch of times over the summer, but Josh never wanted to. So it's taking everything out of me not to razz him about how he likes to do things when they're his idea, but not when they're mine.

As we head over, I don't bother asking him who's going to be there—and neither does Nick. I'm pretty sure it will include Alex, JT, and Darren. They travel in a pack. And then who knows after that? *Everybody* could mean a million different things.

Turning in, I'm relieved to see that today *Everybody* is just guys. I like to board, but I'm not great. I sure don't do any impressive grabs or flips. I count at least ten kids from our grade, and so far none of them look like a budding Tony Hawk either.

At first no one seems to notice or care that we're here. Josh stops and scans the crowd for a second, I guess looking for his best opening. Alex finally waves us over, and Josh approaches in his typical Josh way, high-fiving anyone who comes within a five-foot radius. "That kid can work a room," my dad once said after a little league awards banquet.

Alex is trying to explain how to do a heel flip to JT, which Alex can apparently land anytime he wants. I keep waiting for him to *do* one, but instead he just keeps talking about it. Darren is on the far side of the park taking a long pull from a water bottle and laughing with a couple of kids, so for now I stay put for the heel-flip lecture.

After a few minutes, Darren's group spreads out and goes back to boarding. They're flying—cutting back and forth across the ramps—and I hate to admit it, but Darren is an awesome skateboarder. He seems to float an extra inch or two above the concrete like he's breathing helium instead of regular oxygen like the rest of us. He knows it too. I can tell by the way he adds a trace of finesse after an especially hard jump or grab and then looks around to see if anyone is watching.

Alex has finally finished his lecture, and we're off. I want to push myself for more speed and zone out everything except the sound of my wheels, but I can't. I'm looking around, checking out the way some people are battling with a trick and others are nailing whatever they try. I keep moving, waiting for my Zen.

After almost an hour, I notice a kid from my math class, Jack, sitting on a bench surrounded by backpacks and water bottles near one of the ramps. It seems like he's been sitting in the same spot since we got here, but I don't know for sure. Jack's eyes are glued on JT, who bails midair on a spin. As soon as JT is back on his board, Jack yells, "Overall a 5.9. Major deductions for the shaky landing!"

JT laughs. "Thanks, man. Tons of room for improvement."

"Over here!" Alex yells, whizzing by. "Gimme a score on my heel flip!"

Jack stands up for a better look and after considering Alex's trick, announces, "Comprehensive score of 7.3 for the self-proclaimed heel-flip expert."

Now everybody's calling out to Jack, asking him to score them. He's fast and furious with the color commentary, a mash-up of a stand-up comic and a sports announcer. I'm laughing so hard that when I go in to pop an ollie, I can barely keep my feet on my board. Jack's remark is, "Moderate degree of difficulty with unnecessary exertion. 6.1."

Nick gets a 7.9 for "original artistry" on a failed Indy Grab.

Josh scores a 5.2 for "excessive use of air."

I sit down to catch my breath. Out of the corner of my eye I see the one person Jack hasn't scored yet. Darren. He's standing off to the side, leaning his board against his leg. He's not laughing, but he's not looking particularly happy, either.

I'm not the only one who's noticed Darren, because just then Alex yells, "Darren, you're the last dude to compete!"

"Yeah, go for the gold!" adds JT.

Darren doesn't move for a second, but then he's off—carving back and forth, faster and faster, catching air, and gliding like he could do it forever. He slows down a little, seeming to head straight for Jack, executes a flawless kick flip, and comes to a stop. He turns to face Jack, sporting his classic, smug grin. I think he's waiting for applause.

Darren's boarding was easily a thousand percent better than what anyone else did. I'm thinking Jack will have to give him a perfect ten, whether he wants to or not.

"8.9," Jack yells, adding, "Deductions for extraneous stylistic flourishes."

I might choke trying not to laugh, even though the other guys are all cracking up. I don't need to give Darren any more reasons to hate me.

Darren steps off his board and walks toward Jack. "Really? Why don't you show me how it's done?"

Jack shakes his head. "Hey, man, it's all in fun. Seriously." He reaches out his hand to shake Darren's, but Darren folds his arms tight across his body.

"Come on. You can use my board." Darren's voice is hoarse. "I'll score you."

Jack shrugs. "No need. I don't skateboard. You know that."

I'm feeling bad for Jack. I know what it's like to be on the receiving end of Darren's attacks.

"For someone who's afraid to try skateboarding, you sure have a lot of opinions about it."

"Let it go, Darren," Alex says. "You're being a jerk."

I don't want to look at Jack. I know exactly how he feels.

But maybe I don't know. Because he's laughing. "I'm not *afraid* to board," he says. "I just don't want to. Never have."

Now Darren will go in for the kill. I'm bracing for it. But instead he starts laughing too. "Stylistic flourishes? How'd you come up with that?"

And then it's over. Everybody's joking around and picking up their stuff to head home. Except me. I'm not doing either of those things. I'm kind of frozen, standing apart from everyone, while I try to decide if Jack's an incredible escape artist or if Darren simply saves his best abuse for me.

Josh and Nick look ready to go, so I start walking toward the skate park exit. After a few steps I realize I don't hear them behind me, and I turn around to see they've stopped to talk to Darren. I'm far enough away to not catch most of what they're saying, but not so far away that they can't see me standing here alone.

With each passing second I feel my body temperature sky-rocketing. I don't want to stand here by myself, but walking back over to them doesn't feel like a great option either. So I pull out my phone and pretend to text.

Finally, Josh and Nick make their way over to me. They're already planning to do this again, and I'm secretly wishing for an early winter that would close the skate park down until spring.

32

You Are What You Eat

I'm looking forward to some quiet during today's Lunch Bunch. With only ten days until the Abner Farms trip, the buzz of excitement around school is impossible to ignore— like a baby screaming on a plane.

But as usual, Olivia has other plans for me.

"I can't help but observe that the elements of your lunch don't vary much," she says, gripping her huge sandwich like it's alive and might somehow get away from her. A chunk of tomato escapes, splattering on our lab table. She swipes it up with her napkin and pauses. "In fact, there's no variation at all."

I turn to look at her, and the electric hue of her neon green T-shirt almost burns my eyes.

Since the first day of these Lunch Bunch meetings, I've been waiting for Olivia to jump into a conversation with her fellow over-achievers. But she never does. And none of them have tried to talk to her, either. So we're stuck sitting together, marooned on our own little lab table island and completely cut off from the rest of the sixth-grade advanced science community. It's a fate that seems to bother only me.

She insists on using scientific jargon whenever she speaks. So far that's only been moderately irritating, but now that she's using her powers of observation on me and my lunch, I think I might lose it.

"Yeah," I say, looking down, "I pretty much eat the same thing every day."

"Interesting."

"Not really." I wish Mr. Butler would start talking. I don't care what Olivia thinks, but I'd rather not have her examining me like I'm an amoeba.

Today Olivia's lunch is relatively normal—a gargantuan sandwich, carrots, oatmeal cookies, and a clementine. But sometimes she pulls out stuff that's downright weird, even by other people's standards—sushi, hard-boiled eggs, black beans, cold hot dogs, snap peas, leftover pizza. The only thing that's the same every time is the *Have a good day* note written in loopy cursive writing on a yellow sticky note.

Olivia stares at my lunch with such determined concentration that I wonder if she's mentally tabulating its nutritional value.

"Hmmm," she says thoughtfully.

"I know. It's boring. I'm sure whoever packs your lunch would be shocked."

"I didn't say your lunches are boring. In fact, I admire the extreme control and predictability. It must free up your mind for more important business."

"What?" No one has ever admired my lunch.

"Some of our greatest American inventors followed a similar approach to eating." She stops and thinks for a second. "I'm assuming you have a limited diet all day, not just at lunch?"

I'm determined not to provide her with any more personal data, but I can't stop myself from nodding. "What are you talking about?"

"Well, Steve Jobs, for starters. He went through phases where he only ate carrots and apples."

"Nothing else?" I ask. My diet is downright exciting compared to that.

"Yeah, for weeks on end. Sometimes his skin turned orange."

"Gross."

Olivia nods. "And Henry Ford was so busy trying to figure out how to mass-produce cars that he didn't have time to bother with meals—so he ate weeds from his garden for lunch. Even made them into weed sandwiches." She peels the skin off her clementine. "I'm surprised you didn't know about them."

I want to ask her some more questions, but Mr. Butler starts talking. Olivia can't open her science fair project binder fast enough. She pulls her sheet of possible topics out, and I hold back a laugh. She must have fifty ideas listed, and most are so complicated that I don't even understand them. Toxicity levels in environmentally friendly detergents. Using digital cameras to measure skyglow. Aquaponics. Aquaculture.

I pull out my own completely blank sheet. I can't think of a single scientific question that I care about—unless I could design an experiment about how to get Lauren to like me again. And I'm distracted by what Olivia just said—because her factoids about Steve Jobs and Henry Ford make eating only one or two things sound like a badge of honor. I don't mind being lumped in with those super-successful geniuses. It's actually kind of cool.

But the more I think about it, the more I realize I'm not like them at all. Their extreme eating was a decision, made because they were too busy or too quirky to deal with trivial details about food.

I've never made a choice to eat like this.

When Mr. Butler pauses, Olivia pops the last piece of clementine in her mouth. "Why do you think someone else packs my lunch?"

Before I can figure out what to say about the notes, she whispers, "I do it myself."

33

FOOD FOR THOUGHT

Same stupid volcano. Same stupid hot air balloons. Same stupid silence. Rob stares at me, smiling like something's funny. Which it's not. I should be hanging out with Josh and Nick. I don't know how many more dentist appointments I can fake, especially since I have perfect teeth.

Finally, I uncross my arms. "I don't need to be here."

Rob stops smiling. "A lot of kids I see don't need to be here."

"Then why do they come?"

"Probably the same reason you're here. Their parents think it could be helpful."

"Well, talking to you isn't really going to be helpful for *me*."

"You might be right." He shrugs, like he doesn't really care one way or the other. "But since you're here again, we could give it a shot."

I shake my head.

"And just so you know, I don't think there's anything wrong with you."

We should report Rob to the authorities for being completely useless. He's basically stealing money from my parents.

"What I *do* know about you is all great. You're smart, athletic, you have friends... Sounds like you do a good job of taking care of yourself." He shifts in his chair a little. "But this one thing's tripping you up."

I look at my shoes, silently questioning whether all those things about me are still true. Lately having friends feels complicated, like I've been dropped into an alternate universe where I can't speak the language and the rules don't make sense. I don't understand why just hanging out with my two best friends isn't enough anymore. And I really don't understand Josh and this stupid squad stuff.

"Your mom's concerned about the class trip that's coming up."

I look up from the floor, which seems to encourage him to keep talking.

"She's afraid your eating might get in the way of enjoying that trip."

I don't move a muscle, silently teleporting myself far away from this nosy double-agent. Whose side is he on anyway?

"How would you like things to go when you're away?"

I don't say anything for a long time, imagining myself at home while every single kid in my class is having a great time in the great outdoors. Finally I say the most honest thing I can about how I'd like things to go at Abner Farms and everywhere else.

"Just regular."

Rob nods like he knows exactly what I'm trying to say.

But then he asks a question that proves he doesn't.

"So what would *just regular* look like for you?"

Rob's a total doorknob. I can't believe I'm going to have to spell it all out for him.

"No hassles. No comments. Eating what everybody else is eating."

"So what you'd really like is to be able to eat more things."

"Maybe."

"Because eating more things would make life easier, or because you really want more variety?"

I shake my head. "I'm fine with what I eat. But no one else is."

Rob thinks for a few seconds. "That's really good to know."

Now I'm wondering if what I just said is exactly true. "I mean I'd rather be able to eat different things, but I don't feel like I'm missing out."

"And I'm guessing that trying new food is pretty difficult for you."

"Impossible," I say, not looking up.

"Gagging? Sweating? Vomiting? That sort of thing?"

I nod.

"That's rough."

Suddenly I panic. "You're not gonna try to make me eat something, are you?"

"Absolutely not," he says, shaking his head. "I would never do anything like that. And I have a feeling you've had plenty of experiences along those lines already."

"Yeah," I say, laughing a little bit even though it's not funny.

Rob doesn't laugh. He seems deep in thought. I guess he's realized my situation is hopeless. But before I can think of something to say to change the subject, he's back at it.

"I'm wondering if there are other ways to make the trip more bearable without changing the way you eat."

"Like what?" I already know where this is going. I might as well humor him for a few minutes. I just have to make it through this appointment, and then I never have to come back. And I can totally bail on the trip too. Mom made me turn in my permission slip so I could "keep my options open," but that doesn't mean I have to actually go.

"Like getting a note from your doctor explaining your dietary needs so you can be sure there will be something for you to eat."

I stare at a spot on the wall behind Rob's head. Now I understand why Mom is willing to blow her money on this guy—she's paying him to repeat the same stuff she tells me at home.

"There will probably be kids on the trip who have diabe-

tes or food allergies and need some type of dietary accom-
modation."

"That's what you don't get," I say, trying not to yell. "I
don't want any special attention."

He waits for me to explain. But I'm sure not telling him
about Darren. And how even my best friends are acting
weird now about my eating. I cross my arms and focus on
the spot on the wall again. Rob shifts gears. "Do you know
that some scientists believe there are evolutionary explanations for what we call picky eating?"

"I hate that word, *picky*."

"Yeah, I agree. I'll use a more clinical term—Selective
Eating Disorder. Have you heard that term before?"

I shake my head.

"It has a newer, longer name, too—Avoidant/Restrictive
Food Intake Disorder—or ARFID—but I think *selective* is
easier to remember. It's used to describe someone, an adult
or child, who has a pretty limited diet—meaning he or she
might only eat foods that are a certain brand or color or
texture. Foods that feel 'safe.'"

"*Adults?*" I ask before I can stop myself. "There are adults
who eat like me all the time?"

Rob nods.

So this is a life sentence, I think, imagining myself falling into
a deep, dark hole.

"My mom still thinks I'll outgrow it. But my dad thinks I
should have outgrown it already," I say, hating the sound of
defeat in my voice.

"Some kids who are very selective eaters when they're
young do outgrow it. But ARFID involves more than just a
limited diet."

"Like what?" I ask, not sure I really want to know.

"Well, some stuff you probably know about. Like feeling
a lot of stress around eating, whether you're eating at home
with your family or out with your friends."

I'm not going to open that up for discussion, so I wait for him to say something else.

"And some kids have trouble gaining weight and growing, but that doesn't seem to be an issue for you."

I nod. I have about a million questions, but I don't want to give Rob the satisfaction of answering them. So I choose the most important one. "So I guess I'm going to be like this my whole life?"

Rob smiles. "Not necessarily. A lot of selective eaters have been able to add all sorts of food into their diets."

The muscles in my neck relax a little.

"But it takes time. And patience—for the person who wants to try new foods *and* for the people in his life."

If Dad's patience is required for me to make any progress on this, I'm screwed.

"And, like most things, before we can work on changing a situation, we have to understand it." Rob looks at me for a second like he expects me to say something. "If it were as simple as deciding to eat new things, I bet you would have already done it."

"Right," I say, imagining Dad sitting here and listening to Rob with me. He'd go one hundred percent ballistic right about now.

"Selective eating is a relatively new field of study." Rob pauses for a second, then continues. "Kids like you are shaping how we understand and treat it."

"Great," I say looking at my shoes. "I'm a real trailblazer."

"Like I was saying earlier, there's actually some pretty cool scientific research out there." Now Rob sounds like a salesman. "Like some selective eaters have more sensitive taste buds than other people. They're called super-tasters."

I look up. That's all the encouragement Rob needs to keep talking.

"Thousands of years ago, ancient people had to figure out what plants were safe to eat and which ones were dangerous.

Most of the deadly ones tasted bitter, so humans may have evolved to be good at detecting bitter tastes."

"That's interesting, but I don't eat leaves."

Rob laughs a little. "Yeah, we don't have to forage for food out in the wild. But it might help explain why some people, maybe even you, have strong sensitivities that make most foods taste plain nasty."

He's surprising me a little. Maybe he's not as stupid as I thought.

"How would I know if I'm one of those super-tasters?"

"There are kits you can buy online."

I take a second to think before I ask another question.

"So maybe that's why I'm like this?"

"It's possible. You might be a super-taster, or your selective eating might be related to genetics or an experience you had when you were younger."

This guy is better at asking questions than giving answers.

"But there has to be some reason," I say.

"Maybe. Or maybe not. We can't always explain why people are the way they are."

"So have you ever met someone like me?"

Rob looks right at me. "Yeah, I've met a lot of kids who have something going on they don't want anyone to know about, like their parents are getting a divorce or their classes are too hard for them. And whatever that secret is, it gets in their way."

"So what do they do?"

Rob takes a deep breath like he's about to say the most important thing in the entire world. "There are only a couple of ways to deal with a secret. You can try to make it disappear, which is pretty hard. You can't stop your parents from getting a divorce, and you can't make yourself smarter."

I know what he means. I can't make myself eat new things.

"Or you release it. You crack it open. Make it public. Once the light hits it, a secret usually loses most of its power."

Rob sits back, waiting for my response.

"I like the first one."

"Make it go away? By getting yourself to eat more things?"

"Yeah, 'cause the second one doesn't really work anyway," I say, so quietly I can barely hear my own voice. "I mean, my own parents know all about my eating, and they never stop making me feel like crap about it."

Rob seems like he's thinking really hard. I guess I've stumped him. Or maybe he's mad because I said *crap*.

"You make a good point. It's not a fool-proof plan."

I nod, just a little.

"And I bet your parents could use some information about what ARFID is all about."

I roll my eyes. "Good luck with that."

Rob laughs. "Okay, well that's my problem, not yours." He leans forward. "But here's the thing—when you go public, then it's on the *other person* to decide if they want to be a jerk. It's not on you to keep the secret."

I look at the floor. "I'm still going with the first one."

34

CHEW ON IT

I don't say a word in the car on the way home. Mom's questions are so carefully worded that it feels like she's reading them from a parenting book about how to interrogate your kid without sounding like a detective. But it's totally obvious that she wants to know exactly what Rob and I talked about. I pretend I can't hear her.

"Why don't you just call the guy and ask *him* how it went," I say when we've finally pulled into the garage. I slam the car door harder than I should.

"And my two sessions are done, by the way," I snap before I stomp in the house.

The info-dump Rob just did on me hasn't made me feel better—and I thought that was a therapist's main job, to make people feel better. I had told myself in the car I was not going to Google *selective eating disorder* when I got up to my room. But of course I do it, cringing as I type the words *eating disorder*—a phrase I'd never imagined would apply to me.

I don't understand a lot of the explanations and definitions, but what I do understand sounds weirdly familiar. I can't decide which is worse—thinking I'm the only eating freak or knowing I'm lumped in with a bunch of other eating freaks. And I don't buy into Rob's optimism that my situation can change.

Before I dive into my homework, I suddenly remember the one thing he mentioned that I was a little excited about. I search *super-taster kit* and order one before I change my mind, using an old gift card I've had lying around. It might be nice to know if I am one. Not that I could change it if I am.

When Maddie and I are called down for dinner, I take the

stairs slowly, dreading more therapy questions from Mom. But maybe she's thinking the same thing, because she's back in the kitchen and my bowl of buttered pasta is waiting for me on the coffee table. It looks like a consolation prize.

I think all the stuff Rob told me this afternoon is messing me up. I wonder if I'll still be right here watching the Disney Channel with Maddie when I'm in high school, shoving pasta down my throat like I'm in a trance. Or worse, maybe I'll be a forty-year-old man trying to cram my grown-up legs under the coffee table while Mom, who looks like a grandma by then, serves me the same pasta in the same bowl over and over and over and Dad hobbles past me with a cane, shooting me the same old dirty looks.

I'm doomed, probably for life. At the very least, I'm doomed for Abner Farms.

It would be great if Dad turned out to be right about all the fresh air and nature triggering such a ravenous hunger in me that I'd suddenly be willing to eat whatever was being served, even if it was something totally repulsive like beef stew. But I can't count on that, and I'm not willing to humiliate myself by trying out his hypothesis. And there's no way I'm giving Mom the go-ahead to broadcast details about my eating all over school.

I don't know why something other people do multiple times every single day without even thinking about it is such a problem for me or why everyone else in the world thinks it's okay to give me a hard time about it. Suddenly a vivid memory bubbles up from my mental slog.

I'm sitting in a shopping cart, small enough to be strapped in and facing Mom, so we're looking in opposite directions. As soon as I spot him, I'm fascinated. I stare for a minute, watching him strain to reach something on a shelf that's not even high, and then I point and yell, "Look at that man! He's so little!"

Mom and I had a very serious conversation in the car on

the way home about how it's bad manners to call attention to people's differences. She acted like I was the only person in the world who didn't know this fundamental rule of human decency. But it turns out that most people, even adults, don't know the rule either—especially when it comes to me and my eating. Like the young me in the grocery cart, most people who don't know me well are overcome by their natural curiosity about what I eat and what I don't. So they ask a lot of questions:

Is that all you're going to eat?

Are you sure you don't want to try this?

Which is generally followed by complete disbelief:

You've really never eaten a hot dog? Or a brownie? Or lasagna?

My answers, or lack of answers, never satisfy them. They usually move straight on to staring and whispering and eye rolling and commentary, like, *This can't be healthy. You're going to starve to death.* And finally, *I can't believe your parents let you get away with this.* I'm pretty sure Mom and Dad hate that last one as much as I do. But they never stick up for themselves. Or for me. And even though they're never on the same page about my eating, they both think I can survive Abner Farms.

But I know the truth. I can't handle two and a half solid days of starvation and torment from Darren and every other kid or adult who gets on my case.

I hear Dad come through the kitchen door. He's going to talk to Mom for a minute before he heads upstairs to change out of his work clothes. I will have less than five minutes to surrender.

When the coast is clear, I carry my bowl into the kitchen. Mom is stirring something on the stove, which works out well because I don't have to look at her.

"I'm not going."

Somehow her silent nod feels like a betrayal. I was expecting a fight.

Maybe she's given up on me too.

35

Dinner and a Show

"I have some scientific business to discuss," I say to Olivia as I drop my lunch bag on the table and sit down.

Just as I predicted, she raises her eyebrows and smiles. I'm finally speaking her language.

"Well, this is an interesting development." She pushes her lunch to the side. "You have my full attention."

Until this morning, the super-taster test kit has been sitting unopened in its brown cardboard box on my dresser, silently taunting me with its promise to reveal something new about my eating habits. But I don't want to find out if I'm a super-taster by myself, or with my family, or even with my friends. And I sure don't want to explain super-tasting to any of them.

I realized last night that the only logical sidekick for this operation is Olivia. She's trustworthy and serious. And because she's my lab partner, she's probably obligated to participate.

I slide my chair close to hers and quietly fill her in on everything I know about super-tasters and how you find out if you are one. Mr. Butler hasn't even shown up for Lunch Bunch yet, and as usual, all the other kids are too busy talking and eating to care about what Olivia and I are doing. I show her the paper strips from the kit and explain how super-tasters are able to taste a substance called PTC—but regular tasters can't. She stares at me with an intensity that suggests she's receiving top-secret military intel.

"So what do we do?" she whispers.

According to the instructions, we should both test ourselves with the test strips and the plain-papered controls, and we shouldn't know which are which. But since we're scientists-in-training, I figure we can skip all those procedural details and get right to it. I take one test strip and hand her another, and we place them on our tongues at the same time.

Right away, I taste something awful. It's bitter and gritty like I've just licked all the freshly cut grass off the bottom of the lawn mower. I try not to make a face, but I can't stop myself from shuddering. Olivia's eyes are shut tight in concentration. I pull the test strips out of my mouth and wait for her.

"Nothing for me yet," she says calmly, her eyes still closed. "What about you?"

My heart's pounding. "You don't taste that?"

She opens her eyes and for a second we just stare at each other.

"Oh my gosh. You *are*, aren't you?"

"Yeah. I think I am," I say, laughing, my thoughts flying in a million different directions.

Now Olivia is laughing too. "Are you okay?"

I nod. I'm not exactly excited, but somehow I'm strangely relieved.

"This is so amazing. Our first real scientific discovery," she says, shaking my hand with pride. Then she bites down on her lip the way she does when she's thinking hard. "I bet you could make this your science fair project."

A familiar dread rolls over me like dense fog, snuffing out any bit of confidence I just earned.

"Nah," I say quietly. "I'm not going public with this stuff."

36

I Scream, You Scream

"Whose house?" I ask Josh as we push through the school doors. We're surrounded by kids calling out to each other while they head toward the bus lines in clumps of twos and threes. Josh doesn't answer me. He's too busy craning his neck in ten different directions, surveying the scene.

"Snyder," someone says from behind me.

I turn to face Albert, who's standing too close and totally invading my personal space. I take a step back, irritated that he's bugging me in front of Josh. His khakis and long-sleeved button-down are suspiciously fresh and crisp for so late in the day. I'm surprised he's not carrying a briefcase.

"What's up?" I ask, motioning for him to move a few feet away with me.

"I've been thinking about a class project, or social event, like you were talking about."

"Great." The muscles in my neck relax a bit. "What've you got?"

He steps in closer again and lowers his voice. "Listen to this. How about Bring Your Dog to School Day?"

I take a deep breath. "I don't think that would fly," I say softly. "For about thirty different reasons."

He winces. "Really? It's original."

"Let's keep thinking," I say, wishing I felt more appreciative of the fact that he came up with an idea. It's more than I've done.

I turn and head back to Josh. He doesn't seem to have noticed that I left. But then he proves me wrong.

"That kid's gonna hit middle age before Thanksgiving,"

he says, rolling his eyes. Even though I've been thinking the same thing for a couple weeks, I'm surprised Josh said it loud enough that Albert might have heard him.

"Dude! Over here!" Josh yells into the crowd. I wait for Nick to appear, but instead it's JT, talking a mile a minute.

"The girls already started walking, so let's get moving," JT says, pulling out his phone.

JT always knows where the girls are—I guess that's one of the perks of having a twin sister.

"Where are we going?" I ask, but they're both too busy texting to answer.

Nick slides in between them. He looks at me and shrugs. I shrug back. As usual, Josh has a plan in the works he hasn't shared with us. I don't remember when it was that we handed over the management of our free time to Josh, but maybe it's always been this way. But now everything Josh orchestrates involves the entire sixth grade. Lately I've started to think it might be nice to be consulted first.

Especially today. With Abner Farms only two days away, I was hoping for a chill afternoon with Josh and Nick before I come down with the phony illness that will prevent me from making the trip.

Finally Josh looks up. "Too nice a day to waste inside. Everybody's going to The Freeze."

Suddenly we're joined by a crowd of guys—Alex, Darren, and a few others I barely know.

"Let's get outta here," Josh says.

We head toward town. Not far in front of us, a cluster of nine or ten girls walks together with Lauren at the front of the pack. Their voices jangle together, amplifying until they dissolve into laughter and then beginning again. While it's nice to be somewhat near Lauren, it's more than just a group of kids that's keeping her from talking to me.

It's a gorgeous October afternoon, sunny and almost as warm as summer. But even on a day like this, I can't shake the bad mood that has settled over me since the election. Plus, sometimes these big group activities wear me out. This one will be no different, especially if I'm the only one not eating ice cream. I'm already running through a list of possible excuses. I could lie and say I just remembered I have an early soccer practice tonight.

We pick up the pace, bringing us closer to the girls.

"Hey," Josh says, nudging me.

He hangs back, so I do too.

After we've fallen a couple of steps behind the other guys, he says, "At The Freeze, just get an ice cream like everybody else."

"You're messing with me, right?" I ask, laughing. But my right hand tightens around the strap of my backpack, and I clench it so hard my fingernails dig into my palm.

He rolls his eyes. "Don't be a baby—just get an ice cream cone. It's not complicated," he says, speeding up again.

"*Baby?*" I repeat.

But Josh is already way ahead of me, yelling, "Hey, JT, you gotta tell me what happened in study hall."

A rush of static floods my ears, sizzling like my brain is frying from the inside out. Josh's command feels both totally random and completely premeditated, like he's decided my eating has a direct effect on his social status. Suddenly I wonder if I'm auditioning for a spot on his stupid squad. Maybe I'm not going to make the cut.

I kick a stone on the sidewalk and send it flying onto someone's lawn. It's bad enough how I'm constantly thinking about what and how I eat, but now it seems like a lot of other people have a stake in it too. Josh has watched me not eat ice cream at The Freeze since we were in preschool. Why is it such a big deal now?

The group is far enough ahead that I could probably turn and walk home without anyone noticing, which feels like a better option than being treated as a bench-warmer. I'm just about to ditch the whole thing when someone yells my name.

"Ben! Dude, move it!" Nick yells. He's trailing the group waiting for me, so I pick up my pace. Darren and Lauren are a few people in front of us. They have veered off from the others and are now absorbed in a quiet, private discussion.

"You okay?" Nick asks when I catch up to him.

"Headache," I say, laying some groundwork for my up-coming disease.

Nick and I walk the last two blocks together, not saying much. We're separated from the rest of the group by a few paces, but it feels like miles. I can hear most of what Lauren is asking Darren about, like how many pairs of shoes to pack and whether to bring an extra blanket and if there might be bears. I'm sure Darren is soaking it all in, basking in her attention. After a few minutes I'm truly feeling sick and turn my focus away from them, only to catch Josh ahead of us trying to manage two or three conversations at the same time.

Nick is watching Josh too. "Just ignore him," he says, not looking at me.

"Yeah," I say, not sure of what I'm agreeing to.

I want to ask Nick if he knows what Josh just said to me, or if he thinks Josh is being a jerk, or if he would consider sticking up for me. But I'm not sure I can handle the answers to any of those questions, so we walk the rest of the without saying much.

The Freeze is loud and crowded like it's a warm summer night. A crabby old lady works the register, snapping out orders to an even crabbier teenage boy behind her. Somehow I've managed to get in line right in front of Lauren and Darren. She can't decide if she wants chocolate chip or bubble gum, and he keeps saying, "Bubble gum's the best," like he's some kind of ice cream expert. She finally settles on bubble gum but then changes her mind again and again.

I hate listening to her non-stop perky chatter with Darren. Each cute little thing she says is like a dagger through my heart. Sixteen days. That's how long it's been since she's said a single word to me. She's completely frozen me out. And I still haven't come up with a single idea about how to redeem myself.

Josh is at the register. I'm wondering if he might be so caught up in his popularity and his ice cream that he forgets about our chat a few minutes ago and I might escape the line unnoticed. But when he turns around holding the biggest, drippiest mint chip cone I've ever seen and looks me straight in the eye, I know he hasn't.

The cashier is even nastier now and hollering at people to not block the door. I'm wishing everyone would leave and head over to the park across the street, but it's clear they're waiting for Lauren and Darren and me.

It's my turn to order, and I have no idea what to get.

The cashier clenches her jaw, and I can almost hear her teeth grinding. Her personality seems more suited for work in a maximum-security prison than an ice cream shop. She glares at me, which must be a signal that she's about to blow.

I'm paralyzed by a crushing panic. It feels like the whole place has gone silent, waiting for me to say something.

"I don't have all day," she growls without moving her lips. Or maybe I've imagined it.

Finally I spit out the name of the only ice cream flavor I can think of. The flavor that sealed the deal on my parents' love. The flavor that is Snyder family legend.

"Pistachio."

Her head tilts to the side. "Not what I would have guessed," she mutters.

"Original," Lauren says from behind me, almost sounding impressed.

I'm momentarily thrilled that she has actually spoken to me, but I'm too stressed to enjoy it or turn around. There's nothing remarkable about what I'm doing except for the fact that I've never done it before. I'm an ice cream fraud—purchasing my cone with as much confidence as I might have if I was trying to buy a six-pack of beer.

I pay, and the teenager hands me my cone. As soon as it's in my hand, I notice two things. First, pistachio ice cream is surprisingly green. Second, it's already melting. One side seems to be liquefying at a faster rate than the other. And there's no way I'm going to do the one thing that could fix it.

After Darren and Lauren get their ice cream, Josh opens the heavy glass door and we all pile out. Nick shoots me a weird glance. I shrug and look away, focusing all my attention on the time bomb I'm holding. When I step outside, I can practically see the hot, humid air enveloping my cone and accelerating its thaw rate.

Green soup is pooling along the lip of the cone, and I watch, mortified, as it oozes over the edge and onto my thumb.

"I've never had cookie dough," Lauren says to Darren between licks of her pink cone. She's working pretty hard to keep up with her own fast-melt situation.

"Wanna try it?" he asks.

She reaches to take it from Darren, and their hands briefly touch, somehow skyrocketing my own frustration into the stratosphere. I'm sure my anger won't help me or my own ice cream situation. She smiles and takes a small taste. I drop my gaze when she catches me watching her.

I'm holding my own cone at a bit of an angle, hoping the whole drippy mess will slide off and hit the ground—the only idea I can come up with for how to get rid of it entirely. Running wind sprints would be less painful than this.

As I wait for it to drop to its early death, Darren walks over to me. His face is blank, but he's definitely up to something. Staring at me, he takes a huge bite out of his ice cream. I don't know what it's like to eat ice cream, but biting into it seems like a pretty aggressive move.

"Pistachio, huh?

I smile. "It's a classic."

He crinkles his nose. "Well, it smells weird."

I have no idea what pistachio ice cream is supposed to smell like. As soon as I bring the cone up for a sniff, I know I've made a huge mistake. But it's too late. Lightning fast, Darren pushes it in my face with such force that a big hunk of it goes right up my nose, stunning me with its oozing coldness. It clogs my nose and drips down the back of my throat. I start to choke and drop the cone. It splatters when it hits the pavement.

"Man," somebody yells, "you got him good!"

I open my mouth in an effort not to taste the pistachio, letting it ooze down my chin. It must look like thick green snot is slobbering all over my face. And even worse, it's in my mouth. I bend down, resting my hands on my thighs and spitting. Hanging half upside-down is not helping my situation, but I can't face the kids who have started to crowd around me. Someone waves a fistful of napkins near my head, and I grab them, desperate to wipe all the sticky goo off my face.

"Are you gonna hurl?" Darren asks in a voice of fake concern.

Still hunched over, I nod, taking note of which direction his voice has come from and shift a bit in that direction.

"Gimme a second," I sputter. The feet around me all take a step back.

"I think he's crying," Darren adds in a stupid sing-song voice, laughing at his own joke.

That's it. I don't care what's all over my face.

I stand up fast, and in one quick motion shove his cone into his own nose.

"Oldest trick in the book." I laugh. "Can't believe I fell for it."

It feels like I might have I hit him too hard. And the fact that he's flat on his butt with blood trickling out of his nose confirms it. Everyone rushes to him, offering napkins—the same ones they were offering me just a minute ago.

I slide past the other kids and offer my hand to pull him up.

"Sorry, dude," I say, but I'm not sorry at all.

Darren looks me in the eye before he grabs Josh's outstretched hand instead. Once he's standing, the blood is gushing more than trickling.

"Tip your head back! Tip it back!" Lauren yells until he does. She stares at me and crosses her arms, pulling them in tight like she's cold.

"Want me to call your mom?" somebody asks.

I pretend I'm busy cleaning myself up, but nobody's paying attention to me anyway. After another few seconds, it starts to feel like the other kids are intentionally ignoring me. Finally Alex turns around and glares at me with cold, flat eyes.

"You think that was funny?"

My chest tightens. "Everyone thought it was a riot when he did it to *me*."

"Maybe *you* need to chill and learn how to take a joke."

Now everyone's paying attention to me. It feels like they're waiting to see what I'll do next. My muscles twinge like they have a mind of their own, and I focus on squeezing the napkins I'm still holding in a death grip. I try to slow down my breathing and look over at Josh and Nick, waiting for them to back me up—but after a second it's clear they're not going to. I guess that shouldn't surprise me, after what Josh said to me about ordering an ice cream in the first place.

No matter what I do, I keep getting pushed closer to the end of the bench.

A second wave of hot, explosive rage surges through my body and threatens to unleash like a storm. Somehow Darren's dirty tricks to make me look bad keep working. It's beyond unfair—like when a player gets thrown off the court for retaliating after a dirty foul. He's ruthless, and I keep falling for his stupid tricks. And he's not just messing with me—he's moving in on my friends and he's already moved in on Lauren. She might not be my girlfriend, but she's way too good for him.

Suddenly my plan for skipping the trip to Abner Farms feels like the worst idea I've ever had. Because maybe there's something even worse in my future if I'm a no-show. Total social obliteration—a silent, solitary existence like in those movies where an untethered astronaut floats through space all alone, slowly running out of oxygen.

Darren's plan is working. I am disappearing. And he's not going to stop until he erases me entirely.

I can't stay home feeling sorry for myself while Darren carries on his campaign to destroy me. I can't make it so easy for him. I have to buck up and go to Abner Farms.

"I'm outta here," I say to no one in particular.

I don't wait around to see if anyone will try to stop me. They don't. As soon as I'm out of the park, I break into a hard run all the way home. I push through the kitchen door and say it before Mom has even turned around.

"I'm going. And I'll take the granola bars."

37

Don't Bite Off More Than You Can Chew

I leave for Abner Farms in fifteen minutes. My about-face on the decision to go unleashed a Niagara Falls of activity for my parents, and the past two days have been a scramble.

Mom has been on a mission to collect all the gear she didn't think we needed to worry about. She's been edgy and snippy like we're expecting houseguests, which is what happens when she's nervous. And Dad's relief that I'm not wimping out on the trip has triggered a doubling down on his pep talks about my manly appetite in the great outdoors.

Last night I pulled out the Abner Farms information packet again. I was positive another read wouldn't yield anything new, but I did it anyway, reviewing the menu for the thousandth time and shuddering at words like *sausages* and *succotash*. For some reason on this read, the word *flapjack* jumped out at me. I was pretty sure flapjacks were in the biscuit family, which is another category of food I don't eat. But I Googled it anyway, and suddenly I realized there might be a way out, or through, Abner Farms. Because flapjack is just an old-fashioned word for pancake. And flapjacks will be served at breakfast on both days.

I've been camped out at the kitchen table for a while this morning, focusing on maximizing my caloric intake by stuffing more of Mom's pancakes into my body than I've ever managed before.

"I knew you'd come around and make the right decision about this," Dad says, gazing at me with pride.

I nod, not sure of which part of his statement I'm pretending to agree with.

He turns toward Mom. "I'm happy to take Ben and his gear to the bus."

I finish off my fifth pancake and wait for Mom to save me.

It takes her less than a second. "Thanks, but I've already made arrangements for Maddie to walk to school with the neighbors this morning." Her cheery voice is super-fake. "So I'll take Ben."

I'm holding it together, but Mom knows the last thing I need is to be trapped in the car listening to another ten-minute speech about *following the pack*—Dad's single piece of advice for fitting in. As far as my eating is concerned, his philosophies have never been very useful. But maybe I'm finally desperate enough to try something new.

My strategy for surviving the next two and a half days—or fifty-four hours—will rely entirely on pancakes (or flapjacks, depending on what century I'm in.) I'm gorging on them now before I leave, and I will repeat the flapjack feast on Friday and Saturday morning at Abner Farms, filling up on water in between. That's as *following the pack* as I can manage. Who knows? Dad might actually be right. Maybe being surrounded by my friends in the great outdoors really will make me hungry enough to eat whatever everyone else is eating.

My top priority is to look like a chill colonist at all times. I have to pull it off. Especially around Lauren, who's probably on the lookout for every uncool thing I might do. And around Darren, for obvious reasons. I don't need to give him one more reason to get on my case.

"Five minutes," Mom says from the sink.

Before I push away from the table, I force a seventh pancake into my mouth. I might have overdone it—my stomach is so full I feel like I could explode. When I get upstairs, I fish around in my duffel to find the bag Mom stuffed with granola bars. She's definitely packed more than the six she promised. There's no way I want to be caught with them, and my flapjack plan is so solid I don't think I need them anyway.

I'd never tell him, but this might be the first time Dad and I have ever been united about anything having to do with me and food. I'm finally appreciating how his intense confidence in me is way more appealing than Mom's constant nagging. Suddenly I'm so psyched about my survival plan that I do the most fearless thing I can think of—something that will guarantee my success away from home.

I take the bag of granola bars out of my duffel and leave it on my bed.

When we get to school, I can't jump out of the car fast enough. Mom has been talking a mile a minute ever since we backed out of the garage, reminding me to brush my teeth and make good decisions and wear bug spray. Before she even puts the car in park, I'm opening my door.

"Hold on. I'll help you carry your stuff."

"I've got it," I say, grabbing my sleeping bag and duffel from the backseat. I cannot allow her to have even a second of contact with Mrs. Frankel, who's standing near the school entrance clutching a clipboard and, most surprisingly, wearing jeans rather than her regular formal skirts and blouses.

Mom yanks the keys out of the ignition. "I see a lot of other parents over there."

"I've got it, Mom. I'm gonna be fine."

Before her disappointment gets the best of me, I flash her a big smile. "Really, Mom. I'm *fine.*"

"Okay then. Well, have a great time, honey." Her voice is squeaky, and I know I'd better get away before she does something weird like kiss me or start to cry.

As I slam the car door shut, I have a twinge of regret about leaving the granola bars on my bed, right where she'll see them. I should have stashed them in a drawer.

But in the time it takes me to walk across the parking lot, I've completely forgotten about it. Instead, I'm focused on doing the fastest check-in humanly possible with Mrs.

Frankel so I can join Josh and Nick over by the buses. "Were you guys the first ones here?" I ask as Nick makes room for me at the front of the line.

"Yup, we wanted to get the prime seats in the back." Josh has a serious look on his face, as if sitting in the back row is vital for our health and safety.

Nick rolls his eyes a little. "We got here before most of the teachers."

Everyone's been so pumped up about the trip that it seems like the ice cream scuffle has been forgotten. At least by everyone except Darren and me.

Once we're settled in the back, me in a seat by myself and Josh and Nick together across the aisle, the impact of eating seven pancakes hits me like a brick wall. As I fall into a heavy, full-stomach sleep, I hear Josh droning on about the tent assignments. We haven't even made it out of town yet, but I already know this trip is going to be great.

38

THE WORLD IS YOUR OYSTER

I'm way more impressed with this place than I expected. Before we've even pulled in, old-fashioned flute and drum music sails out from behind some trees to greet us. We pile off the buses, and staff dressed in old-fashioned clothes unload our bags from the luggage compartment. Our teachers direct us to a huge circle of split log benches surrounding a fire pit. Once we're all seated, the band—three guys in full colonial costumes—marches through an opening in the circle and stops dead center.

The oldest one looks like he's my dad's age. He takes a little bow and announces, "Welcome, travelers, to Abner Farms. I am John Conrad. Our community, which you will now call home, was established in the year sixteen hundred and ninety-four."

His voice booms like thunder, and even though I really want to turn around and check out the buildings around us, I feel like I'd better pay attention.

"Travelers, please accept our hospitality. It is my hope that your hard work and openness to our way of life will benefit us all. And now we will commence living together in this great new land."

Somewhere behind me, not close but not too far, a cannon goes off. After we shake off our initial startles, we cheer.

"Quiet, please," Mr. Conrad says in a more normal voice. He takes off his wide-brimmed hat and wipes his brow. "I can't keep up this formal vernacular for too long."

I'm kind of relieved he's not going to do the fake-colonial routine for our entire trip.

"We're glad to have you kids, and I'm sure this is going to be an adventure you'll never forget. But before we get going, we have to review the schedule and the expected behavior out here at Abner."

I wish we could skip ahead to the tent assignments. I'm almost positive I'll be grouped with Josh and Nick because a form in the information packet asked who we wanted to bunk with. There were spaces for up to five names. I only wrote two, but I'm sure Josh filled out every single line. Now that I'm thinking about it, maybe I should have used all the lines too.

"Let's start with the most important thing. Real colonial living was hard and frightening most of the time."

Mr. Conrad pauses, I guess so we can imagine some horrible, scary scenarios.

"Fortunately, survival isn't an issue at present-day Abner Farms." Mr. Conrad laughs at his own joke, and I'm thinking that for me, survival might actually be a real concern.

"But in order for us to have a positive camp experience, the same spirit of cooperation and community that our forefathers and foremothers used still applies," he continues. "If you see someone who needs a hand, jump in and help— whether it's on your job schedule or not."

He stares out past us and into the woods, crosses his arms, and tilts back on his heels like he's being especially thoughtful about what he's going to say next. "I want to be clear, this isn't summer camp."

His voice has dropped an octave or two. If he's trying to intimidate us, it's working.

"Goofing off, especially if it jeopardizes safety, is not tolerated here. I will not hesitate to send anyone home who cannot follow our rules. And since you all received our rules as part of your information packet, I assume you are clear on what they are."

We all nod, as if we're under a spell. Nobody wants to

cross this guy. All I want to do is get moving so I can start checking this place out.

Abner Farms is nestled in a clearing, surrounded by woods on three sides and a lake on the fourth. On the far side of the fire circle is a covered open-air pavilion with about twenty picnic tables. There's already a little fire going under a huge black pot, and I try not to imagine what it might hold.

On this side of the fire circle is a gravel path that curves under a carved wooden archway reading "Tent Row." In the distance is the lake, which sparkles like a million tiny mirrors behind an impressive stone lodge that seems to stand guard over this whole place. An ornate wooden staircase leads up to its huge wrap-around porch with at least a dozen black rocking chairs.

On either side of the lodge are fields. The one on the left looks like a baseball diamond, and the other is set up for archery. Behind me is a cluster of three small cabins. Hand-lettered signposts indicate that one is Mr. Conrad's cabin, one is an office, and the last one is for the nurse.

I think Mr. Conrad is probably sick of the sound of his own voice by the time he finally finishes his lecture about schedules, rules, and protocol. He's so worried about us getting lost or hurt that I'll be surprised if we ever get to do anything beyond being trapped in this circle, listening to him talk.

"And now for the tent assignments. When you hear your name, head over to the buses to retrieve your gear."

Everybody perks up. The girls are fidgety. A few are actually holding hands, like they're waiting to hear if they'll get a spot in the last lifeboat off the *Titanic*. Directly across the circle from me, Olivia sits alone, staring intently at her lap. Anyone watching would guess she's so nervous about her tent assignment that she's unable to lift her head. But I'm pretty sure that tucked behind her backpack is a book, probably about astrophysics or astronomy.

Mr. Conrad never had a hope of holding her attention.

I scan the crowd, trying to find Lauren—and then I spot her. Her hair is pulled back in two long braids with little blue bows at the ends. The girls she's sitting with—Tiffany, Rachel, and Claire—all have braids too. It must be a colonial thing. Maybe she can feel my stare, because suddenly she looks over at me. When our eyes meet, she looks away.

Nick elbows me as he gets up. I guess I didn't hear my name called. Josh is up and moving too, and I'm psyched to hear Alex and JT's names. But my pancake-stuffed stomach lurches like a go-cart when I hear the one name I was hoping to dodge. As Darren walks past me and straight toward Josh for a high-five, I'm pretty sure he rolls his eyes a little.

I need a game plan.

39

LOSE YOUR LUNCH

When I show up with my stuff, Josh is already waiting on the steps of our tent and grinning like a fool. It's bigger and sturdier than I expected—the tent sits on a raised platform under a huge pitched tarp, anchored on all sides by wooden supports. The back and side flaps are rolled up, giving us an awesome view of the lake—which is bordered with bright red and yellow fall leaves.

I'm out of breath from casually sprinting over here, determined to choose a cot as far away from Darren as possible, but I'm momentarily blown away by how cool it all is.

"Sweet," I say as I push past Josh on the stairs.

There are three beds on either side. Josh has dumped his stuff on the farthest one back on the left. I grab the first one on his side, closest to the entrance, leaving the middle cot for Nick. Suddenly I'm feeling better, knowing I have my own little corner.

As soon as the other guys arrive, a bell starts ringing from the dining pavilion as a signal for us to head there for lunch. Darren bee-lines for the farthest cot on the right, across from Josh, dropping his stuff and announcing, "I'm *starving*." Glancing at me, he adds, "Can't wait for some genuine colonial grub."

Or at least I *think* he glances at me. Before I can decide, everyone's rushing past me to head off to lunch. Darren bumps into me—hard—on his way out, and now I know I'm not imagining any of it.

Nick is standing outside, waiting for me.

"I'll catch up. I'm gonna grab a sweatshirt," I say, thinking

about how to put some space between Darren and me. I'm
in no hurry to see our first Abner Farms meal up close and
personal.

I rummage through my duffel until I find my blue sweatshirt and slowly head out of the tent. My pancake plan is
working so far—I'm not even hungry. But I haven't really
thought about exactly how I'm going to handle all the other non-flapjack meals. Mr. Conrad made it pretty clear that
we're supposed to stay together, so hiding out in the tent
until lunch is over is definitely not an option. I can only hope
that by the time I get over there, all the food will be gone.

Heading down the dirt path, I try to make it look like I'm
walking rather than downright stalling. But I've only made it
a couple of yards when I'm busted.

"Hello there, young man," someone says from behind me.

I turn, grateful to see it's not Mr. Conrad but an even
older guy in faded jeans and an army green flannel shirt maneuvering a huge black wheelbarrow filled with firewood. As
he pauses to catch his breath, five or six logs tumble out. It
occurs to me that I may not have to figure out the next move
of my not-eating plan—because it just landed at my feet.

I reach down and start stacking the logs in my arms to
carry them, ignoring the way they scratch through my sleeves.

"Thanks for your help. I guess I've overestimated the
capacity here."

"No problem," I say, and then I remember how Mom
always says that expression is rude. "Glad to help."

"Heading toward lunch, I presume?"

I nod, hoping he can't sense my lie.

"I'm Ben Abner," he says, reaching out his arm to shake
hands and then chuckling since my arms are full.

"I'm Ben too." I say. "Ben Snyder."

He lifts the hand grip of the wheelbarrow, and we start
walking.

"Ben, you make a fine apprentice."

"Wait," I say. "Is this your place?"

"Yup, my great-great-great-grandfather settled here. The wife and I live back yonder." He nods backward. "On the lake, just past Tent Row."

The clatter of dishes is getting closer. I have about a million questions I'd like to ask Mr. Abner, but for now I've got to stay focused on the problem of lunch.

The path curves, and up ahead the dining pavilion is buzzing with activity—a few of our teachers are still in line for food and others are already clearing their plates. Kids are crowded around the picnic tables, laughing and eating like they're at a party. Josh and Nick haven't noticed me. They're sitting with the other guys from our tent, making so much noise that I wonder if they're trying to be obnoxious. Staff dressed in colonial clothes are tending to the fires and scraping out huge black kettles. My best bet is to keep chatting with Mr. Abner until all the wood is neatly stacked.

"So if you're the boss, why are you working so hard?" I ask.

He laughs a loud, bellowing laugh that I hope doesn't draw any attention as we head past the food line and toward the pile. "Keeps me young, I guess."

I'm relieved my conversation is entertaining Mr. Abner. If he's enjoying himself, he might let me help him until lunch is over.

Suddenly, the heavy smell of roasting meat hits me in the face. Its stench is sharper and denser than anything my mom ever cooks at home. Before I remember to hold my breath, the smell is in my mouth and has become a taste so thick and revolting I start to gag. My need to drop these logs and run for miles and miles is so strong and convincing that my legs are actually twitching.

But somehow I continue to follow Mr. Abner past the food, around to the far corner of the pavilion, and back to a small shed. The smell is still making me fight back ob-

scene images of maggots floating in the liquefied garbage
that sloshes around the bottom of our trash cans at home. I
mentally scream at myself to calm down, and I tilt my head
toward my chest and try to breathe in the clean smell of my
sweatshirt.

Mr. Abner sets the wheelbarrow down and turns, arms
outstretched to take the logs from me, and the expression on
his face tells me I don't look so good.

"You okay, Ben?"

I nod, knowing if I open my mouth, I will hurl.

"You'd better head over and get yourself some lunch before they run out."

I nod again and walk out of the pavilion, far away from
everyone, until I reach a clump of bushes. When I think I'm
safely out of view, I bend at the waist, resting my palms on
my thighs, and wait. I'm panting like I've just run a race, but
after a few seconds the feeling passes and I slowly stand back
up.

But I'm frozen in place—there's no way I can get myself
to walk back toward the food, but I have no legitimate reason
to be out here by myself. I'd like to make a run for the buses
and maybe hide out in one for a little while, but it's too risky
to sprint through the center of camp where there's no cover.
I'm staring at my bus, thinking about how cool and quiet
it must be in there, when I notice someone stepping down
from it holding an enormous cardboard box.

I've never been so happy to see Mrs. Frankel in my entire
life.

I run toward her, and she sets the box on the ground.

"Mr. Snyder, I see you're taking the suggestions about
being helpful to heart."

I pick up the box. "Where are we headed?" I ask, praying
it's not back near the food.

"Right over there, where we started this morning." She
points to the campfire circle. "If you've already eaten, you

can spend a few minutes helping me organize these things."

As we pull out dozens of colored bandanas and several big stacks of papers, I congratulate myself on dodging the first non-flapjack meal. It's only going to get easier from here.

40

Top Banana

Twenty minutes later, my enthusiasm is fading.

We're all back on the log benches, and Mr. Butler is standing in the middle of the circle talking about team building and making new friends. Suddenly it's perfectly clear that we're not going to be choosing who we work with on *anything* while we're here, because every single detail has been prearranged by the teachers. And even worse, Mr. Butler explains that our teams are assigned by science class and our orienteering partners will be our lab partners.

Olivia smiles at me from across the circle.

I want to hide. I didn't come all the way out here to hang out with Olivia. My mind races as I mentally compose a passionate speech in which I remind Mr. Butler that the colonists journeyed to America in search of freedom and self-determination—not to be bossed around; that in the spirit of colonialism, we should be able to choose our own groups and our own project partners. At the end, I'd yell, "Give me liberty or give me death!"

But instead, I'm handed a stupid purple bandana. I have no other choice, so I tie it around my neck. On the plus side, I'll be spending a lot of time with Lauren. But on the negative side, I'll be spending the same amount of time with Olivia and Darren.

According to the schedule, my afternoon will consist of the dumbest of dumb colonial activities, starting with sewing a leather pouch at the lodge, followed by quill and ink writing, and ending with supper prep. At some point today there's something called *rounders* that seems promising, since it meets on the field. The clang of a bell indicates when one activity is over and the next one begins. Josh and Nick, in matching red bandanas, don't look back as they race toward wood splitting. They're going to be wielding axes while I'm threading a needle. Life has never been more unfair.

I stand up slowly, not eager for my sewing lesson. Olivia barrels toward me, and I realize in a split second that things could actually get worse. I'm sure she assumes that our lab partner status means we're going to do everything together. I slip behind a group of other purple bandana girls headed toward the lodge in an effort to dodge her.

A few yards away, Darren is scanning the crowd, and I know in the pit of my stomach exactly who he's looking for. Once he spots Lauren, he rushes over to her. I watch, dejected, as they walk together.

Someone comes up on my left and I turn, not surprised to see Olivia. She's panting a little from catching up with me. I pick up my pace and stare across the lawn at the archery field, where a luckier group of kids is about to learn something cool.

"I've got something for you," she says, reaching deep in her sweatshirt pocket.

Alarm bells go off in my head. I have no idea what might be in there, but whatever it is, I'm sure it's creepy weird. Like a frog. Or a love letter, written in her own made-up language. There's no way I'm going to take whatever she's offering, especially in front of the rest of our group.

"Uh, wow. That's great, you know, but I don't need anything right now," I say as I try to race up the steps to the lodge. "So could it wait until later?"

"I guess. I mean it's up to you." She slows down.

For once she's picking up on social cues like a regular human. I try not to think about how offended she looks. I don't know why she keeps following me around. She's interfering with my ability to keep track of Lauren, who is now pulling

Darren next to her as we all grab seats at a huge wooden table. Just when I think I'm safe, Olivia reappears and plops down way too close to me, announcing that she certainly hopes we will not be using real animal skins for this activity.

After only a few lopsided stitches, I'm sure I won't ever trust my leather pouch to hold anything valuable. But I focus on what I'm doing and pretend to concentrate, mostly so I don't have to watch Lauren and Darren whisper and smile at each other.

I have to be patient while I wait for the right opportunity to turn things around.

41

Winner Winner Chicken Dinner

"Listen up!" Mr. Conrad yells.

We're all huddled around him on the field, with most of us hoping this next Abner Farms activity will be more fun than the last ones. I hope I never see another quill pen.

Mr. Conrad is losing his voice. But he's determined to describe, in painstaking detail, how to play rounders—which he says is the colonial version of baseball. As far as I can tell, the main differences between rounders and baseball are that rounders is played with a wiffle ball and a small wooden stick the batter carries around the bases—or *posts,* as they're called—and that each team only bats one time, running through their line-up over and over until every player has made an out. Theoretically, I could bat fifty times and the game would go on forever. The team with the most runs, or rounders, wins.

Most of the regular baseball rules about making an out apply to rounders, as well as a couple of extra ones—like dropping the stick while running the bases, overtaking another runner, and trying to steal before the ball has left the pitcher's hand. But I'm not worried about making an out.

I daydream while Mr. Conrad talks about scoring, because it seems unnecessarily complicated—especially compared to modern-day baseball. Besides, I'm too busy imagining how far the ball is going to sail when I crush it. This is my first chance to amaze Lauren by doing something truly heroic—like making a game-winning home run.

Mr. Conrad divides our purple group in half, which works

out well for Darren and the other guys from science class he was standing with. But Lauren had wandered a few feet away from Darren for a perfectly timed minute, putting her on my team. I'm pumped, imagining all the ways I will blow her mind with my athletic ability.

Immediately there's a problem with my plan. Our team is up first, which makes it impossible for me to make the game-winning homer. But I figure I can still make a memorable hit—maybe I'll get it all the way into the lake.

"I'll pitch," Darren announces with his usual cockiness.

Of course he's volunteered for the position that will make him the center of attention. I study his form as he takes a few underhand practice pitches—or *bowls*, as Mr. Conrad keeps calling them. Weirdly, batters can still get on base, even if they don't make contact with the ball, as long as they make it to the first post without being *stumped*.

As the game gets going, the girls on my team are screaming and cheering like it's the Olympics. It seems like they actually paid attention during Mr. Conrad's speech, because they all make it to the first post. Two guys on our team forget to run after they've missed the ball, instinctively dropping their heads and handing the stick to the next player.

I hang back, wanting to bat at the bottom of the order so I can make sure everyone who's on base gets home. Lauren bats ahead of me, and she doesn't even try to hit the ball—instead she sprints to the first post as soon as the ball leaves Darren's hand. The pitch goes right between the catcher's legs, giving Lauren plenty of time to run. Right away Darren is teasing her, demanding that she's called out. Lauren is obviously satisfied with her strategy, and I try not to laugh—especially when Mr. Conrad comes on the field and says, "That's not really in the spirit of the game." But he doesn't take Lauren off her post. Now I'm even more determined to send her home with my big hit.

Darren's face twists into a scowl as I step onto the batter's square. His first bowl bounces before it gets to me, and Mr. Conrad yells, "No-ball!"

I take a practice swing, which feels a little ridiculous considering the size of this wooden stick, but I bet it looks intimidating to Darren, who's in a lose-lose situation—either he bumbles the next pitch and I get a walk, or he feeds me a decent one and I annihilate it. I'm counting on the latter.

I choke up on the stick, get my feet in position, and stare him down. I hear a couple of kids yell, "You've got this, Ben," and I know as soon as it leaves his hand, they're right.

I swing so hard it's possible I've dislocated my shoulder. I look toward the sky, and that's when I realize I've missed it. Whiffed. I'm so stunned I can barely hear the crowd screaming at me. As I start to run, I watch as Darren snatches the ball from the ground and barrels over to the first post. I'm out, but he walks over and tags me, hard, at my hip anyway.

"Nice hit," he says under his breath.

I wish the ground would crack open and suck me into a gargantuan sinkhole, never to be seen again. But I don't have that kind of luck today.

"Six and a half rounders for the first team," Mr. Conrad yells in a hoarse voice as we take the field.

We're all bummed about how quickly we made our outs. This prehistoric game is harder than it looks. I grab a spot in the vicinity of where third base should be, and wish I had a baseball cap. The sun is low, blazing in my eyes, and I guess we have about forty-five minutes of daylight left. I'd like this stupid game to be over, but our next activity is dinner prep—and I'm not in any hurry to do that either.

An edginess has begun to overtake my concentration. I'm sure it has a lot to do with my pathetic at-bat, but it feels like something else too. Everything is starting to irritate me, including Lauren and her BFFs, who are yelling dumb cheers from the outfield.

My complicated maneuvers to avoid Olivia all afternoon

have paid off—I almost forgot about her. But now she's up, and even though I can't hear what she's saying to Mr. Conrad, I'm sure from the way they're both looking at the muddy wiffle ball we're using that it's some sort of criticism about the authenticity of our rounders experience.

She's holding up the game. As I start to mentally review all the ways she irritates me, I realize what else is bothering me. I'm hungry. Not in a desperate, urgent way, but in a firm, threatening way—as if my stomach is making an announcement over the loudspeaker at school: "Benjamin Snyder, please report to the principal's office immediately."

This is not a great development. I've been counting on having a full stomach until tomorrow. I thought Mom's pancakes would hold me over.

Olivia has somehow stumbled over to the first post. No one from her team is cheering her on, which doesn't surprise me. For a second, I actually feel a little sorry for her. But I also hope she's called out before she makes it over to my side of the infield.

Darren is up, and his entire team, minus Olivia, is cheering for him like he's a rock star. I know he knows how badly I want him to miss, and I look down and smile for a second, hoping nobody notices. But when I look back up, the ball's coming right at me—a screaming line drive, possibly foul. Before I even think about it, I'm airborne, my arm stretched across the front of my body until it's almost popped out of its socket. I've snagged the ball, and I crash back to earth, savoring the sting shooting from my palm up toward my elbow. I stay on the ground for a second longer than I need to, waiting for the cheers from the outfield and mentally assessing the gravel digging into my other arm.

"Awesome catch, man!" somebody yells as I get up, and even Olivia is clapping—probably because she doesn't understand I just got one of her teammates out. Or maybe because she does.

I swipe most of the gravel off and take a quick glance across the field at Lauren, anticipating her admiration. She's fiddling with her braids and not looking my way. I'm not even sure she saw my catch. But the simmering irritation smeared across Darren's face tells me it's already seared in his memory. For now, that's good enough.

We're winning, but the game is close and their next batter is a talented kid I remember from Little League. His hit sails through the outfield, and Lauren and her friends scramble after it. He's fast, moving like a cheetah, and it feels like everyone on both teams recognizes the problem with his speed right away—because according to the rules, he can't overtake another runner or they'll both be out.

And he's gaining on Olivia. She's blissfully unaware of what's happening, completely oblivious to the yelling and screaming about how slow she's moving toward the next post. Her gait is so cautious and awkward that she looks like a grandma trying to chase a bus down the street.

I start to yell, too, hoping maybe Olivia will hear *me*, her trusted lab partner, telling her to pick up the pace.

But it's Darren's voice she finally notices, shouting, "Come on, snotlick! What's wrong with you?" Olivia turns her head toward him in disbelief and trips, her face splattering down in the dirt. But the batter can't slow down, so he leaps over her like a long jumper.

I sprint to where Olivia lies in a mangled heap and drop to my knees next to her. "Olivia! Are you okay?"

She's motionless, and I'm thinking she might be paralyzed or dead. After a second her arms and legs start to move, and she sits herself up. I'm relieved she's not crying, but as soon as I register that thought, her eyes fill up and tears tumble down her face. Mr. Conrad barks orders about finding some ice, but no one else seems to care about Olivia—which strikes me as pretty crappy.

I hesitate but then put my arm around her, the same way

I do with Maddie when she gets hurt, and say, "It's okay" over and over. But I don't take my eyes off Darren. I haven't heard anyone call Olivia that name in years, and I'm surprised he even knows about it since he didn't go to our elementary school.

From out of nowhere Lauren appears and crouches on the ground next to us. She sighs in disgust. "I can't believe what just happened. It's not worth getting hurt over a stupid game."

Lauren and I help Olivia to her feet, but she says she's dizzy. I keep my arm around her as Mr. Conrad points out the nurse's office on the other side of the fire circle.

"I'll take her," I say to Mr. Conrad. I glance over at Lauren, thinking she might offer to come too. She's smiling at me, just a little. It's enough to make my heart blast off to the moon and back.

A few kids clap as Olivia and I walk off the field. When I get close enough, I glare at Darren and say, "At least *she* got on base."

42

STEW IN IT

Beef barley stew. Succotash. Cornbread. Chocolate Pudding.

Beefbarleystewsuccotashcornbreadchocolatepudding.

It's been on repeat in my head ever since I realized I was hungry. I've been sitting on the nurse's front stoop for at least twenty minutes, pretending to wait for Olivia. Hopefully I've been here long enough to have missed the food prep work. Finally the nurse comes outside and tells me Olivia is taking a little nap, so I should leave and catch up with my group. I'm out of options, so I drag myself toward the pavilion. On the other side of the fire circle, some kids are already starting to show up for dinner.

Beefbarleystewsuccotashcornbreadchocolatepudding.

I'm sure this is a particularly disgusting menu, even for normal eaters. Earlier today somebody in our tent said that succotash is a wet combo of corn and lima beans—gross by any standard. There are a bunch of foods I wish I could eat because it would make life easier—like pizza and burgers and hot dogs and birthday cake—but tonight's menu items have never made it on my list.

The closer I get to the pavilion, the more deflated I feel. My dad's predictions about the great outdoors sparking an appetite so monstrous I'd eat whatever's being served now seems as unlikely as my ability to sprout a tail, morph into a squirrel, and buzz up a tree. This morning while I was stuffing pancakes down my throat at home, I was sure I could pull this off. But now that confidence has shriveled up into a small, hard knot in my stomach, pulsating with each step and taunting me with its warnings of danger and starvation.

I've got to get my head on straight before I face the reality of dinner. I run through some battle-tested tactics I've used before when facing impossible eating situations, but I'm so keyed up that my thoughts crash into each other like bumper cars.

As I sort through my arsenal of survival maneuvers, I pull my top strategies to come up with a five-rule plan.

Rule #1: Show No Emotion. Staying calm is nearly impossible when I'm hungry or tired. But if I act stressed out or upset, it might encourage more attention.

Rule #2: Avoid Suspicion. The momentary victory of keeping something off my plate is more than offset when someone notices its absence. I'm better off accepting a serving of something than to keep my plate empty, even if I never take a bite.

Rule #3: Initiate Mental Lockdown. Sometimes I have to turn off my own brain. Left unchecked, I can make bad food situations worse by letting my imagination run at full throttle. So when people are eating terrible things near me, I have to try to limit my thoughts to something harmless—like trying to remember who I was with when I saw each *Star Wars* movie.

Rule #4: Plead the Fifth. Try not to say anything about my eating that's likely to trigger further questions or a discussion about what I eat and what I don't and why. It's best to stick with a one-line explanation. Generally it's a gargantuan lie, like, "I'm not hungry" or "I already ate." I've learned the hard way that the worst possible thing to say is "I don't feel well." It usually attracts unwanted adult attention.

Rule #5: Abort the Mission. In only the most desperate situations, when my sense of self-preservation is so damaged that the only thing I can think to do is escape to the bathroom and hide out until the meal is over.

On some desperate occasions, I've tried some other pathetic moves I found online. Like numbing my taste buds with cold water before taking a bite (doesn't work). Or drying my tongue with a napkin to render the sense of taste less effective (just makes the food taste worse and interferes with swallowing). The riskiest move in the not-eating playbook is the choice of last resort: hiding food in my napkin, which is really nothing more than a stalling technique and only effective until I stand up and have to dispose of the evidence. If the situation is hopeless enough to even be considering any of these options, it's better to give up and retreat.

I'm as ready as I'll ever be.

It looks like my group has finished the work. They're hanging out on the far side of the pavilion. I'd like to get over there and blend in before an adult asks me to do something.

But I can't pull it off. A tall, official-looking woman in a brown colonial dress and apron is looking for me.

"Ben Snyder?" she calls to me.

I nod and walk over to her, and she gets right down to business.

"I'm Mrs. Larsen, and I run the kitchen here. I understand you were otherwise occupied earlier when your group did food prep. So I saved a couple jobs for you, one to be done before you eat and one after."

"I need you on water duty right now, and then you'll be my silver watchman during cleanup."

She nods in the direction of a picnic table holding at least a dozen metal pitchers. On the floor nearby is a stack of plastic dish racks filled with glasses.

"Get going," she says. "You only have about five minutes till it gets wild in here."

My relief about this water-pouring job is so intense I want to high-five Mrs. Larsen.

The pitchers are icy to the touch, and I wonder if Abner Farms has an old well nearby, pumping our water from the same aquifer the colonists used. But there's no time to ask or even think about it, because I have to get to work. I fumble around for a minute or two, trying to figure out the best way to get the glasses out of the racks and onto the table and filled with water in the least amount of time.

After a few attempts, I decide the best thing to do is to line up the glasses really close together and then make a continuous pour down each row. I guess there are some benefits to outdoor dining. I'm also thinking ahead, planning to offer to refill these pitchers that I'm being rather careless with. Hopefully that water well is really far away.

Mrs. Larsen glances at me, a look of surprise flashing across her face as she notices the puddles under the table. I'm ready for her to yell, but instead she smiles and looks away.

Kids are starting to line up for dinner, and I watch Mrs. Larsen give a nod to the other apron-wearing ladies manning huge pots of food. I switch over to one hundred percent mouth breathing.

A glass of water is the last thing to grab at this colonial buffet, so I have a couple of minutes to piece together a survival strategy while I wait for my first customers.

I try to think clearly, but hunger is messing with my concentration. Several variables are working against me, but I need to stay calm. I try to channel the attitude of an airline attendant directing passengers during an emergency landing.

I consider the biggest problem first: I'm wicked hungry. Breakfast was ten hours ago, and my next breakfast is at least fourteen hours away. I'm a little light-headed and definitely edgy. But before I cave into a full-blown panic, I remind myself that, according to a recent Google search, it would take thirty to forty days for me to actually starve to death—maybe even longer with proper hydration. I've never needed guidelines for eating in public so badly.

I do a quick review of the next four rules: *Avoid Suspicion, Initiate Mental Lockdown, Plead the Fifth, and Abort the Mission.* The words blow around in my mind, feeling flimsy and weak. I am definitely in over my head.

With each passing second, my chances of skipping this meal are diminishing. A few guys are already headed toward me for water, and I watch in horror as one kid accidentally tips his plate with one hand while he reaches for a glass with the other, resulting in a reddish-brown streak of beef stew gravy-grease dripping onto the concrete. My mind explodes with sickening interpretations of what the brown splash on the ground looks like—and before I can torment myself for too long, I initiate *Rule #3: Initiate Mental Lockdown*, desperate to turn off my own brain. Sometimes math is the best option, like counting backwards from five hundred by sevens.

Just when I start to calm down, Albert shows up at my side and says one word. "Beanbags."

"Huh?" I ask, desperate for him to leave me alone but also understanding he won't until I hear him out.

"Replace all the desk chairs at school with beanbags, so we can learn in comfort."

I pretend to think about it. "Interesting," I say. "I'll give it some thought."

It's enough positive reinforcement to send him on his way.

I'm resigned to the fact that once my water duties are over, I'll be forced to take a plate of steaming food that might as well be puke and sit with my friends—and Darren, who is busy with his own dinner-related job somewhere around here. I'll have to be ready for whatever questions and insults he hurls my way. He is going to be all over my case when he realizes I'm not eating at all.

I'm only feeling lukewarm about my rules right now, so I consider what my threshold for pain and humiliation will be for *Rule #5: Abort the Mission*. If it gets to that point, I might as well go home. Mrs. Larsen marches over and hands me a plate of food. "Go ahead and eat, and as soon as you're done, check in with me at the clearing area." She points at a row of black industrial garbage cans.

As soon as you're done sounds promising.

43

BOTTOM OF THE BARREL

My plate holds a swampland of soupy muck. If I make one misstep on the way to my table, I will disrupt the soggy equilibrium and drip it onto my shoes—or even worse, my hands. Balancing requires I do the one thing I want to avoid—look at my food.

My mind zigs and zags, ignoring my Mental Lockdown command as I try to figure out what the ridges running down each little grain of barley look like. After a second I know—butt cracks. I start to laugh but stop myself when I arrive at our table. I need to put my game face on before I sit down.

There's a spot between Josh and Nick, almost like they saved it for me. My relief fades as I set my plate on the table, realizing I am sitting directly across from Darren. Everybody's talking, and for a second while I unfold my napkin and put it in my lap, I entertain a brief fantasy involving Darren being snatched by a pack of vultures, his screams fading as they fly off into the woods.

Suddenly I remember that water is my best weapon to fight hunger. I reach for my glass and start gulping, hoping it will trick my stomach into feeling satisfied.

"You got the lumberjack portion," Darren says, his eyes darting up from my plate to meet mine.

My left leg starts doing that nervous jittery thing where it bounces about a thousand times a minute. I rest my hand on my knee, pushing so my heel stays on the floor. But as soon as I take it off, my leg starts up again, shaking like the paint cans in the mixing machines at the hardware store.

I plunge my fork into the middle of my plate and smile, careful not to look at what I've stabbed. "Yup."

If I even consider the possibility of putting the fork in my mouth, I'll puke. I'm frozen in place, waiting for something to happen.

"So what's the holdup?" Darren asks, his mouth pulling into a scowl. "Can't wait to see you dig in."

Everyone is staring at me. My eyes are tearing up, and that's what tells me I'm in deep trouble. Maneuvering through a high-stakes dining situation is bad enough—but doing it this hungry is impossible. I'm jumpy, trapped, and too grossed out. My stomach is gurgling and stretching, as if a live animal is trying to claw its way out. Usually hunger pangs come in bursts and then stop, but these roll out like waves, determined to drown me.

I need to create a distraction.

I put my fork down, watching a lone carrot slime its way through the gravy and past some lima beans. Turning to Josh and his completely empty plate, I say, "Wow. Are you gonna eat the table too?"

The old Josh would have jumped into some stupid banter with me, but new Josh is already scanning the crowd, probably plotting his next social move. He's barely heard what I said, and he's definitely not going to help me create a diversion. Nick seems to be intentionally ignoring me—the way I try to ignore Maddie when she's embarrassing me.

Darren, on the other hand, is mesmerized. "Aren't you eating?"

"Not hungry," I say, shrugging and holding his gaze.

"Really?" he asks. "We were all starving." Darren looks like he's deciding whether to let it drop or not. He doesn't. "Not even the cornbread? It's pretty good."

I glance down at my plate, again hit with a burning taste crawling up my throat. I study my slice of cornbread, noticing it has actual kernels of corn in it, protruding from its crevices like zits. I look up again, willing my face to hide every single emotion I'm feeling. "Nope."

Darren leans back, clasping his hands behind his head like he's in charge. "I'm thinking you've never tried cornbread."

It's a challenge—and if I wasn't so hungry and ready to jump out of my skin, I might have a clue about how to respond. I go with *Rule #4: Plead the Fifth* and don't say anything, which I guess is as good as admitting he's right.

"I'm just sayin', how do you know you don't like it if you've never tried it?" Darren is laughing like he's a comedian, and a couple of the guys chuckle along. Josh and Nick aren't exactly laughing. They actually look as mortified as I feel. But they're not making a move to help me out, either.

"What's the deal?" I ask. "You want mine?" I grab the cornbread off my plate, careful not to touch any of the wet crud it was sitting in. I hold my arm up, as if I'm about to throw a pass.

Darren shakes his head. "No offense, dude. I was just asking."

It's time to engage *Rule #5: Abort the Mission.* I don't know if I've been sitting here for two minutes or two hours.

"What are you, my mom?" I say, standing up and grabbing my plate. My breathing is ragged, like I've just run a mile.

I head toward the garbage cans, questioning whether things are now better or worse.

I've only taken a couple of steps when Darren yells. "Hey, cornbread!"

Keep walking, I tell myself, staring at the far end of the pavilion.

"Cornbread!" He's louder this time, and a few people turn around to see what's going on. Everyone else is still seated, so it's clear I'm the moving target. I pause, knowing the absolute worst thing I could do is turn around and face him.

The whole place has gone quiet, like we're under a spell, and I'm pretty sure this is what Darren has been waiting for—the moment when he has everyone's attention. "You're a freak!" His voice cuts through the silence. "A cornbread freak!"

An eruption of laughter echoes off the wooden rafters, and a sharp, angry pain tears at my side like I've been punched. Only Darren could make the word *cornbread* sound hilarious.

As promised, Mrs. Larsen is waiting for me by the garbage cans. She glances down at my full plate and hesitates for a second. I'm sure she's wondering if she should give me some sort of lecture about how the colonists didn't waste food. But instead she takes the plate out of my hand, and using her thumb to hold my silverware, slides the entire pile of muck into a garbage can.

"Personally I think it's ridiculous to use real silverware when we could use plastic, but I'm in the minority," she says, tossing my fork and knife into a plastic bin. "So it's your job to make sure we don't lose too many of them."

My mind is still reeling from what just happened. I'm eyeing some uneaten bowls of pudding on a table near me and considering whether I should pick one up and drop it on Darren's head. Logically I know that's not a good idea, but I'm so worked up with starvation and rage that it's hard to tell.

Mrs. Larsen looks at me blankly. "Understand?"

"No," I say, following her gaze down to the garbage. Then it hits me—she actually wants me to save the silverware from drowning in succotash and beef barley hurl.

"What?"

"Don't worry, you don't have to reach in there or anything." She points to a stick with a net attached to one end. "You can fish 'em out."

I stare at Mrs. Larsen. A few strands of damp hair are sticking to her neck. "Is this a joke?"

"Absolutely not." She hands me the net. "It helps to remind them before they dump their scraps."

Mrs. Larsen rushes away, leaving me standing open-mouthed and hyperventilating. I lurch to one side, knocking against the garbage can, which wobbles for a second, threatening to overturn. As I steady myself, the stink of its contents engulfs me.

If there ever was a time to admit defeat, this is it. I've overestimated my ability to endure the lethal combination of colonial living and Darren's harassment. I'm debating whether I should leave now and make a run for the nurse's cabin. But before I can leave, the first group of kids shows up with their dirty dishes.

"Silverware in the bin!" My voice is high-pitched and panicky.

"Settle down, cornbread," somebody says, and the laughter that follows reminds me of cackling witches stirring their brew. I force out a laugh of my own, surprising myself with the sudden realization that I'm *not* completely out of gas—I might still have a shred of fight left in me. I just have to wait for the right chance to use it.

My new nickname has spread through the pavilion like the flu, with each kid who says it thinking he's a genius. A couple of them try to be creative by acting like they're going to puke into the garbage can. I laugh along with that too, pretending they are the first ones to think of it. I don't look in to see if anyone has actually dropped a piece of silverware, but I keep reminding everybody and acting like this is the most fun I've ever had.

Somehow my determination to keep standing here is stronger than my disgust for what's happening right under my nose. In between people, I hold my breath for as long as possible, then when I'm about to burst, I turn away to grab some fresh air.

I've finally gotten the hang of the breathing and not looking and laughing at my own expense when Lauren brings her plate over and I lose track of everything.

She smiles and whispers, "Are you okay with all this *corn-bread* stuff?"

I nod. "It's no big deal," I say, wishing it were true.

"Okay, well, I'll see you at the campfire." She flashes me a smile. This is the moment I've been waiting for. But I'm too hungry to enjoy it.

"Right," I say, trying to smile back. But I'm laser-focused on Darren, who is now three or four people back at my garbage-dumping station. I want her to leave, to be far from what is about to happen, and I'm relieved when she finally walks away.

I know what Darren is going to do, and I bet he knows I know too. He looks me straight in the eye and dumps what's on his plate into the can, including his silverware.

"Oops, cornbread. I guess you'll have to take care of that for me."

I plunge my net into the sludge, concentrating only on the flash of silver floating on the top, and I pull the net through the heavy wet slop until I hit the solid rubber side of the garbage can. I yank the net up higher than I need to and flick my wrist, splashing Darren with an obscene combination of gravy and chunks of soggy vegetables. It's worse than I expected. The front of his sweatshirt is covered, and a lima bean is stuck to his cheek.

"Oops," I say.

It's nice to be on this side of all the laughter, but Darren's glare tells me I might have gone too far. And the looks Nick and Josh are giving me from the back of the line tell me the same thing.

Darren wipes his face with sleeve of his sweatshirt before he walks away, seemingly oblivious to the way other kids move away when they see him coming.

The teachers are directing everyone to head over to the fire pit in the middle of camp. I need to finish this job without thinking about my own sweatshirt, which I'm sure is splattered with gravy and mush. As soon as the last kid has been through the line, I look down and start to retch. I sprint out of the pavilion, where I gag behind some bushes. The dry-heaving squeezes my empty stomach and wrenches the muscles in my sides and lower back. Finally the glass of water that was supposed to shield me from hunger spews out, bitter and burning in my throat.

I peel off my sweatshirt, grateful that the T-shirt underneath is still dry. I wad the sweatshirt into a ball and hide it in a nearby bush. I'm shivering—from hunger, cold, nausea, and a little bit of satisfaction.

Lauren is sitting with a horde of girls on the logs around the fire pit circle. When she sees me, she waves and slides over to an empty spot. I sit down next to her, and she nudges me with her shoulder.

"You know what?" she asks, her eyebrows furled like she's deep in thought. "I like cornbread."

"Thanks," I say, weighing out the different meanings of what she's telling me. I'm pretty sure they all mean she likes me.

"And I was really impressed with how you helped Olivia this afternoon. I didn't know you two were such good friends."

I am facing the most critical moral dilemma of my life. I helped Olivia without thinking about it because it was the right thing to do. I also tried to ditch her a couple of times today. So I don't know if Olivia and I are really friends. And I don't know if I want to be. But I might be okay with Lauren thinking Olivia and I are friends if it makes her like me again. I don't want to commit either way, so I nod. And that nod seems to be sufficient for Lauren to jump to another subject—Darren's latest name for me.

"It's kind of a *different* nickname," Lauren says, deep in thought. "Why did Darren start that cornbread stuff anyway?"

"No idea. Just Darren being a jerk," I lie. I'm craning my neck, looking around for Josh and Nick. Honestly, I'm more interested in their thoughts about what happened back there with Darren than Lauren's.

Lauren is going off on a tangent about nicknames. Nicknames she's heard. Nicknames she thinks are cute. Nicknames she wishes someone would call her. I nod like I'm taking it all in. She's a human wind-up toy, unable to stop until all her energy has been depleted.

I spot Josh first—he's standing in the middle of a big group of guys who seem to be angling for position next to him. Darren, who has ditched his sweatshirt, too, is off to one side. Darren looks calm, like he's on autopilot or something, and I have no idea whether that's a good sign or not. Nick is standing on the other side of the group, and when I see him he nods like he's been waiting for me to notice him. He raises his eyebrows and tilts his head toward the other guys—and Darren. Nobody else in the world would be able to decipher what he's trying to say, but I hear him loud and clear: *What were you thinking back there?*

I shrug in return, which seems to sum up the entirety of my thoughts right now.

Jack walks past us with a few girls. "Hey, cornbread," he says, slapping my back.

I laugh but Lauren doesn't. "Don't worry about it," she says. "By tomorrow everybody will be talking about something else."

It occurs to me that Lauren probably hasn't heard about what I did back at the slop bucket. I have to jump on this golden opportunity to narrate my own story before someone else does. I turn toward her and whisper, "I have to tell you something." I know the whispering will get her attention. She scoots closer.

"What?" Her eyes are huge. I can tell she's trying to mirror my serious tone, but an excited smile is pulling at her mouth.

"He's got some obsessed attitude with me," I start, nodding my head in Darren's general direction.

I'm half-hoping Lauren will jump in with a complicated theory of how I trigger a crushing insecurity in Darren, complete with all the reasons why. But she just nods.

As I mentally sort through what to say, choosing and discarding words at lightning speed, I feel like an NBA player taking the ball down the lane, bobbing and weaving, looking for my shot. My goal is to present myself as a reluctant hero, standing up for myself—and not as an irrational garbage-throwing monster. And I have to do it without mentioning food.

"So right after you cleared your plate, well, Darren brought his—and he *accidentally* dropped his silverware in the scrap bucket so I *accidentally* spilled wet food scraps and garbage on him when I got his silverware back out."

"Gross," Lauren says thoughtfully.

"Yeah, totally gross." I wait, letting it sink in.

"But you had to do *something*. I mean you've gotta *defend* yourself."

I'm liking Lauren more and more.

"I don't know what his problem is," she says, shaking her head.

Honestly, I don't either. Tonight I might have beat him at his own game, but there's still a lot of colonial living ahead of us. Glancing back at Josh and Nick, I wonder if I should be hanging out over there too, instead of explaining myself to Lauren. Even though I don't want to admit it, I can't help wondering if either of them has my back on all this or if I'm in it alone. For the first time ever, I wish I was part of an official squad.

Everyone sits down, and Mr. Conrad marches in front of the fire circle to announce a special Abner Farms surprise: we're going to make s'mores, despite the fact that real colonists didn't have marshmallows or graham crackers or chocolate bars. As if on cue, Mrs. Larsen and the other food-serving ladies arrive holding trays of s'mores supplies.

"You can't really have a campfire without s'mores," Mr. Conrad says, more enthusiastic than what seems appropriate for an adult. "It's an American tradition."

Everyone's excitement about another thing I don't eat makes me feel like running off into the woods. The only bright side is that maybe Lauren will let me roast hers—I'm actually a great marshmallow-roaster because I take my time. Unlike most people, I'm in no hurry to eat my creation. But when Mr. Conrad starts leading us in corny camp songs, I know I'm in dangerous territory. I'm crashing. I'm way too hungry, and I'm starting to seriously doubt I can make it another day and a half here. Scanning the crowd, it's clear that I'm the only one here who's not having a great time.

Maybe Darren was right. Maybe I am a freak.

44

RUNNING ON EMPTY

My fingers are gooey from roasting Lauren's marshmallows to perfection. As the guys and I walk back to our tent, I'm struggling to follow the conversations going on around me about tomorrow's orienteering competition. I give up trying and focus instead on the sound of gravel crunching under my feet, and I realize I'm struggling to keep up with the other guys. It feels like everyone else is running. Worried I might puke again, I hang back a little. I'm relieved when Nick does the same.

"You okay?"

"Yeah," I say, grateful for the dark.

"Don't let him get to you," Nick says.

"I'm trying not to. But that kid's a piece of work."

"Or maybe you're making a big deal out of everything."

"What are you talking about?" My voice is sharp and defensive. "He's out to get me."

Nick stops walking. "I'm talking about the thing with the cornbread. And the garbage can. And the ice cream the other day. Nobody's out to get you. But seriously, if you keep this crap up, no one's gonna want to hang out with you."

"Got it," I say, needing to shut this conversation down.

We walk the rest of the way in silence, but my thoughts about what he just said are deafening. Nick didn't say it out loud, but it sure feels like he's calling me out on the way I eat, which has never happened before. A long time ago Nick and Josh asked me about my eating, but it hasn't come up again. It's never been a big deal.

But now I guess it is. Somehow my eating habits are more

than a minor inconvenience—they're a liability. And when Nick said no one's going to want to hang out with me, I think Nick might have been talking about himself and Josh.

By the time Nick and I climb the steps to our tent, our bunkmates are already coming down, pushing past us and headed to the showers. I'd do almost anything to skip the shower and crawl into bed, but I'd probably get hassled about stinking up our tent with BO—so I rummage through my bag until I find my bathroom stuff and towel.

Nothing makes sense. Here I am at Abner Farms, surrounded by my entire sixth-grade class—including the two guys who are supposed to be my best friends—but I've never felt more alone.

45

BOILING OVER

Judging from the amount of noise blasting from inside, the Abner Farms boys' bathroom is the scene of a raucous party. From where Nick and I stand outside the entrance of the dressing area, it sounds like a few raccoons have been locked in a metal garbage can. We head in and each grab a stall to change into our bathing suits. A consensus was reached last week by the sixth-grade boys regarding showering: real men shower in shorts.

It seems like everybody's managed to get as clean as possible in the least amount of time, so when Nick and I head back to the area where the showers are, it's already clearing out. There's nothing refreshing about the experience—the water smells suspicious and the soap dispensers are all empty, so I wash my entire body with shampoo and rinse off at warp speed. Nick and I grab our stuff and make our way back to the dressing area, where now a massive towel-snapping brawl is underway. A few minutes ago, Mr. Conrad included towel-snapping on his list of things we are not allowed to do in here, which must be what gave everyone the idea.

It's an all-out war. Battle cries bounce off the walls, echoing into the night like a prison riot. I'm sure the whole thing will be shut down by some ticked-off adult very soon, but in the meantime I slide around the periphery of the room to avoid the middle, where the most intense rat-tailing is going on. My daily hand-to-hand combat quota was already filled back at the slop bucket with Darren.

I'm one step away from the safety of a locked bathroom

stall when I hear it—a crack so pure and decisive it takes a millisecond before I realize I've been hit. A burning pain screams from my Achilles. I look down, expecting to see a gaping hole where my ankle used to be.

The place has gone quiet like someone hit a mute button. The only sound is the whistle of a shower someone left on. I turn around slowly, certain Darren is standing behind me.

He is. And he's holding both ends of his towel, forming a twisted loop that rests against his leg. It's the perfect weapon, rolled tight and ready to attack again.

"Nailed you, cornbread. That's payback."

The welt at my heel pulsates like a heartbeat. I stand completely still, staring at Darren and willing my ankle to hold my weight. I'm breathing too hard. My anger feels dangerous, possibly requiring a warning label like *FLAMMABLE, HIGH VOLTAGE,* or *BIOHAZARD.* Knowing I can't physically rip into him, I start to let loose with an avalanche of accusations—but instead of chewing him out, the sound that comes out of my mouth is more like a sob. I clamp my lips together, refusing to suffer the humiliation of crying.

Before my body can completely betray me, I lunge at Darren, knocking him to the ground. All around me, guys are yelling, egging us on like this is the UFC. I'm on top of him and about to take my first punch when someone yells, "Conrad's coming!"

Suddenly, Josh and Nick are pulling me up off Darren and back toward the stalls. A couple of other guys yank Darren off the floor.

"What in God's name is going on in here?"

Nobody answers.

"I asked a question, gentlemen. *What* is going *on?*" Mr. Conrad turns full circle, studying everyone. Most of the guys are looking at the floor, shifting their weight side to side like they're about to run a race. But a lot of them are staring at me.

Mr. Conrad follows their gazes and approaches me. He

stands close enough that I can see right up inside his nose. My breath is still uneven, giving me away.

"Care to explain?" he asks. His voice sounds like a growl.

"Nothing, sir. Just messing around." I force myself to look up from his nose and directly into his eyes.

"Somehow I think there's a little more to it than that," he says quietly. He turns back to the group. "Everybody finish up and clear out. Lights out in twenty minutes."

We all stay frozen in place until Mr. Conrad has left the building. Josh and Nick are still standing behind me, ready to back me up. And from the way Darren keeps looking over at us, I'm pretty sure he realizes we're a package deal. If he wants to start anything up again, he'll have to deal with all of us. Finally, he gathers his stuff and walks out.

Josh rests his hand on my shoulder, in a fatherly, coaching kind of way. I'm thinking he's going to give me some pretty good props for my retaliation—or what was about to be my retaliation. "Seriously, man. Was that necessary?"

I laugh and turn to face him. But his expression tells me he's not joking.

I glance down at my ankle. It's bright red. "Did you see what he did to me?"

I'd also like to tell them about what he did to Olivia earlier today, but I don't have the energy to explain it.

"Yeah. I did. He got you good," Josh says. "Like you said, he was messing around. *Everybody* was messing around."

"Come on, you saw him," I say, looking at Nick. "That was more than messing around."

Nick shrugs. "He's a jokester. He's obnoxious, but like I said before, you can't let him get to you."

"Thanks," I say in the most sarcastic voice I can muster.

I lock myself in the stall and slowly get dressed. The bathroom is empty now, but just in case, I wipe my face hard with my towel so no one can tell if I've been crying. Honestly, Josh and Nick's digs sting worse than my ankle.

I open the stall door, knowing that walking into the tent alone will be even more embarrassing than what just happened with Josh and Nick.

When I get back, I head straight for my cot and climb into my sleeping bag, tuning out all the conversation going on around me. Nobody's even trying to talk to me anyway. I toss and turn, searching for the clues about how a day that started off so strong ended like this. I've overestimated my own stamina and underestimated Darren's. And I don't know if a tower of flapjacks is going to get me back on track.

46

SINK YOUR TEETH IN

I'm awake before anyone else. Soft light creeps in where the canvas flaps of our tent meet, creating long, skinny sunbeams on the floor between the two rows of cots. The air is crisp, and my breath billows like steam from a train when I exhale.

My first thought of the day is almost identical to the final thought I had before falling asleep last night: I'm barely surviving my stay at Abner Farms. The only thing I have going for me is that I'm almost halfway there. Technically, the midpoint of the trip will be at ten this morning—at hour twenty-seven out of fifty-four—but it's close enough now to call.

I'm sure that any minute now, somebody's going to pop in here and tell us to get up. But in the meantime, I'm content to lie here listening to the other guys snore. I try to psych myself up with the knowledge that I've made it this far. And that pancakes are in my immediate future.

Mr. Conrad yells a cheery "Rise and shine" from outside our tent, and Josh pops right out of bed. He pulls open the flaps on our side, and it's a completely perfect day—chilly but not cold, blue sky, and no wind. It's got to be a good sign. Suddenly even the prospect of spending all morning with Olivia feels workable now that I'm this close to having a full stomach.

We're all up and scrambling, trying to find our clothes and shoes and notebooks for the orienteering course. I'm definitely the most alert and with-it of the six of us, I guess because I've been awake the longest. I'm dressed and ready first, and from the slow-mo way the other guys are moving, they're going to take a while. I hop back on my cot for some lounging while I wait.

The first time Darren shoots me a look, I try not to give it a thought. But the second and third, time it's harder to ignore. I figure he's still ticked about what happened at the slop bucket, and I decide that when I have a chance, I'll take Nick's advice and say something low-key to prove I'm not letting him get to me. Maybe that will set him straight. But no matter what, I'm not going to get worked up like last night.

I don't know if near-starvation has changed my brain processing or something, but I'm actually feeling okay about the day ahead of me. I'm itchy to get moving in the direction of breakfast, but I force myself to stay on my bed maintaining a chill demeanor while Nick empties his entire duffel on the floor in search of clean socks.

When Nick is ready he looks over at Josh and the other guys, and it's pretty clear he wants to wait for them rather than leave now with me. With each passing second, it's harder for me to sit still and contain my out-of-control hunger. I can practically taste the first bite of pancake. I think if I were to open my mouth, I'd drool like a dog.

It feels like we've been waiting hours, even though it's only been a couple of minutes. Finally everybody looks ready. I stand up and say, "Let's move."

"Hold on." Darren's voice has an edge to it. "I need a minute." He sits on his cot and slowly leans over to tie his shoe.

I guess I'm the only one who notices his shoe is already tied. I watch as he unties it and then ties it again. He glances up at me as he switches feet. I translate his sneer into a hundred different messages, all of them hostile, while I force my face into a relaxed expression. I might have to revise the laidback approach to interacting with Darren today and instead just avoid him.

Josh makes the first move to head outside, and the rest of us follow him. Darren is the last one out, and it takes every ounce of self-restraint I have not to yell *Come on already!* At the bottom of the steps he pauses and looks right at me, but I stare past him and don't give him the satisfaction of seeing me get irritated. Nothing can sink my mood this morning.

"I forgot something," he says, turning to go back in.

I wait for one of the guys to call him a diva or ask if he remembered to put his lip gloss on, but no one does. And I'm not going to, either.

Once we're all walking to breakfast—me at the front of the group and Darren at the back—the tension evaporates enough for me to follow the conversation.

I hope Lauren was right about my nickname being yesterday's news, but as I step into the pavilion, someone yells, "Yo, cornbread!" from the breakfast line. I raise my arm and smile like a thick-skinned politician.

The guys and I take our own places in line, about thirty kids from the front, and my mind starts racing. It's not only the disturbingly strong smell of eggs that's freaking me out. It's the realization that I haven't actually been through the line yet. I escaped lunch yesterday, and my dinner plate was handed to me after my water-pouring job. Until right this second I had assumed that as I moved down the line, I'd politely decline everything until I reached the pancakes. But it looks like everyone ahead of us ends up with an identical plate of food. I can't make out what's on it, but I don't see pancakes. Panic sweeps through my mind like a brushfire in August.

My feet are moving, but the voice in my head is screaming words much worse than *crap*. The line goes faster than I expect, and suddenly I'm standing across from a cheery-looking old lady who is pouring what looks like glue on my plate.

"Our grits are good. Everybody tells me so," she says in a reassuring voice, spooning a huge glop in the middle of my plate. The next server drops two almost-burnt sausages hanging from sticks on the mess.

The clump of grits oozes across my plate. It's mesmerizing in a horror-movie kind of way. As they slime near my thumb, the next lady drops scrambled eggs on the one remaining dry spot on my plate. I look ahead to see what atrocity is coming next, and realize I wasn't totally wrong about the most critical aspect of breakfast at Abner Farms—the last cheery old lady is serving pancakes. Little tiny pancakes. Smaller than the circumference of a soda can. And she's doling them out in twos.

My two microscopic pancakes, dangling from a huge serving fork, are headed straight for my mountain of scrambled eggs. Without thinking, I thrust my right hand out, directly under her fork, and they fall into my palm.

I look up and smile. "Thanks."

A couple of kids snicker but stop when they notice the look of intense displeasure on the pancake lady's face.

They are lighter than a piece of bread and smaller than any pancake I've ever seen, even smaller than the silver dollar pancakes on children's menus. I hold them carefully, like I would a baby bird. I'm tempted to shove them in my mouth as I walk to our table, but I know I must eat them slowly, savoring every bite.

I sit, place my pancakes on my napkin, and take a deep breath. There's no way they will sustain me until tomorrow, but I don't want that realization to ruin the experience of eating them. I tear off part of the top pancake, stunned to realize the bite-sized piece between my fingers is actually bigger than what's left on the napkin. I bring it to my lips, take in its familiar scent, and pop it in my mouth.

My taste buds explode in celebration. I'm so relieved to be eating that for a terrible second, I think I might cry. The second piece is in my mouth before I've finished chewing the first, and I squeeze my hands together under the table before they can grab the other pancake.

Josh is talking about some outrageous dream he had last

night. He has everyone's attention, and I force myself to turn my head in his direction so it seems like I'm following along. I also use it as a chance to see if the pancake lady is still standing at her post. Maybe there are a few extras. But she's gone, and the huge silver tray holding the pancakes is gone too.

I rip the second pancake into fourths to make it last longer. I'm willing myself to wait as long as possible before I put the next piece in my mouth when Darren interrupts my train of thought.

"Cornbread, you look like a rabid squirrel over there, eating with your paws."

I laugh first. And loudest. And longest. Not because what he said was particularly hilarious, but because I don't know what else to do.

Nick nudges me. "Dude, you look nuts."

"Squirrel. Nuts," I blurt out between hiccupping giggles. I keep laughing even though no one else is. Even though nothing about my situation is even remotely funny. I'm wicked hungry—dangerously hungry—and I'm surrounded by food. But not the right food. For a millisecond, I remember some old poem about *water water everywhere and not a drop to drink*.

Nick nudges me harder this time. "Seriously, cut it out."

He's sitting very still, but his eyes dart around our table in some sort of warning. The guys all stare at me, studying me closely like they're witnessing a crime. I am now swimming at the very bottom of the food chain, and I can't think of a single thing I can do to change my situation.

"I'm outta here." I grab my napkin and stand up to leave. I don't bother to clear my plate.

But I'm not laughing as I walk out of the pavilion and into the sun. I figure one of the adults will stop me, but no one does. I keep walking, past the fire circle and up the lawn toward the lodge. The lake is glassy and still, glistening under birds swooping overhead. My shoes are getting soggy from the morning dew, but I keep going, wondering what kind of trouble I'll face when I get caught way over here by myself.

Half the porch is completely shaded, making the black rocking chairs almost invisible. I decide that's where I'm headed, where no one can see me. I take the steps fast and dart to the right side of the porch, where I slide into the farthest chair. I unwrap the napkin, shove all four quadrants of my second pancake in my mouth at the same time, and start rocking slowly to calm myself down. I try not to think about the scene I just made at breakfast and the fact that I feel so edgy and weird. It might really be time to give up and go home. A two-night, three-day field trip is way beyond reach for me. I should have known better.

I rock and watch the rest of my class zigzag into the fire circle and take their seats on the log benches. Every few seconds someone shouts or laughs, and even though I can't make out exactly what anyone's saying, it all annoys me. I keep rocking and brooding in defeat, and a heavy exhaustion settles over my body. Just as I close my eyes, I faintly hear a car.

I look toward the pavilion and see that a minivan has pulled up on the back side. I watch as Mr. Conrad jumps out. Today he's dressed in overalls, and from where I'm sitting he looks more like a farmer than a colonial settler. He opens the back and starts pulling big baskets from the van, setting them near the shed where the wood is stored. As he turns, I see what's in the baskets. Apples. Red apples. Hundreds of them.

I'm up and moving before I even know what I'm doing. I hoist myself up on the back corner of the porch railing, looking for a way down that will keep me in the shadows. The drop is only six feet or so, into some bushes that have leaves rather than prickers, so I fling myself over the ledge and brace myself for the fall. Somehow I manage to land on my feet, and after I shake off the mulch and dirt, I shimmy around to the side of the lodge, eyeing the distance across the path to the trees on the other side. I'll be out in the open for a second or two, but I'm willing to risk it.

My sprint is silent but quick, and when I'm safely camouflaged by the edge of the forest, I take a deep breath. I stay a couple of feet inside the tree line, watching for sticks that will snap and give me away as I try to remember what else we learned in Scouts about walking quietly in the woods. Of course we weren't practicing to be thieves back then.

After Mr. Conrad pulls away in the van, I make my move. I creep over to the closest bushel, grabbing the first two apples I touch, and slide back into the woods. When I'm safely out of sight, I shove one in my sweatshirt pocket and take a closer look at the other one. My fate rests on whether this is the right kind of apple—Red Delicious.

But it's definitely not. It's too round. Red Delicious are more top-heavy. And the color of this one is duller than what I'm used to. But it's in the family of red apples, and maybe that's close enough. I've been thinking I'd eat them here in the woods, then walk back through the pavilion to the fire circle as if I'd been there the whole time.

But now that I'm holding the stolen apple, I realize I've overlooked the most obvious thing: I only eat apples that have been peeled and sliced. So I have pretty much risked my life for no reason. There's no way I can snoop around in search of a sharp knife. That would really get me in trouble. I yank my arm back like I'm about to chuck this worthless apple deep into the woods, but then I stop.

I might be able to make it work.

I can't think of a time I've tried to eat something because *I* wanted to. There have been plenty of times I've been forced. Or bribed. Or shamed. And it's always worked out the same way. Choking. Gagging. Puking—once right on the kitchen table. Dad had been so insistent about getting me to try mashed potatoes. "Come on, bud," he said. "This is gonna

blow your mind once you know how great your mom's potatoes are." I knew it wouldn't work. But I tried anyway—and
then blew chunks of potato and pretzel and grilled cheese
everywhere, even right on Dad's plate. He didn't say a word.
He just got up and walked upstairs. But maybe this is different. Maybe with no pressure and no spectators, I can do it.

The apple is hot in my hand. I rub my thumb against it,
feeling its smooth, even surface. I keep thinking *apple apple
apple*, trying to keep my mind from imagining what else it
might feel like. I bring it to my face and gently touch it to my
lips. It's waxy like a candle, and I have to tell myself *apple apple
apple* again before my mind gets too creative and comes up
with something revolting.

There's no way I'll be able to eat the peel. I'm going to
have to rip it off with my teeth and spit it out. And I don't
have much time—the noise from the pavilion is dying down.
I notice the apple is almost oily, and suddenly my mind is
far away. I'm at Nick's house on his ninth birthday, when
his grandparents came all the way from Florida, and I'm
staring at his grandpa's bald, oily head. And now the word
I have carefully avoided so far is right there. Skin. An apple
has skin—like a person. Like the oily, shiny skin on Nick's
grandpa's head.

I close my eyes and bite into it. The crunching noise is
deafening and violent, as if I've actually taken a bite of a
bald skull, and then I'm spitting and gagging, trying to get it
all out of my mouth. Bits and shreds are stuck between my
teeth, and I pick them out with my nails.

I've made a decent hole. I go in at the same spot again,
using my front teeth to scrape more of the peel off and letting the pieces drip out of my mouth in drooly bits. Finally,
I've reached the fruit. I take a bite and hold it in my cheek,
desperate for it to taste like an apple at home, sliced into
identical slivers and splayed across a plate.

I chew once, realizing instantly that this apple is softer

and mealier than any apple I've had before. It's mushy in my mouth—not crisp, and not as sweet. But the flavor is similar to a Red Delicious. Or maybe close enough. I chew again and again, determined to swallow the bite.

But I can't.

After a few seconds, I bend over and spit it all out, ready to avoid my own shoes when I puke.

Surprisingly I don't get sick. So I stand back up and take one last look before I fling it into the woods, listening for the satisfying thump it makes when it lands. The second one goes even farther.

I'm back to the reality of looming starvation, but I'm feeling strangely okay. Actually, better than okay. I just did something I've never done before.

And the best part is that I'm the only person in the whole world who knows about it.

47

Hits the Spot

Olivia is pumped. I can tell by what she's wearing—cargo pants, a camo shirt, a fanny pack, a safari hat, and binoculars—and by the way she elbows me every time Mr. Butler gives our class another tip about the orienteering course.

I'm trying not to be too bothered by her outfit and instead focus on how I successfully slipped back into camp after my apple adventure. Nobody noticed.

"Remember, the map has all the information you need—the scale for distances, the terrain, the markers, and any other clues you might need to get around."

Olivia's arm shoots up. "And the scale is the same as what we used in class, right? One centimeter for every one hundred meters, right?"

Mr. Butler nods. "Yup, everything is the same as when we practiced on the field at school. Setting the map with your compass, taking a bearing, pacing your distance."

Olivia nods along.

"And remember, even though this is a *race*, you have to pay attention. If you don't know where you're going, you're wasting valuable time."

Ever since Mr. Butler told us about the orienteering course, Olivia has been obsessed with winning. The competition is perfectly matched to Olivia's favorite things in life—science, details, and being bossy. Right now having her as my partner doesn't seem so bad. I won't have to worry about anything.

"And what's the most important rule?" he asks us for the thousandth time.

"Don't go near the water," we answer in unison.

"All right. Check to be sure you have your compasses, pencils, whistles, and score sheets."

I don't even pretend to check. Olivia has got us covered.

"In a minute, each lab partner team will be escorted to its individual starting point. There, you'll be given an envelope containing your map. The sound of the dinner bell will signal you to open your envelope and start the race. I'd suggest spending a few minutes studying your maps before setting out."

Olivia is shifting her weight between her feet, back and forth like she's doing a weird dance. A few weeks ago I would have thought it meant she needs to go to the bathroom. But now I know she's just excited.

Mr. Butler is pretty excited too. He's rambling through the instructions that at this point we all know by heart. "Ten stations. Ten punches on your score sheets. Ten single letter clues. You'll be disqualified for working the checkpoints out of order. Cross the finish line when you've unscrambled the letters to spell a colonial word."

Nobody's listening to him.

"We're running the course four more times today, so don't move anything out there or it will impact the next group. The winning team with today's lowest overall time will be announced before dinner tonight."

Olivia and I are assigned to Mr. Conrad, who will take us to our starting spot. As soon as we're out of earshot from the rest of our class, Olivia turns to me and says, "You might have to ditch the sweatshirt."

"What?" I ask.

"It's bright *red*. You're too easy to spot."

"This isn't hide and seek. It doesn't matter if people see us."

"Technically, you're right. But we don't have to advertise where we are, either."

"Okay, you're in charge. Let me know when I have to ditch it," I say, trying not to roll my eyes.

After a few minutes of walking straight into the woods, probably not far from where I threw my apples, Mr. Conrad stops. "Station Seven is right here." He points to a small orange and white flag on the ground next to a metal box.

There's nothing to do but wait until we hear the bell. It seems like a good time for me to score some points with him by asking more about Abner Farms.

I throw out the first thing I think of. "I've been wondering what you know about the families who settled—"

Olivia cuts me off before I've finished my question. "Ben, when the bell rings, get the letter clue out of the box and punch our score sheet. I'll start on the directional calculations."

It looks like Mr. Conrad's trying not to laugh. I guess I'm immune to how ridiculous Olivia sounds when she's in science mode, because it doesn't even seem weird to me anymore.

Finally the bell clangs, and Olivia rips the envelope containing our map from Mr. Conrad's hand.

"Good luck," he says, turning to leave.

I open the box as fast as I can. Official orienteering competitions have official punch pliers to mark the score sheets, but it looks like we're using craft hole punches similar to the ones my mom uses for making scrapbooks. I punch a tiny star into the seventh square on our sheet and write the letter P on the bottom of the page while Olivia copies down our next coordinates.

Olivia is beyond excited. "Can you think of a ten-letter word that starts with a P?"

"No, I can't." I'm trying not to laugh. "And besides, it might not start with P. There's just a P in the word."

"Good point," she says, clearly disappointed that we have not already solved the puzzle.

She's busy with her compass, setting up for our next stop. She doesn't ask for my help, and I don't offer.

"Oh, I almost forgot." She reaches into her fanny pack and rummages around. "I've been trying to give you this since yesterday."

She tosses something green my way. I recognize it midair.

The shiny wrapper of a packet of Nature Valley Crunchy Oats 'n Honey Granola Bars.

I'm so shocked I can't say a word.

A hundred images flash through my mind like I'm flipping past channels on the TV too fast—the bag of granola bars Mom packed but I took out; Dad's arms resting on his knees, insisting that fresh air is all I need; beef barley stew; Darren yelling, "Cornbread!" from our table; two miniscule pancakes dangling from a fork.

My plan, so clear before I arrived at Abner Farms, has not yielded much success. In some ways, I'm more exposed than ever. Considering how desperately hungry I am, it's almost ridiculous that this little green packet of potential salvation is causing a full-blown moral dilemma for me. The confidence I had when I left the granola bars on my bed at home has shriveled into oblivion. But somehow this feels like giving in.

"In order to win, we *both* need to be energetic and alert," she says.

I don't move.

"Well, aren't you gonna eat it?"

I picture myself biting into one of my stolen apples a few minutes ago, holding it inside my cheek and forcing myself to taste it. Suddenly I understand that if I define success on this trip by what I've eaten, I guess I've failed pretty miserably. But in terms of challenging myself, I'm doing way better than expected. And whatever I do right now won't change that. I rip the wrapper at the top, pull the first one out, and take a satisfying bite. The relief is instant.

"I've been a little concerned about how you'd manage

here—you know, with your particular diet." Olivia pauses. "I can't have you passing out on the course."

"Is this what you were trying to give me yesterday?" I ask, suddenly feeling a little guilty.

"Yes. I noticed your altruistic maneuvers with the firewood during lunch. Seems like you haven't eaten much since you got here."

I can't decide if Olivia is a stalker or not, but I'm so grateful to be chewing that I almost don't care. "Thanks," I say. "Really."

I'm sure she hasn't heard me. She's scribbling numbers in her notebook like a fiend. I close the metal box and stand up. I'm already eating the second bar, feeling like I can actually detect my body returning to some sort of physiological equilibrium.

"Compass," Olivia says, holding her palm outstretched like a surgeon demanding a scalpel.

I hand it to her, and she positions it on the map.

"We need to take two hundred and four paces at seventy-four degrees," she says, pointing further into the woods. "The terrain looks flat, but we should watch for fallen logs and branches."

We start walking, counting our steps out loud like we did during practice at school. I'm so relieved to have eaten that I'd probably follow Olivia anywhere. We're at step seventy-two when a question occurs to me. "Weren't you worried about getting caught with contraband food?"

She stops and stares at me open-mouthed. "We can't talk and count at the same time."

I stop too. "I'll count and you answer."

"Seems risky." She scrunches up her forehead in thought.

"I can count. I promise." I take a step and whisper *seventy-three* to prove it.

"No, I wasn't worried." She waits a second, I guess to be sure I don't mess up. "No one would ever suspect me of breaking rules." I nod and whisper *seventy-four, seventy-five.* "Actually, I manage to get away with a lot. In some ways, I draw too much attention. And in other ways, I'm almost invisible."

"I'd like to be a little more invisible myself," I say, shoving the wrapper deep into my sweatshirt pocket. *Seventy-six. Seventy-seven.*

"Which kind?"

"Which kind of what?" I ask. Then, to reassure her, I count *Seventy-eight. Seventy-nine.*

"Which kind of *invisible*?"

"I don't know what you mean." *Eighty. Eighty-one.*

Olivia bites her lip, making her look uncharacteristically shy. I keep counting.

"There are a few different kinds of invisible," she says. "I've been all of them."

Eighty-two. "What are they?" *Eighty-three.*

"Well, there's the kind when no one notices you. It's like you're not even there."

I nod. *Eighty-four. Eighty-five.*

"And then there's the kind when they see you but they ignore you, like they go out of their way to avoid you."

I drop my gaze down to my feet, studying my steps as if my observation of them is mission-critical. I have a sudden vivid memory of Olivia at the end of a lunch table last year, sitting alone. Was that just one day or every day? *Eighty-seven. Eighty-eight.*

"And then there's the kind when you don't care anymore about what anyone sees. Or what they think they see."

It's out of my mouth before I can stop it. "You care about what your friends think, though." *Eighty-nine. Ninety.*

"I don't have any friends."

Her statement hangs between us like a thought bubble in a comic strip. She's not apologetic or even embarrassed. Just matter of fact, in her typical Olivia way.

Ninety-one. Ninety-two. Ninety-three. I'm moving my lips,

but no sound is coming from my mouth. For some weird reason, I start thinking about the swing set in our backyard. When I was little, I believed I could fly simply by launching myself into space from my swing. I was sure that when I reached maximum swinging speed, I could jump off and be propelled into space. A tugging shudder of the metal posts signaled when I'd reached peak altitude. I readied myself by pulling my left arm through the chains holding the swing and pointing it toward the galaxies, but in my final approach— every single time—I'd chicken out at the top, knowing I had missed my chance.

And that's what I do with what Olivia has just said. I bail. I keep counting as we walk, but I don't disagree or act like it was a joke. And I don't say the one decent thing I could say to the person who basically saved my life with two granola bars.

Ninety-eight. Ninety-nine.

"One hundred," I announce really loud—like it's a celebration of some sort.

"I'll count now," Olivia says. Before I can agree, she's at one hundred and one.

48

Smart Cookie

We've hit six out of the ten checkpoints in less than an hour and mastered the art of counting our steps silently. It seems like we're doing well, but there's really no way of knowing. So far we haven't seen anyone else. I'm perfectly happy taking orders from my orienteering drill sergeant, but rather than basking in her bossiness, Olivia is getting snippy.

"I wish we had a vowel. I mean you can't even begin to unscramble a word without a vowel," she says when we retrieve the next letter from its box.

I don't say anything.

"T. C. P. N. P. R. It's completely unsolvable."

"Come on, you're the smartest kid out here. We're gonna win. I promise." I hope I sound reassuring.

I guess I've completely blown her away with my confidence, because Olivia stops walking. "Oh no."

"We're doing *fine*."

"No. No way." She's staring at the map, open-mouthed.

"What?"

"We're going the wrong way."

"I'm sure we're not. Let me see," I say, walking back to her. Honestly, I haven't been paying much attention beyond doing what I'm told, so I doubt I'll have any valuable insight. I take the map out of her hand anyway.

"Right here." She points to some notes. "I reversed these numbers. It's not seventy-two degrees. It's *twenty-seven*."

"So let's backtrack and start this one over."

"We'll lose too much time."

Olivia is breathing hard. Her face is getting blotchy. I am not exactly sure what hyperventilating looks like, but this could be it. I glance down at her fanny pack.

"Do you have an inhaler in there?" I ask.

"No!" she practically screams at me. "I'm just upset. It's not like me to make a—"

She pauses. I don't think she can say the word.

"This is fixable," I say, trying to sound calm. "We'll turn around and start over from our last checkpoint. No big deal."

My relief at not being the one who screwed up is making me sound more considerate than I actually feel. I've got bigger things to worry about than winning this stupid race, but I know it means a lot to Olivia.

"That's the problem." A tear slides down her cheek and past her nose. "I think we started out in the right direction, and then I switched after we took a water break. I'm not sure I can even find the last checkpoint."

She points at the spot on our map where she marked Station Two. "If we don't know where we are, I don't know how we'd get back there."

I don't want to say the word "lost," but I'm kind of wondering if that's what she's telling me. Losing the race doesn't bother me, but having to blow our red emergency whistles so the teachers can rescue us does.

I grab the map again, ignoring the numbers she's scribbled in the margins. Instead I study the topography, spinning in a slow circle.

"That's it," I say, pointing a few hundred yards away.

"That's *what?*"

"The hill right there. That's got to be the highest point on our course—and based on the contour lines on the map, I bet it's right here." I point to the spot on the map.

Olivia nods. "We haven't had any fluctuations in elevation. I think you're right."

"So we'll take a bearing from the north side of the hill—"

Olivia jumps in. "And then we can get back to Station Two."

"Yup," I say proudly.

"But we're still losing time."

"Yeah, I know," I say. "We're being too careful with our pacing."

Olivia rolls her eyes. "There's no such thing as being too careful when it comes to measuring distance."

"Okay, hear me out. We've been pacing at a walking speed. If we double our speed, we can make up time."

"At the cost of accuracy. No thank you."

I take a deep breath. "It's our best shot. For winning."

"We'd need to adjust for the change in gait. And we didn't practice for that."

"See that stump over there?" I ask. "I'll run, you walk, and we'll have a formula for our new pacing."

Olivia pauses for a second, probably because the thought of *me* telling *her* what to do is so bizarre. And then we're off.

Once we've calculated our new pacing rate and I've convinced Olivia that we should be using the map to identify useful terrain on our path, we break into a run.

"I'm quite impressed with your understanding of feature identification," Olivia says in between gasping breaths as we race to our last checkpoint.

She's struggling to keep up with me, but she's not complaining—so I pick up the pace another notch.

After going back to fix our mistake, we manage to hit the next three checkpoints at lightning speed. But Olivia's still not satisfied.

"I hope the last letter isn't another vowel," she wheezes.

I can't help but laugh. "A few minutes ago you were begging for a vowel. Now you've got three."

The sound of voices startles us.

"Duck," I say, grabbing Olivia by the arm.

It's too late. She was right about my red sweatshirt.

"Well, if it isn't team cornbread," Darren yells from a hundred feet away. His lab partner chuckles along. "Haven't you two given up yet?"

"Actually, we're almost done," I lie.

Olivia nods. The blank expression on her face tells me that dishonesty is way, way out of her comfort zone regardless of the circumstances. I assume she's also thinking what I'm thinking.

Darren and his partner were the first team to be called from the fire pit, which means they started at Station One. We started at Seven. Since we all had to go in order to ten and then start back at one, they're either running the course exceedingly fast or they're breaking the rules by working out of order. Based on how little Darren pays attention in class, I'm betting on the second one. They're cheating, and Olivia knows it too. But there's no time to prove it.

"Yeah, same here," says Darren's lab partner as they walk toward us.

"Put the papers in your pocket," Olivia whispers.

I slide our score sheet and map into my sweatshirt pocket without taking my eyes off Darren. Olivia pulls a wrinkled-up paper from her fanny pack and smooths it out.

"We're not letting them cheat off us," she whispers again. It sounds more like a growl.

I don't say anything. The last thing I need is another confrontation with Darren—especially with Olivia as my wingman.

"You've got this, right?" she asks.

I'm not sure what she means. Does she think I'm going to challenge Darren to a duel or something? Before I can question her logic, she rips off her safari hat and chucks it on the ground.

"I've *had* it!" she yells.

"We don't have any evidence they're cheating," I say through clenched teeth.

Does she really think Darren can be scared away that easily?

"You," she yells, pushing her finger into my chest, "are the worst lab partner in the history of collaborative science!"

I turn to her. "What?"

"You heard me, Ben Snyder. I've been telling Mr. Butler for weeks that you're holding me back with your dim-witted mistakes and careless calculations."

I'm frozen in place.

"So *go!*" she shouts, pointing wildly in the direction we were headed. "Go wander through the woods by yourself. *I'm* headed to Station Six, and *I'm* gonna win this race."

I hold back a smile. Olivia is smarter than I ever imagined.

"Well, if that's what you want," I say, hoping to sound offended.

"Try not to get lost," she hisses, tossing the compass at me. She turns on her heels and marches away.

Darren snickers. "Cornbread, you've hit a new low in loser-world."

I wait for them to follow her. And then I run, as hard and fast as I've ever run, to Station Six. Of course it's another vowel. I add a second E to our list. T. C. P. N. P. R. A. E. I. E.

Before I can worry about the mystery word, I have to find Olivia. I take another look at the map, deciding that the easiest way to track her down will be to make my way toward the lake and follow the shoreline back, even if it is against the rules. I'm sure Olivia is leading the cheaters toward the finish line. I rip my sweatshirt off and wad it into a ball. Now I really don't want to be spotted.

There's no real footpath along the lake, but I sprint anyway, hurdling over tree limbs and branches. I can make out what must be Mr. Abner's cabin in the distance, and something about our conversation yesterday hits me. *Ben, you make a fine...* I stop and pull out our score sheet.

A second later I'm running like it's for Olympic gold. As

soon as I see the lodge, I start yelling Olivia's name. When she finally responds, I yell, "Meet me at the finish line!"

The finish line is really just Mr. Butler, standing with the other teachers in the fire circle, each holding a stopwatch. I'm barreling toward him like a runaway train, scanning the edge of the woods for Olivia.

She sprints out of the woods toward me, and I yell, "Pen! I need a pen!"

We stop right outside the circle, and I write the mystery word across our score sheet.

APPRENTICE

"You're first," Mr. Butler says as we hand him our score sheet.

Olivia and I collapse onto the ground. We're both laughing and talking at the same time, putting together our stories about how we pulled off our victory. A shadow darkens our faces and we look up to see Darren standing over us. A familiar uneasiness snaps me back to reality.

"Cornbread, you and your nerd-pal outdid yourselves. Bet you've worked up a real appetite."

He walks away before I can even begin to think of a nasty response. Suddenly winning a dumb science competition feels like a pathetic thing to be excited about. Olivia seems to have missed the entire exchange. She's sitting cross-legged, picking up pebbles, inspecting them, and tossing them aside.

"Ben, I have something to tell you," she says.

As I look at her, I finally take in the complete weirdness of her safari-themed outfit, which I had temporarily overlooked out on the course. I don't want to be on the receiving end of her strange private thoughts, but I can't make myself get up.

I cross my arms and try not to look irritated. The only thing that will make this moment even more awkward is when Olivia starts spraying her inner secrets all over me.

"Are you ready?" she asks. "This is important."

"Sure."

"Ben," she says looking up at me with a serious expression.

I wish she'd stop saying my name. It's creeping me out.

She takes a deep breath. "When you finally become an expert in being yourself, navigating the world gets a whole lot easier."

"Thanks." I pull myself to a stand, signaling our conversation is over.

"Think about it." She looks back down at her hands, and I take that as an opportunity to make my getaway.

49

Two Peas in a Pod

Our purple bandana science class is meeting during lunch for a lesson in identifying plants native to Abner Farms. The upside to this mind-numbingly boring lecture is that brown bag lunches were distributed at the pavilion, which saves me from enduring another sickening sit-down meal. Plus, the rush of sitting next to Lauren on the warm lawn drowns out Mr. Butler's boring talk about woody plants, ferns, and grasses.

Tomorrow morning we'll be sent out in search of these various plants with our lab partners. Mine is scribbling notes and interrupting Mr. Butler with very specific questions about plant classification, so I think it's safe for me to chill.

I haven't even bothered to open my own brown bag. Based on what the other kids are scarfing down, I can tell it's a pretty basic lunch—a sandwich, a bag of chips, an oatmeal cookie, and an apple—the type of lunch I'd usually call *stuff I don't eat*. But since I actually bit into and chewed one of those apples earlier this morning, I modify my description a little—to *stuff I don't eat and an apple I don't like*. Most people wouldn't understand the difference, but there is one. It's like the difference between the patter of raindrops at the window versus being outside without an umbrella. Either way, it's raining. But it's more real when you're getting wet.

From our picnic spot I can see most of Abner Farms, and if I close my eyes and ignore Mr. Butler, I can imagine what this place was like a couple hundred years ago. I'm picturing men on horses heading out for a hunt, children playing rounders, and women baking bread. Lauren nudges my leg with her foot, bringing me back from my colonial daydream.

"You're sleeping," she whispers, trying not to laugh.

Now I'm trying not to laugh too, which strikes us both as hilarious.

Mr. Butler shoots us a look. "Pay attention, please."

The other person shooting us a look is Darren. He's sitting way off to the side by himself, wearing a sore-loser pout and glaring in our direction. But I'm completely mellow right here next to Lauren, and for once it's easy to ignore Darren.

I tap Lauren's foot with mine, and then she does it back to me, and we go along that way back and forth until Mr. Butler says, "Mr. Snyder, enough."

It doesn't feel like enough. I bet I could watch our feet play this game forever. And we've been having so much fun that I don't think Lauren even noticed that I never ate my lunch.

I'm a little disappointed when he finally runs out of things to say about plants and tells us to throw away our garbage and head over to the pavilion so we can learn how to make candles.

I recognize this is a great chance to get rid of the granola bar wrapper that's still in my sweatshirt pocket. Lauren is telling me how excited she is about candle-making, and I nod along. We stand up at the same time and in one quick motion, I pull my sleeve over my right hand and shove it into my pocket. Then I grab the wrapper and slide it inside my sleeve.

Lauren pauses for a second and I say, "That's cool," which seems to encourage her to start talking again. As we walk toward the garbage bin, I reach into my lunch bag and, using my thumb and forefinger, push the wrapper out and grab my apple.

"Want this?" I ask her.

"Thanks," Lauren says, taking it out of my hand. "Mine had spots."

She smiles and takes a huge bite. As I watch her, I'm not

thinking about oily bald heads or the sensation of apple stuck between my teeth. I'm thinking Lauren is cute. Really cute.

"Gross," she says as we drop our bags in the trash. "It's too soft."

I understand exactly what she means.

A wind rips past us, and the temperature feels like it drops by ten degrees.

"I'm gonna grab a jacket," I tell Lauren. Retrieving my beef-barley-stew-splattered sweatshirt from the bushes is actually my primary objective. This seems like a good time to take care of it.

"I'll save you a seat!" she says, smiling as if she just thought of it.

Even the most ridiculous activities are bearable if I'm sitting next to Lauren.

I head toward Tent Row, casually checking each bush, but my mind is somewhere else. I'd like to catch up with Josh and Nick—I haven't seen either one of them since I went AWOL at breakfast this morning.

They have had it easier than me simply because they're in the same red bandana group. And since the entire activity schedule at Abner Farms has been driven by a preschool col-or-coding system, they've been inseparable ever since we got here. They've already done wood-chopping and archery— and I'm about to make candles. Sometimes this whole colonial experience feels like a ploy to force us to "step outside our comfort zones" and "meet new people"—the two main objectives behind every middle-school-sanctioned activity.

Our purple bandana group is on the fast track for becoming experts in colonial housekeeping. They'll probably have us wearing bonnets and aprons before it's all over. Mr. Butler has promised we'll get to try everything before we go home, but I bet we'll run out of time. Either way, by tomorrow afternoon I won't care anymore. My Abner Farms nightmare will have ended.

Not that I'm complaining. The steady climb to almost-dating status has added an unexpected bonus to my Abner Farms experience, even if a lot of it feels like being trapped in a stuck elevator. And even though in some ways this seems like the longest two days of my life, when it comes to Lauren it feels like time here moves at warp speed. It would take weeks to spend this many hours with her if we were at home and just seeing each other at school and on weekends.

A goofy grin spreads across my face as I think about how *right* we are together—which sounds like a corny thing an adult would say. I can't even explain it to myself, but I try to make a mental list of other things that go perfectly together. All I can come up with is stupid stuff about food. Like peanut butter and jelly. Or eggs and bacon. Or cheese and crackers. It's funny, but not really funny, that even I use food similes when really all those foods make me want to barf.

Finally I've got it: a pair of mittens. Fuzzy, warm, and snug. Lauren and I are like a pair of mittens. Definitely not the most romantic thought, but it works for me.

Just as I'm about to give up on finding my sweatshirt, I spot it. I get as close to the bush as possible, bend down to fake-tie my shoe, and in one quick motion yank the sweatshirt out. I stand up and look around, but nobody's watching. It reeks, even worse than last night, and I try to remember if I packed an empty garbage bag for wet clothes like Mom kept reminding me to do. She must have told me more than ten times.

As I walk under the Tent Row archway, I realize I'm in the homestretch. By this time tomorrow, I'll be sitting on the couch eating a twenty-pack of McDonald's nuggets and watching the playoff game with Dad. My overall colonial experience has been far from ideal, except for three highlights—hanging out with Lauren, outsmarting Darren on the orienteering course, and my hunch that Olivia and I won the big competition.

I have just one more dinner to survive. Tonight is a Thanksgiving-type turkey feast—the most gruesome of all food-focused holiday menus. I can barely tolerate watching my own family gorge themselves on all that soggy muck and mop up chunks of gravy with their dinner rolls. Why recreate that kind of misery out here in the woods? What I do have going for me tonight is freedom from the watchful eye of Mrs. Larsen. Since my group has no dinner-related chores, I might be able to arrive late and sneak out early.

Fortunately, no one is around when I get to our tent. I take a second to enjoy my private view of the sun just beginning to set before I pull my duffel up on my cot. My stuff's a total disaster—even by my own standards. If I didn't know better, I'd think a wild raccoon had rummaged through it. I've got clean clothes mixed in with dirty ones, but it doesn't matter. Mom is going to wash every last thing in here. But after a few seconds, I find the trash bag my mom packed for wet or extra-dirty clothes.

Once the toxic-waste sweatshirt is bagged, I slip a light jacket on, grab a baseball hat, and toss my duffel back on the floor. I check my watch—only two minutes to get my butt in the seat Lauren is saving me at candle-making.

50

ROTTEN TO THE CORE

I tear through the pavilion but screech to a halt when I realize Mrs. Larsen has already started her candle presentation. Everyone's backs are to me, so no one notices my late arrival—including Lauren. She's seated at the far end of a table up front, but there's no saved spot for me next to her. Because that dirty weasel is sitting there instead.

I take a seat at an empty table in the back and wait for Lauren to turn around. After what feels like an eternity, she finally does. She shrugs and rolls her eyes in Darren's direction. I'm sure that as soon as I disappeared, he made his move. Still, it's a little surprising Lauren let him get away with it. I shrug back, not sure what my shrug means, and she shrugs again, seemingly trying to hold back a laugh when Darren suddenly glances her way and notices us communicating in our private shrug language. There's something completely satisfying about Darren's inability to interrupt our silent conversation.

But he doesn't give up. Turning back to the table, he leans in and makes some comment that cracks everyone up. Even Lauren. I wait for her to look back to me, but she doesn't. I'm beating myself up for wasting time on a dirty sweatshirt and creating this opening for Darren. I have to play smarter.

If he wasn't in hot pursuit of my almost-girlfriend, I might actually admire Darren's determination. He slides closer to Lauren on their bench and brings his face right next to her ear, then whispers something long and drawn-out. I sit completely still, barely even breathing, and watch as she whispers back. Lauren is captivated by Darren, and from way back here there's nothing I can do about it. He's a cold-blooded fraud, sweet-talking her with his lies, and she's not making any effort to escape from his slimy grasp.

Jealousy surges through me, boiling over like a pot forgotten on the stove as I watch, powerless. I study my surroundings, searching for evidence of a zombie apocalypse—or any other colossal redistribution of reality that could explain Lauren's sudden return to a fascination with my nemesis.

Mrs. Larsen asks for two volunteers, and Darren reaches for Lauren's wrist, raising their hands together. It's a Hail Mary pass. A half-court buzzer-beater. A pulled goalie. And even though I'm practically quaking in my desperation to see him fail, he doesn't. Rather, he holds her hand tight as they make their way to the front. Lauren doesn't even try to pull away.

By the time I'm dipping my stupid strings into the stupid wax, my hands are actually shaking. I replay all the clues Lauren has been giving that she's into *me* and kick myself for letting my guard down. Maybe I've misinterpreted Lauren's attention. Or even worse, maybe she's been playing me the whole time.

Olivia slides in next to me and sizes up my lopsided candle. It looks like a broken finger, but she refrains from her typical commentary. "I'm a little nervous," she says, picking wax off her cuticles. "Some of the afternoon groups finished the course really fast."

I'd completely forgotten about the orienteering award. It takes every ounce of self-control not to yell, "*WHO CARES? I'VE GOT BIGGER THINGS GOING ON HERE!*" Instead, I let her ramble on while I watch Lauren and Darren dip their candles. They take their candle-making very seriously, admiring each other's progress between dunks.

Finally, Lauren turns around and looks at me. And now that she does, I don't know what to do. She smiles—not her regular super-sparkly smile, but a quieter smile. And when our eyes meet, she holds my gaze.

I don't know what it means or what I should do in response that could possibly express what I want her to know. But for one second, I'm simply relieved to have her attention.

And then Darren notices. I can't hear what he says to her, but I recognize the word *cornbread* on his obnoxious lips. Lauren looks away and laughs.

Olivia has witnessed the whole thing. She reaches for my crooked candle and whispers, "Let's get out of here."

We carry our creations to the drying area, where Olivia writes my name next to my scrawny candle and I follow her out of the pavilion. The sun is hidden behind the lodge, and it's even colder now. Wordlessly, we walk toward the fire circle and sit down. After a few minutes, she says, "Well, that was a surprising development."

I nod, unable to string any coherent words together.

"I'm not an expert in the world of social interaction, but there's something highly irregular about what just transpired with Lauren and Darren." She pauses, then adds, "Especially in light of what happened to me yesterday in the rounders game. I thought she had written him off for good."

I nod again and take a seat next to her on a log. We're conspicuously early for the evening announcements and the orienteering awards presentation, but I don't care. We sit in silence for what seems like forever, shivering and waiting.

Finally, a few people start to trickle in. Olivia pats me on the knee, the way my gran might. "I'm sorry," she says.

The irony of Olivia Slotnick taking pity on *me* is almost too much to bear. But at least I have someone on my side. She sees Darren's actions for what they are—a series of attacks that keep succeeding in holding Lauren's attention.

"But I do feel the need to point out that this rivalry between you and Darren feels a bit inappropriate." I turn to her, open-mouthed. I have no idea what she's trying to say. "Lauren isn't a prize to be won. And treating her like one makes you and Darren both look like Neanderthals."

"Maybe keep your opinions to yourself," I say without looking at her. But a part of me wonders if she's right.

I force myself to stare straight ahead at the burnt-out ruins of last night's campfire. My need to know if Darren is still glued to Lauren is like the most ravenous hunger—desperate and gnawing—yet I'm afraid to look. The rising hum of kids chattering and yelling as they arrive is becoming impossible to take.

Just when I think I'm about to totally lose it, I see Albert headed straight for me, probably with another idiotic idea. I look at him blankly, willing him to pitch his latest plan as fast as possible. This one must be exceptional, because he sits down on my other side and leans into me, whispering, "A DJ booth in the cafeteria."

I don't bother to respond.

"With club music. And maybe lasers."

I nod and pat him on the knee, borrowing Olivia's move and hoping he understands it to mean our meeting is over. Thankfully he leaves, but then Josh and Nick stagger past me laughing so hard they can't even walk normally. A couple of guys on the far side of the circle call out to Josh, and they head that way without even bothering to look for me.

I'm not sure which is worse—being ignored by Lauren or forgotten by my best friends—but it's clear that my social standing has plummeted into an abyss. Was it just a few hours ago that I told Olivia I wished I were invisible? It looks like my wish has been granted. A cold emptiness settles over me like a misty rain. All my big plans for this trip are unraveling. I might actually leave Abner Farms in a worse situation than I arrived. And being iced out of Josh's squad might be the least of my worries. Because I think there's a chance I'll never be on anyone's squad ever.

If I had any fight left in me, I might consider moving to a different spot. I'm just not sure where I'd go.

"You'll feel better in a minute," Olivia says. "After we win."

51

A BAD EGG

The stream of kids surges in. I spot Lauren and try to catch her eye, but Darren and his whispered jokes have completely hijacked her attention.

"Hey, come on over here!" somebody yells.

I recognize Josh's voice right away, and my relief is gargantuan. I turn, knowing he's calling for me to join them, but as I begin to raise my arm in response, a gut-wrenching realization hits me like a freight train—Josh isn't even looking at me. He's yelling for Darren. And Lauren. They wave and then weave between logs and other kids, pushing their way over to Josh and Nick at the back of the fire circle. When they finally make it, Josh and Darren high-five each other like long-lost brothers.

I turn back around to face front, pretty sure the shock of what I've just witnessed shows on my face. My stomach clenches like I've been kicked.

Olivia has missed the whole thing. She nudges me and points at Mr. Conrad, who is sporting his stupid colonial garb from yesterday morning.

"I think it's starting," she whispers, not looking at me.

I don't answer. My mind is racing. Have Josh and Nick really traded me in for that jerk? Maybe I should give up on having friends and dedicate my life to soccer. I could be the next Messi or Ronaldo.

Mr. Conrad saunters to the center of the circle and sets a brown paper grocery bag on the ground. His face is set in a serious scowl as he scans the crowd, seemingly searching for someone. For a second I'm distracted by his weirdness and

I follow his gaze, almost feeling pity for his unknowing victim. He looks past Olivia and me, hesitates, and scans back our way. When Mr. Conrad finally turns his attention to the crowd, his eyes nail me.

Olivia glances at me. "What in the heck was that all about?"

I shrug. "Maybe he was trying to find us because we won?" I don't sound convincing.

Mr. Conrad clears his throat dramatically and starts in with his irritating old-fashioned colonial voice. "Hear ye, hear ye. Let's settle down, please. I have some important announcements."

Even though he's not looking at me anymore, I feel weirdly nerved out. My mood is tanking.

"When I welcomed you young travelers yesterday morn', I reviewed our rules and policies regarding our shared survival as settlers in this new land."

Mr. Conrad's over-the-top role playing was mildly amusing yesterday, but now it's just annoying.

"We have had an *unusual* amount of rule infractions since your arrival, and I am sure you and your teachers do not wish to jeopardize future expeditions from your school."

He walks to one side of the fire circle, thankfully farther away from me, and raises his arm for effect. His whole performance is strange, like he's starring in his own badly written play. Olivia lets out a sigh, obviously bugged about waiting for the orienteering announcements. She slips a paperback book out of her fanny pack, tucks it out of sight behind the folds of her sweatshirt, and starts reading. It's getting dark, but the lack of light doesn't seem to bother her.

My frustration is morphing into all-out rage, but there's nothing I can do about Darren or my friends or Lauren while this idiot entertains himself with all this stupid colonial chatter.

"Here at Abner Farms, our philosophy is consistent. We want our participants to recognize that all behavior impacts the health and safety of others." He takes several dramatic steps back to the center of the circle.

"In colonial days, rules were not arbitrary." Mr. Conrad keeps talking. "Rather, they ensured the collective well-being of the entire community. Therefore, we follow a public system of justice—in which all members are made well aware of the regrettable behavior of their neighbors."

I turn halfway around to check out our teachers' reactions. Mrs. Frankel has her hand over her mouth like she's trying not to laugh, and I think I catch Mr. Butler shaking his head a little.

"Not to fear, young settlers. We do not propose a public whipping or stockades for such violations." He chortles at his own joke, then pauses, waiting for someone else to laugh along with him. No one does. "Rather, we endorse an increase in chores as a suitable punishment for less serious crimes. And of course, banishment for the more serious. Banishment meaning being sent home." He pauses for dramatic effect. "So, to start, last night we endured some widespread noise disturbances, from the tents as well as the boys' showers."

I get a little sick feeling when he mentions the showers, wondering if he knows about my attack on Darren. That would be some completely warped justice if *I* got in trouble for what happened last night.

"Punishment for this will be an earlier wake-up time tomorrow morning by fifteen minutes for all campers." Everybody groans. "That time will be spent packing up, sweeping out the tents, and collecting rubbish. And the time will go even earlier if tonight is not quieter. Colonists need their rest."

So far, this is not so bad. But I still have an uneasy feeling.

"Next, the green bandana group seems to have dodged cleanup duty after breakfast this morning." He saunters back to the middle of the fire circle. "Again, this is not to be dismissed. Colonists must rely on each other in sharing the workload. The green bandana group will be responsible for the unfortunate task of cleaning out our campfire pit before supper."

The muscles in my neck relax. This guy is an over-blown actor with no real material to work with. My mind wanders back to the more pressing problem of Darren's magnetic attachment to Lauren and my friends. I twist in my seat to get a look. When I spot them, my stomach lurches. Lauren's hand is resting on Darren's shoulder as he whispers in her ear. She's completely captivated, nodding every few seconds in agreement with every despicable lie he's spewing.

All at once, something Mr. Conrad's just said starts nagging at me. It's the word *rely*. I have the sudden sick realization that no one here has my back. Josh and Nick don't. They've been hassling me about Darren since we got here, telling me over and over not to let him get to me. I bet I've been kicked off the squad before we even got it going.

Mr. Conrad's irritating voice pulls my attention back to the fire circle. "Last, and this is by far the most serious, we've had a significant violation regarding food."

Within one second, the management of my bodily functions goes haywire. My internal barometer rockets up to high alert. My legs start to twitch like they want to run, but I'm glued to my log. Sweat pours into my eyes, and I look at the ground to avoid Mr. Conrad's gaze. Now it all makes sense. He knows about the apples. Or the granola bars. Or both.

Olivia closes her book, suddenly paying attention too.

The distant chirp of crickets sounds like a warning, and I try to remember if I heard them earlier. I imagine my dad hanging up the phone after Mr. Conrad relays the news. I can already feel his sharp disappointment in my inability to act like a normal kid. My mouth is completely dry, and I try to swallow but it feels like the back of my throat is stuffed with a wool sock.

"This is not simply a matter of disregard for our policies. It's a safety issue as well. All sorts of wild animals roam around here. And of course there are modern-day concerns about dangerous allergies for certain campers."

Mr. Conrad reaches into the grocery bag with the fanfare of a magician, pauses for a moment, and then whips out a large clear plastic bag jam-packed with candy bars and wrappers. Olivia and I both sigh in relief.

"Would anyone like to claim these?" Mr. Conrad's challenge hangs in the air.

After a few seconds of complete silence, a humming restlessness races through the fire circle, growing louder like an approaching swarm of bees. Kids whisper and crane their necks to eyeball each other, searching for a guilty face. I twist around on my log, checking out the crowd. Only a special kind of idiot would be dumb enough to bring candy to Abner Farms.

"I would advise the person or persons responsible for smuggling and consuming this contraband to confess now, of your own volition. If you do so, the consequences may be less severe." Mr. Conrad's eyes look like they might pop out of his head. He probably lives for this colonial disciplinarian stuff.

The crowd hushes in anticipation. I almost feel sorry for the kid, whoever they are.

"Well then." Mr. Conrad closes his eyes and shakes his head in fake defeat. He stands motionless for at least thirty seconds, in what must be a move he has rehearsed in front of a mirror.

When he finally opens his eyes, they bore into mine. "Mr. Snyder."

I freeze as if a sniper's laser is pointed at my head. "*What?*"

"Come with me," Mr. Conrad commands, then turns to leave. "You and I will head over to my office, where we'll call your parents."

Quiet chatter builds like a wave, crashing around me. The

word *cornbread* echoes in my ears, and a thunderous roar pounds at my temples. Suddenly, I understand.

I've been set up. And there's no way out. Darren has masterminded the perfect plan to annihilate me.

"That stuff isn't mine." I can barely choke out the words.

"I retrieved the contraband from your duffel this afternoon."

I glance toward the carved wooden archway that reads Tent Row, trying to piece together how this case against me was put together. It might as well say *Death Row.*

I'm sure Darren has covered his tracks so well that even the FBI wouldn't be able to connect him to his dirty work. The memory of my ransacked duffel bag flashes through my mind. Accusing him won't accomplish anything.

I'm totally screwed.

"Let's go, son." Mr. Conrad's voice is rough and impatient.

He walks toward me. Every ounce of my being understands I must escape. My head twists back and forth, searching my surroundings for impending danger, but there's none—no tsunami rising from the lake, no inferno raging through the trees, no hungry lion ready to pounce. Instead, I see something even more terrifying—kids turning away from my gaze, their embarrassment for me too much to bear.

I stand and take a step, but as soon as I do, the ground seems to shift under my feet and my knees buckle. Mr. Conrad reaches out to steady me. My body feels strangely heavy and wobbly. The combination of extreme hunger and being falsely accused of a crime is making me lightheaded.

"Cornbread's going down!" Darren's taunt cuts through the air.

"Are you all right?" Mr. Conrad's hand is warm around my arm, but I refuse to lean into him.

"I'm fine," I snap and pull my arm back.

But I'm not fine. A few hours ago I was lying in the sun next to my soon-to-be girlfriend. I was about to win the orienteering competition. And I was within eighteen hours of completing my first real trip away from home, on my terms.

Now I've lost everything.

No. I haven't *lost* everything.

It's all been ripped away from me by that scumbag.

A pressure surges through my body, demanding to be released. Suddenly my legs are moving on their own, carrying me toward the far side of the fire circle. Faces are blurred, and sounds are jumbled. Someone starts to yell, over and over, "You're gonna regret this!"

It takes a second for me to recognize the voice as my own.

I can make out Darren's face as I get closer. He's flanked by Lauren on one side and Alex on the other. I'm only a few feet away, swinging my arm in anticipation of my first punch. He's strangely still, that sinister smile smeared across his ugly face. I clench my fist and pull my arm back, but Josh steps in front of me. "Ben. Cut it out."

Nick appears on my left just as the heavy hands of an adult grab my shoulders.

"Yeah, pull it together," Nick says, so quietly I'm not sure I've heard him right.

"Okay, this is entirely inappropriate," Mr. Conrad barks, turning me away from Josh and Nick.

Stares zing at me like arrows coming from all sides. I swipe my face with my sleeve, certain that every single kid here knows I'm crying.

"No!" I yell. "That stuff isn't mine!" My body shakes and convulses as an ice-cold sweat drips down my back.

"Let's get you to my office."

Mr. Conrad tries to steer me between the logs and out of the circle, but I jerk away and stumble. Nick holds out his arm and I reach for it, but as soon as I've regained my balance he pulls away. Nick's face is blank, like he doesn't even recognize me, and I understand I've finally been defeated. This is likely to be the moment seared in everyone's minds when they remember our class trip to Abner Farms—The Inquisition and Public Shaming of Ben Snyder. People will be talking about it for years. And whether they get the facts right or not, the most shocking part of the story will always be that when I had a chance to face down my enemy, I failed. And when I should have defended myself, I caved.

Can I live with that?

I turn back to Mr. Conrad and look him straight in the eye. "I've got something I'd like to say."

"You've done quite enough already," he says.

"No," I say louder. "I'm innocent, and I can prove it."

Mr. Conrad motions for some teachers to aid him in corralling me. His hand tightens on my arm, and I wonder if he's going to pull me away like a prisoner.

I'm going to have to work fast.

My entire sixth-grade class is riveted by my desperation, and some kids shift in their seats for a better view. On the other side of the circle, people have scooted farther away from Olivia like she's contagious. Despite the darkness, she hasn't taken off her safari hat. She gives me a thumbs-up.

"You need to lawyer up, dude!" somebody yells out.

A few people snicker, but I'm too mad to care. My chest is tight, barely containing my pounding heart.

"Enough," Mr. Conrad yells. "Could someone..." He looks behind him for backup.

His momentary release gives me just enough time to squirm away. I turn around to see if any other adults are approaching as backup, but our teachers are frozen in place. They look mortified. Maybe they're shocked to see me in such a mess. Or maybe they're considering all the legal and ethical ramifications of getting involved.

Mr. Conrad must have noticed the same thing, because he takes a step away from me.

This is my chance, but for a moment I'm paralyzed like a dog that's been chained out in the sun for days, starved and

tortured by his owner. Now that I'm free, I don't know what
to do. All I know is that I've been ruined. Darren has been
single-minded in destroying me since his dirty slide tackle
at soccer tryouts a couple of months ago. He's stolen my
almost-girlfriend, my friends, and now my reputation. Fury
bubbles back up, exploding like fireworks in my head. For
a second I consider going after him again, but the look on
Josh's face tells me I'd have to take him on first.

A sudden thought hits me. I can't reclaim what's mine by
attacking Darren. And there's no way to erase what's already
happened. Finally, I know exactly what I need to do. I do my
best to stand tall and face the sea of eyes on me.

"Look, this is really nobody's business," I start, my voice
stronger than I expected. "But fine. Here it is."

Mr. Conrad holds his hands up, as if to stop me.

"Let the kid talk!" somebody yells.

I try, but I can't recall a single thing that therapist Rob told
me about how to crack a secret open. I'm in a free-fall without a parachute. I take a deep breath, determined to make my
voice loud and strong. "I can't eat most of the things other
people do. I'm a picky eater—like a *really* picky eater. Literally
there are only ten things I eat."

Saying these words out loud—and to my entire class—is
more nauseating than taking a bite of that mushy apple earlier today, but I plow on.

"This is a real thing—it's annoying and embarrassing and
I can't do anything about it. It has a fancy scientific name
called ARFID, and if you want to know more about it, ask
me. Or Google it." I pause and turn, staring into Darren's
stink eyes. "*Some* people are spending a lot of energy trying
to figure out what's going on with me and food, and I've
been wasting a whole lot of time trying to hide it."

No one moves. A complete silence has blanketed Abner
Farms. Even the crickets have stopped chirping. I'm thinking
of something we learned in Scouts—a sudden, quiet stillness

is a sign of an approaching tornado. Maybe this is a bad idea.

I clench my jaw and force myself to look at my classmates. Lauren is glued to Darren's side. Her mouth is squeezed shut, and her arms are crossed so tight she reminds me of a collapsing star that's burned through its fuel. She shakes her head, possibly in warning, but more likely because she hates me for trying to kill her new boyfriend.

I have no choice but to finish what I've started.

I turn to Mr. Conrad. "Just so you know, those aren't my candy bars. I don't eat candy bars. You can ask anyone. Call my parents. Ask my friends. They're not mine."

"He doesn't eat candy bars," Nick says from behind me, and everyone laughs, probably because it sounds so ridiculous. I guess from now on, I'll be the butt of every joke.

Mr. Conrad's take-charge demeanor is back. He turns to the crowd. "Okay, folks, show's over." He places his hands on my shoulders and guides me away.

I jerk away from him with my last ounce of energy, and walk away with him. I don't know what I was expecting my confession to yield, but obviously it was a waste of breath. Because Darren is still sitting in the fire circle, and I'm being dragged away like a criminal. If anything, I've made things worse. It's official now—everyone knows I'm a freak.

As we pass the last clump of kids sitting on logs, someone asks, "What just happened? Did that kid just come out?"

"Yeah," another kid chuckles. "Out of the refrigerator."

Mr. Conrad walks so fast I can barely keep up with him. Neither of us says anything. I count my steps like I did this afternoon with Olivia, hoping to wipe out the reality of what has happened.

"What exactly have you eaten since you got here?" His voice is softer now, like a worried grandpa.

"Two of the smallest pancakes I've ever seen in my entire life," I say, and we both chuckle a little.

This might be my last laugh for a long time.

52

SIMMER DOWN

"Nancy, I've got a customer for you!" Mr. Conrad calls through the open door.

"I know this one," Nurse Parker says, smiling. "He brought in a rounders casualty yesterday."

"First order of business is to rustle up some dinner for Ben." Mr. Conrad looks at me and pauses, I guess waiting for me to say something. But I don't. "I'll let him fill you in on what he needs."

Yesterday when I walked Olivia into Nurse Parker's office, we learned that this is the only staff cabin at Abner Farms with a full kitchen and a guest suite. At the time I wasn't thinking of myself as a potential guest. But here I am.

Mr. Conrad turns to me. "And, Ben, I'm going to give your parents a call to let them know what's going on. You won't be sent home, but you can't participate in camp activities until Nurse Parker has cleared you. For now, you'll stay here."

I nod, desperate for him to stop talking. If he doesn't recognize the injustice here, I don't want to listen to him.

Mr. Conrad leaves without saying goodbye, and I have an urge to crawl into the guest room and never come out. But before I can do anything, Nurse Parker nods in the direction of a chair.

I plop down, exhausted.

"How can I help?" she asks.

The last thing I want to do is talk about my eating issues again, but once I spit out the truth about being a picky eater, she's all business. She asks me about whether I've been drinking water, the last time I peed, and how I feel overall.

She looks in my mouth, pinches a little skin on the back of my hand, and declares me "not so bad."

What's totally weird is that she doesn't ask me a single question about what I *have* eaten in the past two days.

I'm sure there's a lecture coming about how my parents should have informed Abner Farms about my dietary needs. But instead she asks, "Can you give me an idea or two of what you might eat?"

If I wasn't so miserable, this might be hilarious—I'm finally being offered food, but my appetite is shot. I couldn't eat a single McNugget right now if Ronald McDonald served them himself.

"Mac 'n' cheese? PB and J? Cereal? Grilled cheese?" she asks.

I don't answer.

"You're not the first kid who hasn't been able to stomach Abner Farms dining."

"Grilled cheese," I say, doubting it will be to my standard. "Please."

She surprises me again. "Okay, I've got Kraft singles, white bread, and a little margarine. Will that work?"

I nod.

Maybe.

53

EAT AND RUN

My watch says six thirty-three. It takes me a second to remember where I am and another second to realize it's morning, not night. A soft glow from the hallway gives off just enough light for me to see my duffel on the floor in the other room.

I didn't mean to fall asleep. After my second grilled cheese and a few glasses of water, Nurse Parker suggested I lie down for a while. She said if I felt okay and peed a couple of times, she'd talk to Mr. Conrad about when I could go back to my tent.

Not that going back to the tent seemed like an appealing option.

There were no good options last night. And there are no good options this morning.

Hiding out in the nurse's cabin makes me a coward.

Going home makes me a quitter.

Ratting out Darren makes me a snitch.

And showing my face in public now that I've admitted I can't do the most basic human thing—eat the kinds of food everyone else eats—makes me a total freak.

I sneak out into the hall and head toward the bathroom, but Nurse Parker spots me right away. She's in her office, sitting in a worn-out leather chair and holding a coffee mug with two hands the way my mom does.

"Well, that was quite a nap. How are you feeling?"

I shrug. It's a complicated question.

"I recommend a shower and clean clothes," she says as I head down the hall.

But a long, hot shower does nothing to improve my mood. In fact, I feel worse. Maybe I should give up and go home. Or better yet, grab my sleeping bag and disappear into the woods, snoozing under the stars and criss-crossing the terrain until I find a secluded spot where I can grow old.

My dream of living as an exiled colonist drifter doesn't last long. Mr. Conrad is waiting for me in Nurse Parker's office.

"Good morning. Sounds like you got some well-needed rest." He motions for me to take a seat across from him on an overstuffed plaid couch. It smells like wet blankets.

"I had a nice chat with your mom last night. I had to reassure her that you're really okay."

He pauses, I guess waiting for me to agree, which I don't.

"She was quite disturbed to hear about this business with the candy bars and offered more than once to drive up here and pick you up."

No way, I think to myself. If I allowed myself to be rescued by my mother, I'd never be able to show my face in public again. I'd become a wolf-man hermit with long fingernails and tangled hair, living in my parents' basement until the end of time. But I don't say that out loud either.

"I'd like to hear your thoughts about who placed the candy in your belongings."

I shrug, my signature move this morning.

"When you were speaking to your classmates last night, I was under the distinct impression you knew who was behind all this."

Apparently Mr. Conrad hasn't been a kid for a long time. I'm sure it's not possible to make him understand how delicate my situation is. If there were a fail-safe way to prove Darren planted the candy in my bag, I'd accuse him in a heartbeat. But there's not. So why bother?

"I have no idea who did it," I lie.

Mr. Conrad's exasperation fills the room like a noxious gas. He rambles on for a few minutes about integrity and the colonial work ethic and accountability, but I tune it all out.

I'm swimming in my own thoughts about how I'm going to face my classmates—including Darren. I figure it's better to know how bad it is today rather than wait until Monday morning at school.

"Ben?"

I jolt back to attention, sure that Mr. Conrad can tell I haven't heard a single word he's said.

"As I was saying, I'm reflecting on the wise words of Benjamin Franklin and that you may be heeding his advice."

"Huh?" I say, wracking my brain to figure out how Darren has anything to do with our founding fathers.

"Do good to thy friend to keep him, to thy enemy to gain him."

"I don't get it," I say, wanting to add, *and I don't really care.*

"Well, simply stated, perhaps you hope this person might be so grateful for your refusal to turn him in that he becomes a friend?"

I don't move a muscle, sure that Mr. Conrad is trying to trick me into something.

"Although there's also the risk of this perpetrator becoming emboldened by his success."

I can't understand half of what Mr. Conrad is trying to say, but I do know that my problem with Darren is not going to be resolved with quotes from old dead guys.

"Thank you for the advice," I say, my voice oozing with phony sincerity. "If it's all right with you, I'd like to head back to camp."

Mr. Conrad frowns and presses his lips tight. "Sounds like Nurse Parker will release you after you eat some breakfast."

54

A JUST DESSERT

I toss my duffel and sleeping bag into the pile behind the buses and walk past the fire circle toward the pavilion. Kids are lined up for breakfast, but it doesn't look like they're being served yet. The scene is identical to yesterday morning—for everyone but me. Just twenty-four hours ago, the biggest problem on my plate was the size of the flapjacks. But now my world has imploded, and nothing will ever be the same.

I spot Josh and Nick, and my focus sharpens like I'm watching them through binoculars. Then they're joined by Darren and Alex. They all seem happy and carefree. I wait, wondering for a second if Nick or Josh are concerned about me, but from watching them now it's pretty obvious they are not. My best friends haven't been disturbed by my disappearance. Nope, they don't even care.

Last night before I fell asleep, I tried not to imagine what everyone was saying about me back in our tent. I wanted to believe Josh and Nick were defending me, telling anyone who'd listen that I'd *never* bring a bag of candy here. But now I doubt it.

Maybe the old Josh and Nick would have spoken up, but lately they sure haven't seen the Darren situation from my side. When I rewind and replay everything that's happened since we got here, it's hard to pinpoint exactly when things went so wrong. The old Ben Snyder never got teased or started fights or stole apples or broke rules. Life always worked out for that Ben.

As I approach the crowd of kids standing in the breakfast line, not one person acknowledges my existence. I consider the distinct possibility that, like Olivia, I've become invisible. My feet are moving, but I have no idea where I'm going. I have no plan and no sense of what I hope will happen. Even though I pretty much felt the same way last night at the fire circle, at least I had the flash flood of hunger and adrenaline pushing me along. Now I've got nothing—no strategy, no direction, no burst of anger or disbelief. Even worse, I have no idea what to expect from anybody else.

A voice rings in my head, so clear and so Olivia that it startles me. *You know, once you become an expert in being yourself, navigating the world gets a whole lot easier.* "That's so stupid," I mutter out loud. Olivia's advice is completely worthless.

A cramp has taken root in my belly, sharp and prickly as a backyard weed and intensifying with each step I take. But I don't stop. I head straight over to Nick and the other guys. Their backs are to me, which seems to offer some sort of advantage—maybe an element of surprise will give me a few seconds to assess the situation.

"Hey," I say, a little too loud.

Josh and Nick turn around first. Nick's face breaks into a huge metallic grin, but Josh is harder to read. I can't decide if his raised eyebrows convey curiosity or suspicion.

The moment Darren sees me, his expression morphs from his regular nasty smirk to an expression of complete shock. "What are *you* doing here?" he asks. "I thought you got sent home."

"No, I broke out," I say in what I hope seems like the most casual response in the history of casual responses.

Darren's eyes slide from me to Josh and back again. He shifts his weight from side to side and it occurs to me that I'm making him nervous. His edginess strikes me as a pretty good sign.

For weeks, my mind has been marinating in a muck of misery and doubt. But now it revs up like a car in the starting grid at Talladega because of one simple realization: I've been playing by Darren's rules. And he's a dirty player—on the soccer field and everywhere else. I've let myself get dragged down to his level, and it hasn't paid off. In fact, for the most part, it's made me look like a jerk.

I handled him on the field. I need to trust that I can handle him off the field too. I'm not playing his game anymore, no matter what happens next.

Especially now that I have nothing to hide.

"So that's it? You're not in trouble?" Darren asks, jamming his hands into the front pockets of his jeans.

"Does it look like I'm in trouble?" I ask. It seems like following his question with one of my own is a pretty good strategy.

He doesn't answer. He takes his hands out of his pockets and shoves them back in again. "Well, just because you don't eat that stuff doesn't prove you're innocent."

He glances around at Josh and Nick and Alex, I guess looking for backup, but no one moves.

"Which part don't you get?" I ask. "The fact that I don't eat candy bars or the fact that the candy didn't belong to me?"

A bunch of noisy girls are making their way to the back of the breakfast line, and we all glance over at them. I spot Lauren right away, and as soon as she notices me her face goes pale—like all the usual dazzle and shine has been drained out of her. She stares at me for a second and then walks over.

"Ben, what are you doing here? I thought maybe you'd been expelled."

"Nope, I'm a free man," I say, forcing a smile. My thoughts scatter in a hundred different directions like a flock of birds startled out of a tree. Lauren seems curious but not particularly happy to see me. After how she acted yesterday, I have no idea what's going on in her head.

Darren, however, is sure Lauren is his ally. Her arrival has renewed his confidence. He smiles at her, draws his shoulders back, and pulls his hands out of his pockets. "Yeah," he says, tilting his head in my direction. "Cornbread was just about to tell us how he escaped."

"Escaped?" Lauren gasps.

I shake my head, preparing to twist Darren's mind around again. "No, they released me 'cause my fingerprints weren't a match."

Darren's mouth drops open. "Are you serious?"

"Don't I sound serious?" It's hard for me to keep a straight face. But my attention focuses momentarily on Lauren. Even though I'm pretty torn up about how she ditched me for that creep, I can't stand to see her speechless and confused. She stares at Darren then looks back at me. "What's going on?"

I turn to Darren. "Anything else you want to say?"

His face turns a bright shade of red. I think all my questions are getting to him. "Well, you *do* eat those Hershey's Kisses. And they're made with the *exact same chocolate* as Hershey's candy bars."

"And there were Hershey bars in the bag?" I ask.

"Yeah." He pauses. "Weren't there? I'm pretty sure I saw them."

"Wow, Darren," I say, holding back a smile. "From where you were sitting at the back of the fire circle last night, I don't know how you could've possibly seen what was in that bag."

Josh and Nick exchange glances and then look back at me.

"And, not that it even matters," I continue, "but Hershey's Kisses and Hershey's chocolate bars are *not* exactly the same in taste or texture or even ingredients."

Darren opens his mouth like a gasping fish then snaps it shut again.

"I didn't bring that candy here. Somebody set me up." I stare at Darren, still and unblinking.

Lauren runs her hands through her hair and takes in a huge gulp of air. "Hold on a second." She turns to Darren. "It all makes sense. *You* did this. *You* set him up. You've been trying to make Ben look bad all along. And I actually fell for it."

"So that's your stupid game, dude?" I ask Darren, glad to drop another question.

Lauren answers for him. "Yup, Darren was all *Ben's a trouble-maker* and *Ben's a freak* and *Ben's got anger management issues* and...."

"Thanks, I've got the picture," I say.

Lauren stops talking for a second, but she's lost no momentum. She takes another deep breath and starts again, faster than I've ever heard her—like a blender running at full speed. "I think we should tell a teacher. Or Mr. Conrad. Or someone."

She turns to Darren. "You can't get away with this."

Then she tugs on my sleeve. "Come on, let's go."

But I don't move. I can hear my own heartbeat. It feels like the rest of the world has floated away and we're the only six people left in the pavilion.

Lauren is unusually silent.

Josh's face is blank.

Alex is studying the floor.

Nick glares at Darren, shaking his head with a movement so slight that it takes me a second to recognize it as a warning sign. Since Nick is such a laid-back guy, I've only witnessed it once or twice in my entire life. Slow, rhythmic head-shaking is what he does before he goes ballistic.

"You're such a scumbag," he says, taking a step closer to Darren. "We should have let Ben beat the crap out of you last night."

Nick winds up to throw a punch, but I grab his arm before he can do any damage. A part of me would love to let go and watch this play out, but the last thing I need right now is more attention from adults.

Josh has been jolted out of his trance. "Seriously," he says, glaring at Darren. "It's so messed up—the stuff you've been doing." His shoulders slump as if his disappointment in Darren is literally weighing him down.

Darren crosses his arms tight over his chest, scowling at me. "You can't prove anything."

"I think I already have," I say.

"So what are you gonna do, fight me?" His voice is a little jittery.

"No, that would be too easy." I laugh.

Josh and Nick and Alex laugh a little too, but their laughs are nervous.

"I'll get Mr. Conrad," Lauren offers again.

"Nope. We don't need him." My voice is cool, and my mind is as clear as a cloudless summer morning. I have Darren right where I want him.

I wait for a long, drawn-out moment before I go on. I hope it feels like an eternity. "This stuff between us," I say calmly. "Whatever you want to call it—this stupid battle we have going on—it ends right here, right now."

Darren squirms. "I don't know what you mean."

"You know exactly what I mean. It means you need to stay in your lane. And I'll stay in mine." I shrug like I don't care either way. "Take the blame for the candy. Or back off. Your choice."

He glances around, looking at Josh and Nick and Alex and Lauren like he'd forgotten they were even here. I'd bet all the McNuggets in the world it's because he's just realized I have four witnesses to hold him to his word.

Nodding, he holds out his hand and we shake on it. I hang on a second longer than I need to, until he looks up and meets my gaze. After I let go, he mutters something and scurries away like a rat.

"Well played," Nick says, patting me on the back. "That kid's a real—"

"I know," I cut him off before he can say it. I'm already staying in my own lane.

Josh and Alex each high-five me.

A surge of relief blankets my body like bathwater, and

before I can even consider what life without Darren on my back will be like, Lauren's small hand is holding mine.

"I'm sorry for believing all those terrible things about you," she says apologetically.

The breakfast line has moved on without us, and now we're last in line. Nick puts a plate in my free hand and gives me a congratulatory grin. Alex hasn't said anything, but whenever I glance his way, he nods in what I take as a sign of approval. I'm feeling so good about what I pulled off with Darren that it takes a second before I realize I'm about to go through the dreaded Abner Farms breakfast line again. Memories of yesterday's disaster begin to bubble up, and I remember how I had to save my flapjacks from the threat of rubbery eggs and grits.

And even though I made a public service announcement last night about my eating habits, I'm not any more confident about displaying them in front of my entire class. I already scarfed down two bagels in Nurse Parker's office, but I decide to test my courage at the next level and stand up for myself.

The first server waves a ladle overflowing with scrambled eggs in my direction.

"No thanks," I say, smiling.

She scowls at me. "Everybody gets served the same."

I pull my plate tight to my chest. "No thanks," I say again.

I repeat my move with the grits lady and the bacon lady, waiting for something to happen. But nobody says anything or challenges me. And as far as I can tell, the world continues to spin on its axis.

When I get to the pancake lady, I hold my plate out, knowing its emptiness won't persuade her to give me extras. My two little flapjacks are a small island of bliss on the otherwise-empty plate. I smile at her anyway, satisfied with what I've got.

Abner Farms has not transformed me into an adventurous eater. But I've pushed myself in a bunch of other ways that feel more important than what I eat. I think I'll tell Mom I'd like to keep talking to that therapist, Rob. He'd probably like to hear about how I used his trick of answering a question with another question to take Darren down.

As we all head over to the table, Albert appears and falls in step between Lauren and me. "Not now, man," I say, trying to nudge him out of position. I don't want him to spoil my victory lap with another one of his stupid ideas.

But it's Lauren he wants to talk to. "When we get home, can I text you?" he asks her. "About some student council stuff? 'Cause I could really use some help."

"Sure," she says, smiling.

I'm smiling, too, as I watch him walk away.

When we get to the only open table, Lauren takes the spot next to mine. Once we've all gotten settled, I reach for my fork and—*splat*—two more flapjacks fall from the sky and onto my plate.

I turn around to find Olivia standing behind me. She's sporting an entirely red, white, and blue outfit like some sort of Yankee wackadoodle. She sets her plate of food on the table and pulls a gold medal ribbon out of her pocket.

"This is yours. We won. You won it for us."

I had completely forgotten about the orienteering award.

"Oh my gosh. Didn't you hear about that?" Lauren asks as she puts her two flapjacks onto my plate next to Olivia's.

I want to say something to Olivia about our win, but I'm distracted by Lauren's flapjacks, which somehow seem too special to eat.

"See you later," Olivia says, grinning.

"Wait," I say. "Want to sit with us?"

"That's okay. I'm gonna go read."

"Come on, we winners need to stick together." I turn back to everyone else at the table. "You guys know Olivia, right?"

Lauren scoots closer to me. "There's room right here," she says, patting the spot to her right. "Oh my gosh," she says again, noticing Olivia's wrist, "that's the most incredible friendship bracelet I've ever seen."

"Thanks. It took me forever."

I figured out a long time ago that Olivia had made the bracelet herself. But as I look at it now, I notice something I didn't really think about before. The woven pattern is both complicated and ambitious—just like Olivia's personality. It suits her perfectly.

Lauren leans over to admire the bracelet and then looks back up. She thinks for a second, and then she asks Olivia, "Would you be interested in helping me start a peer tutoring program at school?"

"Absolutely," Olivia says.

Nick stretches across the table, and without saying a word drops his flapjacks on my plate. As soon as they hit, Josh and Alex do the same. I nod a thank you. Now I've got an even dozen, and my plate looks like the mystical flapjack feast I had imagined would sustain me for two and a half days.

From behind, two more pancakes land on my plate. A look of alarm crosses Nick's face, and I turn around to see Darren right behind me. My stomach drops. Maybe this was all too good to be true.

"Maybe we should call you flapjack."

Everyone is still, waiting for my reaction. Even Darren has tensed up.

"Nah," I say smiling. "I kinda like cornbread."

As soon as I've said it, I start to laugh, and after a second, we're all laughing—the kind of contagious out-of-control howling that makes kids from the other tables stare like we're from another planet.

Nothing at Abner Farms has gone the way I'd planned. But as I look around the table, I realize it's all turned out better than I ever could have hoped. And Olivia makes a good point—navigating my world might be getting easier.

I jab my fork into the stack.